L. M. Labat

The Sanguinarian Id

Night to Dawn

Night to Dawn Magazine & Books LLC
P. O. Box 643
Abington, PA 19001
www.bloodredshadow.com
ISBN: 978-1-937769-44-4
Copyright by L. M. Labat 2015

Illustrator: L. M. Labat
Editor: Barbara Custer

In dedication to L. A. Schexnayder, S. F. Schexnayder, Dr. C. A. Gramlich, Dr. C. LaCabe, A. Jenkins, R. Bechet, Dr. S. Clunis, M. T. S. Davis, B. J. Frank, P. M. Davis, S. C. Davis, M. Thompson, B. M. S. Bigard, J. A. Stengl, and D. Pierson.

****

In memory of M. Ferbos, L. C. Ferbos, Jr., and L. C. Ferbos, Sr.

Table of Contents

Chapter One
The Dominion

A book fell from the shelf. An old man arose from his chair. His bones creaked as he picked up the fallen literature. His white, tangled hair draped past his shoulders like cobwebs. His ragged nails scraped along the book's spine. A fireplace burned brilliantly in the room with a peculiar green flame. The man smiled wistfully as he stared into the fire. His appearance was that of a frail, elderly gentleman. However, his posture was erect and as solid as a battalion. He sat back in his chair with his book secured in his hand. This man was a royal of wisdom. Like an eccentric millionaire, he would become lost in his multitudes of lore. He read, "Nothing is defined as nonexistence and the absence of significance. The duality of this word is vast. While the word can describe the absence of quarrel and strife, the word can easily conjure discord, anger, and misery."

He closed the book. Sighing listlessly, he twiddled his bony fingers across the back cover. He leaned towards the fireplace and watched the embers dance amidst the ashes. Even though he was deep in thought, the man's gaze was focused and quiet. He asked himself, "Why is one's life so easily downfallen by this nothing?" The man was adrift in his memories. He pondered the word's meaning.

He placed the literature back onto the shelf. As he looked about his study, his eyes smiled upon seeing his collection of books, his legions of cognizance. Within the mountain's stone walls, this was his solitude. Away from the rest of the world, he was content in his undying study. Hordes of papers were stacked alongside the walls. He searched through the papers and skimmed through his columns of handwritten notes.

"What is this unstableness linked to?" He folded a page corner as he reviewed his notes. "Certain words, such as trigger words, spark past memories or sensations that are linked to an inner vault. Numerous words play as triggers to hidden expressions, emotions, and buried memories. After the trigger is pulled, the spark fades. A person may ponder the origin of all the joys, tears, and thoughts they've experienced. This inner mental vault is comprised of many levels of consciousness." He analyzed his notes. "But, where does the spark come from?"

With spider-like limbs, he reached to the top of a shelf and carried down a large, weatherworn notebook. He flipped to the middle of the book to a damaged photograph. He read the notations to himself, "In the 1800s, there was an extraordinary intellectual named Sigmund Freud. This man is known as the Father of Modern Psychology due to his dedication to the human subconscious, personality, dreams, and his creation of Psychoanalysis. Over time, Freud developed The Personality Structure.

"The Personality Structure represents the judgment and the want of the mind on a day to day basis. The most potent and domineering level of this structure is the Id." The man reminisced in his notations. "The spark is the Id."

He chuckled, remembering his studies. "I remember now. The Id is the deepest, most instinctive, and most powerful desire of the mind. The Id wants instant gratification. When something piques its interest, the Id springs forth to make itself known. Its ubiquitous cravings are constantly forming new demands. When it wants, it feeds. When feeding, it wants. It's a never-ending cycle of more."

He closed the book and placed it onto the table. He thought about the human brain, the Id, and the meaning of nothing. He stared into the fireplace. As he stood, in his shadow, the emerald flames quivered with fear. He swirled his fingers in the hearth's flame. Neither his skin nor sleeve caught fire. "If left unchecked, a person's Id can consume its keeper and bombard every hindrance until it gets what it wants. It has no remorse, no guilt, and no mercy. It will never stop."

He snuffed out the light and listened to the fire scream. The firewood wailed and crackled under the dying flames. He smiled. "What if the Id wants nothing?"

****

A stately manor illuminated in the night. In front of a forest, the manor's windows reflected the swaying pine trees. The dwelling's red brick walls were surrounded by pink and yellow rose bushes as apple trees enclosed the gardens. But even within the lush abundance, the flower's colors and delicate scents were capsized by the manor's stale occupants.

The house's air was thick with tobacco. From corridor to corridor, the maids dusted lamps and large family portraits. In a dimly lit hall, a young man ran after the lady of the house. "Madame, I implore you. Don't do this. She's only a child!" he said.

The woman stormed down the hallway. Her white, silk dress fluttered behind her like a snow flurry. "That child is the only thing keeping me from my right. I'm not tolerating this anymore." Her words were stern. "She has to go."

"What will your husband think, Elizabeth?" the young man asked.

"Shut up, David. That old bastard's too busy with his stocks." Being married to an experienced stockbroker, Elizabeth grew bored and obtuse with riches. As the years passed, Elizabeth found leisure in controlling the lives of others. Being an associate of Elizabeth's husband, David knew too well the lengths of Elizabeth's cruelty. However, as hard as it was, David tried to retain his composure since he was the subordinate in the relationship. As she looked at David and her servants, her peridot eyes blazed with intoxication and envy. She glanced at the painting of her husband above the mantelpiece. "He doesn't notice me anymore." She sneered at his image and threw the painting to the ground. Her eyes were filled with hate as she gouged her nails into the canvas, shredding the portrait's face. "If he's having an affair with his money, I'll have one with

5

mine once she's gone."

David stopped walking after her. His dark hair covered his eyes. "That's not the only thing you're having an affair with."

Her voice soured. "You sicken me." The one thing Elizabeth hated more than lacking power was seeing vagrants behave as if they had dominion. "You forget yourself too often, David." She adjusted the ring on her finger. "If you try to blackmail me, I'll tell your master that you took advantage of me. God knows how much he's waiting to rip you apart."

David clenched his fist. "You lewd bitch! You came onto me!"

"But, you still played along." She rubbed the top of her ring. "Don't be an infant, David. You knew what you were doing. If you didn't, you wouldn't be so good at it." David's face reddened. She snickered at his modesty. She continued, "For the matter at hand, you will help me get rid of that girl. Her expenses are burning a hole in my pocket."

David pushed her away from him. For the past few years, Elizabeth took in a sickly relative. The girl was very young, her wants were small, but her medicine was expensive. However, the girl's expenses were nothing compared to Elizabeth's frivolous nature. Elizabeth was a notorious spendthrift.

"You burned your own pocket!" David shouted. "If you didn't spend so much on Teresa, you'd have more money." Teresa was Elizabeth's stepchild from her husband's first marriage. Sharing a likeness in character, Elizabeth fulfilled Teresa's every whim. In return, Teresa made sure her father returned the favor. In the manor, those two could do no wrong. In both their minds, Elizabeth's blood relative was unimportant. "Teresa is not your blood! The other girl is!" David raged. "You can't just sell her for reimbursement."

Her laugh was prissy. "Teresa is my little princess, and I'll be damned if I'm going to let a tramp like you lecture me on finances. Getting back to the task at hand, I'm not going to sell the girl. The only way I can get her part of the inheritance is through the pronunciation of her death. After that, my Teresa can get whatever she wants."

His face grew pale. "Devil! You're a bloody devil! I'll have no part of this."

Elizabeth grabbed the letter opener from the desk. She plunged the blade into David's shoulder, and shoved him against the wall. Blood streaked her snowy gown.

David paused. Biting his tongue, he pulled the blade out of his flesh and threw it to the floor. His blood seeped back into the wound. Within a matter of seconds, the entire gash was healed. The only remaining damage was a rip in his shirt. Elizabeth scowled at him. "Do not patronize me on who embodies the Devil. Of all people, you hold your tongue! You accuse me of my demons when your hands are stained with buckets of men, women, and children's blood. You stand there, with your pressed shirt and shined shoes, slandering my ways when your master makes the whole of Gehenna look sanctified!" David averted his eyes. Elizabeth took out a key from inside her blouse.

"Is that your husband's skeleton key?" he asked.

"I had copies made," she replied. She opened the door.

In a small bed against a wide window, a little girl slept. The little girl coughed. A tangled mess of black hair and a rosy cheek peeked from under the covers.

"She's knocked out," Elizabeth said. "I had the doctor give her a sedative. Get her out of the bed, and bring her to the attic." David wiped a tear from his eye. "What's wrong now?"

David cried, "She's just a baby."

"The little bitch started bleeding a few days ago. She's practically a woman," Elizabeth replied. "But, I'm the main lady of this house."

David's temper rose, "You're the whore of this house." She slapped him across his face. Her garnet ring sliced his cheek. David wiped his face. His wound healed instantaneously. "You believe that people wouldn't be suspicious of a missing child?"

"All of my servants, guards, and doctors agree with my decision." The more money Elizabeth received, the more her employees' salaries increased. She looked at the girl. "Her illness isn't my doing. She's been getting severely weak as of late." Elizabeth's doctors couldn't diagnose the child's disease. The little girl kept wasting away, coughing, vomiting, and sneezing. "With her medical records already in place, her death will seem natural."

The little girl twitched in her bed. David picked her up. From her face to her feet, the child's body was covered with sweat. Her fingers were tightly curled into her palms. David sensed the mystery disease deteriorating the child's body. A tear fell from his face onto her head. She was so innocent. Elizabeth opened the door. "Are you done?"

He held the little girl close to him. "I should've never stepped foot into this house."

"Remember, I know what you are," she said. He walked out of the room. Elizabeth locked the door behind her. "I have no qualms with exposing you *and* your master."

David read the identification bracelet on the little girl's wrist. From her own petty and spiteful reasons, Elizabeth demanded that the child's name be changed. He hated that woman. David's tears soaked into the locks of the child's hair. He wiped the sweat from her brow. "Forgive me."

****

Outside, far into the distance, a shadowed figure stood quietly under the trees. At a glance, this entity appeared to be a veiled augur. But, as it gazed beyond the walls of Elizabeth's mansion, the creature became more irate and ethereal. It had a soft voice. But, its words were still and as abyssal as death, "Beware the contents of your mind. You will not approve of what you find. Do not resurface the sunken chest lest you suffer Macbeth's rapture unrest. Halt the key unlocking the cage, or you will suffer a blinding rage. Scribes and scrolls of Golgotha and gore bewitch even Poe's forgotten lore. Agony and aching cram every crease as God's creation of man contorts into beasts. Guilt and shame roar through one's cries as they inflict themselves mirroring Oedipus's eyes. Wrath and anger sends teeth and claws until it dismembers its hindrance with blood in its maw. While writhing and scratching, the mind starts to change as politics and reason become deranged. Cease the opening of Pandora's Box, or else your world becomes a paradox. Your right will be left while your outside is in as the blessings around you reveal to be sin. There are reasons why your mind outcasts the shadows and specters of your past. Heed my words, and leave this place. Keep your innocence intact. Not erased. Remember my warning. And, God forbid you face your demon, the Sanguinarian Id."

Chapter Two
New Arrival

Within Europe's late nineteenth century, marvelous medical miracles came into existence that augmented the intellectual to new horizons. Doctors of all fields were admired for their dedication to health and humanity. However, as their accolades increased, these professionals grew fat with entitlement while their patients starved for love. With speedy developments, the human brain, in its entire splendor, spiraled dangerously into the new era of indulgences that forked the path between masterpiece and monstrosity.

****

A group of young women sat on the cold floor. In dirty hospital gowns, they picked and ingested lead paint chips from the wall. Persistently, they crammed more debris into their hungry mouths. Drool covered their cracked fingernails. With muted expressions, the nurses smoked like locomotives at their corridor stations. They watched the self-poisoning, but did nothing to help. The nurses reacted solely when the clock struck seven. The chimes notified them to administer the medication.

In the joining corridor, more patients wandered aimlessly. Whimpering like beaten dogs, most patients wore restraints over their mouths and arms. Others fiddled with their gowns as they stumbled from side to side. No matter what they were doing, the inhabitants complemented each other with the same dead-eyed stare against the barred windows.

The doctors were devils. They prodded, scraped, and teased the flesh with their instruments. Like foxes, the doctors lured people into their examination rooms with wide-toothed grins and false promises. None of them were in harmony with their patients. These mechanized madmen were fluent with their hands and calculations. Their utensils were never bare. These men constantly wrapped their fingers around their equipment's silvery curves. They comforted the metal exteriors like newborn children. The wives of these doctors had sullen lives, wishing their husbands would caress their thighs the way they did their clipboards.

The patients knew no humanity. The kind gazes they saw reflected off foggy spectacles before the serum blacked out their minds. That was if they were lucky enough to have the straps off their foreheads. This was Halcyon Asylum.

****

Screams filled the corridor! A man with ripped sleeves bolted through the door at the end of the hall. Two burly guards grabbed his arms and back. The man screamed louder as he twisted his body to escape their grip. "Liars!" he shouted. "Liars! All of you! Where is she?" One of the guards wrenched the runaway's arm. Something snapped! The man fell hard to his knees in pain.

"Keep him there." a voice said. The guards stopped, and looked behind them. A doctor walked up to the scene. His lab coat was a tapestry of bloody fingerprints. "Specifically, didn't I inform you two to not injure the patients?" the doctor inquired.

The man yelled at the physician, "Where is she?"

A guard punched him in his diaphragm. "Shut up!"

The doctor snatched the back of the guard's hair. He dug his fingers into the scalp. "Didn't I say *not* to hurt the patients?"

The guard nodded submissively, for the speaker was Dr. Alrich Strauss, leading physician at Halcyon Asylum. The doctor released his grip and ordered them to restrain the runaway's hands. The guards obeyed, and returned to their posts.

The man painfully looked up towards the doctor. His mouth quivered. "Where is she? What have you done with my girl? I'm worried about my daughter." The man laid his head upon the doctor's feet. He pleaded, "Please. Dr. Strauss, where is my girl?"

Towering over Mr. Geneva, Dr. Strauss removed his foot from underneath the man's head. He looked at him blankly. "Mr. Geneva, I can assure you that your daughter is in good hands."

"But, where is she? You said that she would be released on the seventh." Mr. Geneva was unnerved by his daughter's absence. Tears ran down his face. "She was supposed to come back to me over a month ago." Mr. Geneva trembled violently. On the verge of a fit, he bit his knuckles as tears flooded his face.

"Mr. Geneva!" The doctor cleared his throat. "Mr. Geneva, your daughter is being taken care of. I am well informed that she was supposed to be released on the seventh, but new issues have arisen." Mr. Geneva was confused. The doctor explained the situation. The amount of professionalism Alrich had doubled in apathy. He shrugged his shoulders. "Mary's hysteria has worsened."

"Why?" Mr. Geneva fretted.

"Calm yourself." Alrich lifted Mr. Geneva to his feet, and led him into a vacant room. Like Mary Geneva, Alrich saw many young women that suffered with hysteria. "After the trauma she's had, this was bound to happen. But, do you think that your behavior would help her? What do you think she would say if she saw you right now? Her father incarcerated in an asylum for erratic behavior?"

Mr. Geneva hung his head in shame. "You're right. She needs me." He began to sob. "It's so hard not to worry. She's all I have."

Dr. Strauss patted his shoulder. "I know. As a father, it's your nature to feel this way." Alrich was a miser of leniency. He understood that Mr. Geneva's behavior was due to his daughter's absence. But, running thin on time, he decided to excuse the misconduct. Mr. Geneva was lucky.

Dr. Strauss fixed Mr. Geneva's dislocated arm and apologized for the guard's rough behavior. Over the remainder of the day, he administered a mild sedative to ease the man's pain and silence the room.

****

Three days passed. Dr. Strauss returned Mr. Geneva's belongings, and summoned a coach to bring him home. Mr. Geneva smiled. "Thank you. Please, take care of my Mary. Have her write to me."

The doctor shook his hand and closed the coach door. The coachman finished grooming the horses. The air was crisp that morning. But, like Alrich's head, the sky was cloudy and loomed with ill weather.

Behind the asylum's front door, a large man stood attentively and watched Mr. Geneva from the shadows. The gray skies reflected off his spectacles.

Alrich beckoned the coachman. "Anthony, a moment." The doctor took out a small, brown pouch from his back pocket, and handed it to the coachman. There was no eye contact. He whispered to Anthony, "Snuff him out." The coachman pocketed his pay. Dr. Strauss waved goodbye to the departing carriage.

The man behind the doors gingerly walked forward. "Is he gone?"

Strauss straightened his sleeve. "He won't be here again."

The man walked down the steps. *"Wünderbar!"* he exclaimed with a thick, Bavarian accent. He adjusted his gloves.

"How's the girl, Mendelson?" Strauss asked.

Mendelson snickered. "Which one?"

Alrich entered the room. "Mary."

Mendelson tapped his chin as he thought. Mary was a lovely name, but, like a school of fish, it was a pain to remember one from the other.

Alrich became irritated. "Mary Geneva?"

Mendelson's eyes widened. "Oh, Mary! She's passed out."

Alrich shook his head. His face turned sullen.

"Why so glum?" Mendelson asked. "You told me she was defective."

Strauss snapped around. "I didn't say you could have her."

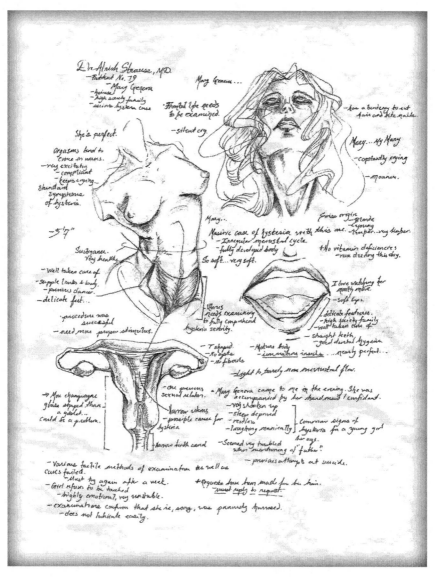

Mendelson laughed. "Don't be so crossed. You said she was defective. Besides, she was bleeding." Mendelson and Alrich shared a deep affinity for women, but Mendelson was insatiable. Greedily, Mendelson took any woman he wanted no matter what condition they were in. However, in respecting a woman's cycle, Alrich never attended the Cardinal's tea party like his friend did. Mendelson continued, "You can have the next girl that comes in."

Obsessing over Mary, Alrich scowled at Mendelson. "I won't forget this. I really wanted Mary."

Mendelson laughed.

"I'm serious," said Alrich. Mendelson followed him through the doors.

****

It rained hard during the following weeks. A powerful storm sat amidst the hills and forests surrounding the asylum. The doctors and nurses were ordered by Mendelson and Alrich to secure the patients as often as possible due to the weather. Thunder crashes and blasts of lightning alarmed the patients. The noises put them into a ballistic frenzy.

Breathing heavily, Alrich stood against the wall. He attempted to strap down a volatile patient. Mendelson walked out the room after the straps were secured. He leaned against the corridor. "What's wrong with you?"

Alrich grasped his wrist. "Fucker sprained my wrist."

"Can you move it?"

Alrich tightened his grip. He clenched his teeth. "Barely."

"Do you think you can handle the others?" Mendelson asked.

Alrich disagreed, "No. I have to tend to my wrist. It may be fractured."

"Go have a smoke." Mendelson tossed Alrich a lighter. "I can handle the rest."

****

The corridors were numerous with tall ceilings. To a spectator, the painted stones, tall arches, and doors were an architectural beauty. Alrich hated the structures. Every day, across scuffed floors, his flat shoes sent shocks up his calves. He sat at the bottom of the lobby staircase like a tired grasshopper. His long legs were bent on the step. He lifted his foot and stared at his raggedy sole in disgust.

The storm continued. Black clouds smothered the night sky as their insides barraged the asylum's walls with hard arrows of icy rain. Alrich fixed his eyes at the window. The room was freezing. The cold intensified towards the front door. He stood up and sat himself next to the window. The glass was frigid. It numbed his fingertips.

Looking at the cascading rain, he remembered Mary. He recalled the tears rolling down her cheek. Mary was such a gentle girl. Alrich reminisced on her freckles and soft locks. Like the window he touched, Mary was clear, clean, and easily broken. But, his joy was short-lived. He soon remembered the look in her eyes when Mendelson made his approach.

Enraged, Alrich tightened his fist and hit the wall. Immediately, he gripped his wrist. He forgot the struggle he endured before.

Alrich may have been the leading physician, but his position was a lie. Acting as an older brother to Alrich, Mendelson helped Alrich out with anything he needed. Everything Alrich had was on account of Mendelson's wealth and connections. Mendelson was a brilliant surgeon. After obtaining his licenses, Mendelson built the asylum. His associates expected him to lead it. But, Freudric didn't want the title's attention or aggravation. So, he anointed Alrich the mask of being lead physician while he silently led from the shadows. Alrich hated being Mendelson's subordinate.

Alrich respected his caliber, but Alrich was jealous of his friend's stealth and precision. With women, medicine, and everything else in his life, Mendelson formed his tactics like a chess game: three steps ahead.

The doctor and Mendelson shared similar tastes. Mendelson became the shadow of any woman that caught his fancy. He never left them alone. Alrich, on occasion, behaved the same way. However, Alrich never hounded women like Mendelson did.

Rubbing his wrist, Alrich leaned his forehead against the windowpane. His breath fogged the glass. The rain slacked. It was drizzling and foggy, but he could see past the gaslights.

Beyond the ghostly lights, the tree line was vast. Everywhere, thick trunked guardians of the forest stood as an impregnable wall protecting their treasures. He stared at their heavily barked branches and wondered, *What could you all be hiding back there?*

Deep chimes filled the lobby. Alrich turned towards the clock. It was midnight. His eyes were tired. His bottom lids were gray and puffy from insomnia. Scratching the back of his head, he gazed into the storm. He wanted to get as much peace as he could before the thunder awoke once more. He wiped the fog off the glass.

Before he lit one of his cigars, he stopped. Something caught his eye. Out in the distance, near the tree line, something white fluttered in the chilled air. Alrich put his face on the glass to decipher the object. It was torn fabric.

His heart quickened. He didn't know why, but the sight of the white fabric excited him like a begging flag of surrender. He dropped the lighter and dashed outside.

He stood underneath the lamps to scan the area. Even though it was drizzling, the rain stung his face like frozen needles. He adjusted his glasses and focused on the thin fabric. It was a lace dress.

He ran off the stone steps. His feet plunged into the soft ground. Mud filled his socks. He studied the unknown being.

It was a girl. The girl in the lace dress lay face down underneath the trees. The forest stood over as her defense. He knelt down beside her. Her hair was packed with mud and dead grass. Flipping her over, he wiped the dirt off her brow. He checked her vital signs. She was breathless and had no pulse. Her limbs limped like shoestrings against his arms. He placed his fingers on her cardiac arteries. He felt nothing. He looked up at the sky. The clouds grew impatient. He placed his ear on her chest. There was a low gurgling in her lungs.

He leaned her forward and hit her back with the palm of his hand. "Come on. Come on. Come on," he muttered. The girl coughed up mud and murky water. At last, she gasped for air.

Mendelson rushed through the doors. He held his dropped lighter. "Alrich!" he called. "What the hell are you doing? Section two needs your help!" The rain fell harder. Mendelson covered his head with his jacket. "Did you hear me?"

"There's a girl here, Freudric!" Alrich responded.

Mendelson looked up. The rain was an onslaught. The thunder boomed. Mendelson dashed towards his friend and grabbed him by the back of his coat.

"Freudric, she was drowning in the mud!" Alrich shouted. "I revived her. She's alive!"

Freudric held the door open. "Just bring her inside."

The doctor wrapped the child in his coat. They retreated into the asylum. The doctor carried the little girl into the lobby, and laid her on the couch. She was so frail. He felt her wrists. "She's barely alive."

"Where did you find her?" Mendelson asked.

Alrich removed his muddy shoes. "By the tree line."

Mendelson started to laugh.

Alrich wiped off his glasses. "What's so funny?"

Mendelson wrung his hair. "I'm a man of my word."

"What?"

"You can keep her. She's all yours." He laughed harder. "I won't bother her."

"You are an ass!" Alrich shouted.

Freudric laughed. Between the two men, Freudric held all the power. With one snap, Mendelson could have Alrich's life destroyed. But, he viewed Alrich as a younger brother. And, due to their history together, Mendelson was never bothered by Alrich's outbursts. "You looked so excited bringing her inside. And, she's just your type: frail, lost, and near death."

Alrich stood up. "That's not funny!"

Mendelson sat next to the girl. "I'm joking! I'm joking," he said.

Alrich glared at him.

Mendelson combed his hair back. He asked Alrich what made him react so spontaneously. Alrich scratched the back of his head and looked towards the floor. Mendelson knew that posture.

"You're thinking of Martha, aren't you?" Freudric asked.

Alrich rubbed his eyes. His nose started to run. He lived a heartbroken life. For every person he saved, countless loved ones were lost.

Freudric inhaled deeply. "I'm sorry for joking like that."

Alrich didn't respond.

Freudric continued to comfort him. His voice was calm and sincere. "Alrich, you can't blame yourself for what happened. It was a long time ago. Things were too unstable."

"Unstable is an understatement!" Alrich clamored. His mind raced with memories. "I wasn't there! I left her all alone!"

Freudric put his hand on Alrich's shoulder. Of all the deaths he's had, Martha's death scarred Alrich the most. He rubbed his temples. "I've tried to forget."

"I have, too," Freudric said. He sat next to the girl. "But, that was dealt with. Remember?"

"I remember," Alrich said.

Even though Alrich endured horrible pain, Mendelson survived the worst. But, through it all, the two grew up together like brothers. They were inseparable. "I'm still your brother." Freudric said. He cleaned his watch. "If I can leave my demons behind, so can you."

Strauss glanced at him. "Have you?"

Mendelson cut his eyes at Alrich. After a few moments he regained his composure. "What are you going to do with her?" he asked, pointing to the girl.

"I'm going to bring her back to health. I need to find out who she is, and try to find her family." Alrich thought about the tree line. *Why was she all the way out here?*

Mendelson stroked her hair. "She's a cute little thing, isn't she?" He looked at her shoulders. They were riddled with bruises. Her wrist was covered in scars and burns. He tilted her to look at her back. It was massively scorched. "Who are you, *fräulein?*" he pondered.

"Whoever she is, she's here now," Alrich said. "I'll try to find a room away from the patients."

Mendelson agreed as he continued caressing the child's hair. The light from the lamps reflected against his blue eyes as his irises shifted in hue. In highly emotional events or sparks of curiosity, Mendelson was known to have his eyes shift in color. To those who knew him, like Alrich, this transition served as a conversational thermostat. To others, however, the change was both cautionary and unnerving. Freudric became infatuated with her presence the more he gazed at her. She was a mystery. Where did she come from? How did she come all the way to the asylum? She had a frightful pallor. Her black hair reminded him of raven feathers.

Alrich returned, holding a ring of keys. "I found a room." He paused. "What are you doing?"

"She's burned," Mendelson said. Alrich leaned forward. Freudric tilted the girl. He carefully pulled down her garment. "Look."

Alrich examined her wounds. He was deep in thought. "How long do you suppose they've been there?"

"I don't know," Freudric replied, laying her on her side. "But, whatever happened, I'd be more concerned on what she'll be like when she wakes up."

Alrich leaned over to pick her up. Freudric stopped him.

"You are covered in mud and God knows what else. Go take a bath." Freudric offered to bring the girl to her room. Alrich agreed, and tossed him the keys. The doctor retired to his study.

****

Mendelson hoisted the girl up into his arms. He carried her to the vacant room. The old staircase creaked beneath his feet. As he walked further from the lobby, the air smelled more of sweaty linen and medicine. The hallways were clear, but the windows were cluttered with greasy handprints.

The room was clean, and, like the bed, it was small. He washed her off. While washing her hair, he felt something odd. Betwixt her locks, there was something hard with a tiny chain. Untangling it, he wiped off the surface. It was an identification bracelet. He read it aloud, "Patient No. 11: Hael. Dr. Admin, MD." He couldn't decipher the rest of the inscription. It was melted. He looked at the bracelet again. "Hael? So, that's your name."

The girl didn't move at all. This child could be held from her ankles, and she would remain a rag doll. Her breathing was normal, but her slumber was alarming. For the rest of the night, Freudric observed her, and searched for any more injuries. He was wide awake. He thought through the proper course to take if anything would go wrong.

The rain slackened. He opened the window for some fresh air. The wind was cold and breezy. He draped another blanket over the girl to aid her warmth.

She coughed. It was a shallow cough, but the sound relieved the worst of his worries. He smiled and rubbed her back. He adjusted her pillow. "Hael, what happened to you?"

Chapter Three
Necessary Assessments

Alrich didn't fall asleep that night. As the pale blue light of dawn seeped through his windows, the doctor opened his cabinet drawer and took out his journal. With a nearly empty inkwell, he turned to a fresh page. He wrote:

April 2, 1872. Mendelson has been by the girl's side since she arrived. I think he said her name was Hael? I don't know. Some kind of gypsy name, perhaps. Judging by her hair and facial features, she's most likely some sort of gypsy. However, I've never known a caravan to lose one of their own before.

Hael is still asleep. The girl's vital signs are weak, but, according to Freudric, she's still breathing steadily. He's always been good with children, but I've never seen Freudric so concerned about a child.

I can't remember the last time I slept. The days are melding in with one another. I understand very well the demands and importance of my duties as a physician. But, for fuck's sake, can I get one damn hour of sleep? A quick nap, maybe?

Alrich closed his journal and placed his quill on the desk. After the ink dried, Alrich flipped through his previous journal entries. Some entries were brief while others talked for days.

He stopped at an ink-spattered page. Unlike his other entries, this page was chaotic. Gobs of black and red ink splashed from one end to the other. All across the paper, his handwriting morphed from fine calligraphy to chicken scratch. The page was a record of an event between Mendelson and himself concerning a series of experiments. But, the angry handwriting and pen slashes made it impossible to translate. Alrich's bloodshot eyes stared at the horizon. He looked down at the muddy ground. He recalled the night before with the little girl. As his thoughts gathered, the memories of his own rabid journal entry and Mendelson's trials slunk back in. He slammed the journal shut. Disgusted, he looked at his schedule as he adorned his vest. When the clock struck, the doctor left to check on the young girl.

****

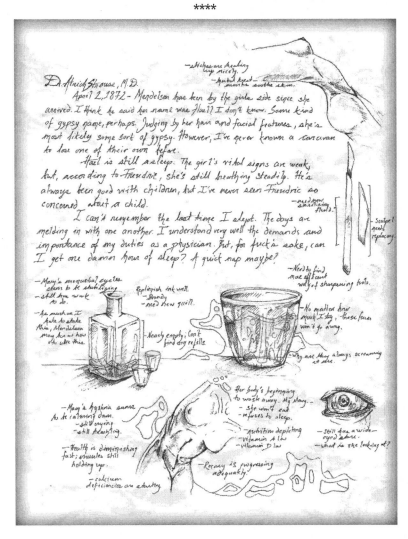

Alrich restlessly tapped his watch. He shook his head. He showed the clock face to his friend. "Is that really the time?" he asked. Freudric paid no attention. He sat quietly as he examined the bracelet. Alrich nibbled his fingernail. "Why isn't she awake?"

Freudric sighed. "Well, she was drowning in mud."

Alrich stopped pacing. "Do you think she's comatose?"

"What do you want me to say?" Freudric shrugged. "We don't know how long she was in that position." Alrich bit his finger and continued pacing the room.

Since he was a child, Alrich had a bad habit of gnawing his fingers when stressed. When his nerves were grated raw, he would unconsciously peel his skin from his cuticles to his knuckles. Alrich's fingers were terribly scarred. He wore gloves to hide his shame. It didn't work. At the end of the day, the dry patches of blood were obvious, and Alrich would need a new pair of gloves.

Mendelson pocketed the bracelet. He tried being optimistic. "I don't think that she was there for that long. The poor thing could just be exhausted."

Alrich remembered his childhood. "She's just like Martha," he said. "Aside from minor features, everything is my sister." Martha was Alrich Strauss's younger sister. Aside from Alrich, Mendelson was the only person who knew Martha's fate. The tragedy happened decades ago, but Alrich blamed himself for his sister's demise.

Mendelson observed his friend. Sleep deprived and teeth clamped down on his knuckle, Alrich was a mess. "Let's see how she's doing," Freudric said. "It's noon. She could be up." They walked to Hael's room.

****

Freudric grabbed the doorknob. The room was unlocked. Mendelson and Alrich were the only two who had the key to the room. Neither of them had checked on the girl during the past few hours.

Alrich opened the door. A nurse was checking for dirty laundry. "Where is she?" Freudric asked.

The nurse paused. She twiddled her fingers around her key ring.

Mendelson told Alrich to search the halls. He asked again, "Did you hear me? There was a little girl in here. Where is she?"

This nurse had the daily job of emptying clothes hampers from the rooms. "I don't know, sir. There was no one else here when I arrived."

This made no sense to Mendelson. For staff safety, all of the rooms in the asylum were locked from the outside. There was no way the girl could've left the room.

Alrich walked briskly from around the corner. Something confounded him. "Freudric, follow me."

"Did you find her?" asked Freudric.

Alrich pointed into the corridor. "Look at this."

Entranced at her reflection, the little girl sat on the ground in front of a large mirror in the corridor. She didn't blink, move, or acknowledge the two at the end of the hall.

"How did she leave the room?" Alrich asked.

Freudric walked up to her. He knelt down, and waved his hand past her eyes. He gently tapped her shoulder. "*Fräulein*, are you alright?" She didn't respond. He waved his hand again, "*Fräulein?*" She was totally still. He stood up. "Is she sleepwalking?"

Alrich shrugged his shoulders. "Most likely."

Mendelson knelt in front of her. "Do you hear me?" he asked.

She was oblivious. Her eyes were fastened and placid. She stared like a dead person.

He touched her arm. "Hael, can you hear me?"

The girl twitched violently. Her eyes snapped towards him. She bit at his wrist. Freudric yanked his arm away. A dim golden hue flickered in his eyes. Quickly, he grabbed her shoulders and held her down.

"Freudric, stop! She's sleepwalking," Alrich said. "If you disrupt her, she could go into shock. Don't disturb her."

"She almost bit me," Freudric said.

Hael stopped thrashing. Her body went limp. Freudric sat her against the wall.

Alrich pushed him. "You shocked her. I told you she was sleepwalking!"

"Quiet." Mendelson pointed to Hael. "Look."

The little girl shook her head. Lethargically, she looked up. Her glazed over eyes shifted as if they were soaked in molasses. She looked at the two men. "Hello." Her voice was soft, but it was very hoarse. "Where am I?"

Dr. Strauss knelt down to her. "You're in a hospital." He helped her up onto a chair. "Can you tell me your name?"

She did not respond.

Mendelson remembered the identification bracelet. He kept it to search for a clearer identity. He handed it to Alrich. "Here. It's not much, but this was on her last night."

Dr. Strauss studied the bracelet. "Is your name Hael?"

She shook her head in confusion before agreeing.

"Are you sure?" Alrich asked.

She stared at the ground, held the back of her head, and nodded.

Alrich handed the bracelet back to Mendelson. "Hael, do you remember anything of last night?" She shook her head. "Nothing?" he inquired.

"No." she replied. Alrich asked her who brought her to the forest.

"Did you bring me here?" Hael asked.

"No," Alrich replied. "We were hoping that you knew."

Her big eyes searched for answers. "I don't know."

Alrich asked her if she remembered where she came from. She didn't know. "What about your house? Parents?"

She shook her head.

He continued. "Do you have any pets? Dolls?"

She remembered nothing. Alrich bit his thumb. He dealt with amnesia patients before. The outcome was never good.

Freudric slapped Alrich's hand. "Stop it."

The little girl laughed. She rubbed the back of her head.

"Why do you keep on rubbing your head?" Alrich asked. "Does something hurt you?"

She continued rubbing her head. "My head feels funny." She rubbed harder. "Ow!" she yelped.

Strauss leaned towards her. "Let me see." She clasped her hands over her head. "It's okay, sweetheart. I'm a doctor. I'm here to help you."

"No!" Hael grimaced. A tear fell down her face like a diamond.

"Don't cry. Let me take a look, and I promise that I'll make the pain stop."

Hael still refused.

Mendelson rolled his eyes and pushed Alrich to the side. He put his hand under her chin and raised her head. She shut her eyes. Reaching into his pocket, Freudric pulled out a necklace. As a precaution, the staff was instructed to remove all accessories from the patients. The storage rooms were filled with jewelry. The necklace was silver and adorned with three sapphire roses.

"Were did you get that?" asked Alrich.

"I confiscated this from a patient earlier today," he said. Before dawn that day, one of Mendelson's patients had those shimmering roses stuffed between her labia. After she passed a surprise inspection, she lodged her head under the mattress, slipped out the necklace, and choked herself unconscious. After confiscating it, Mendelson sterilized the necklace.

As Mendelson shook the chain, the jewel roses made a lighthearted twinkling sound. Curiously, Hael opened one of her eyes. After seeing the sparkling, iridescent blue, she pawed at the roses. Mendelson teasingly moved the chain so that her little fingers barely touched the edges. He smiled at Alrich. "This works every time."

Alrich scoffed. "Bribing patients doesn't make a good doctor."

"No," Mendelson smirked, "but it does make one hell of a salary." He continued teasing Hael. "You want this?"

She nodded and reached for the roses.

Mendelson laughed and pocketed the necklace. "Let's make a deal. I'll give you the necklace if you show me what's hurting you."

She paused. Her hands slowly retreated as she contemplated.

"You know, there's a lovely woman down the hall who'd love to have this."

"It hurts right here!" Hael interjected. She pointed to the back of her head.

He adorned her with the necklace. "Was that so hard?" She fiddled with the roses. "Be a good girl, and let the nice doctor see what's wrong. Okay?" She shook his hand in agreement.

Mendelson stepped to the side. Alrich rolled his eyes and proceeded with the examination. Like handling thin pieces of glass, Alrich carefully combed through her hair. He jolted. There was an open gash beneath her feathered locks. The wound was deep and cauterized around the edges. The doctor paled. *"Mein Gott!"*

"What's the matter?" Mendelson asked, leaning inward. Like a rabbit gawking in open space, Freudric's eyes dashed back and forth from the wound to his friend. He whispered, "How is she still conscious?" The doctor had his hand over his mouth. By the size of the gash, she should've been comatose or dead. They were baffled.

Alrich patted Hael's shoulder. "Good girl."

Hael tugged his coat. "I don't need any medicine, do I? I hate needles."

Besides his nervous tick, Alrich kept his emotions undisclosed. However, this situation pushed his discipline. "No. No medicine at all," he said, smiling. "But, for now, go with the nurse. She'll take care of you. Nurse Brimfield!"

The clacking of hard soled shoes reverberated against the walls. Within moments, an elderly woman with silvery bouncing hair ran into the hallway. "Nurse Brimfield, please escort Miss Hael into her room." Alrich turned Hael around so the nurse could see the wound. "Make sure she's warm."

"Shall I give her some of my special tea, Dr. Strauss?" the nurse asked.

"Good idea. Make it a tall glass."

Beyond the scores of infamous tools within his arsenal of control, Brimfield's tea was the nectar of Strauss's garden. Nurse Brimfield, like the majority of his employees, had sketchy pasts. With a drunkard father and her mother trialed as a witch by the church, Ondine Brimfield paved her way out of poverty and an early death. At age thirteen, Ondine's mother was sentenced to hang. Ondine postponed her mother's execution by drugging the accusers with home brewed herbal tea. Her tea was concocted from plants out of her mother's notebook. The plants she picked were seen as bewitched since they brought upon heavy sleeping spells to whoever drank their essence. With their warm tea upon the scaffold, the executioner and her mother's accusers fell hard to the cobblestones, breaking their necks. But, Ondine's victory was short-lived. Once the courts found replacements, her mother was hanged, and officials searched for the culprit. By that time, Ondine was gone. Later on in her years, she was discovered by Dr. Strauss and Mendelson. Together, they perfected her tea to the point where they could craft whatever sleep they desired.

****

Hael sipped the tea. Steam delicately wrapped around her face. Golden, honeyed drops dripped from the side of her mouth. Swiftly, sleep took over her. Ondine laid Hael down, and rubbed her back.

Dr. Strauss entered the room. "Is she asleep?"

Ondine nodded. Ondine had never shown fondness of children. But, the nurse had a questionable look about her. Her expression was kind, almost motherly. Alrich never saw Ondine like this. "What's wrong?" Alrich asked.

Ondine paused. "I'm just remembering my mother's stories."

"Which stories?"

She smiled faintly at Hael. "She's like a changeling. She was found near the woods. No one knows where she came from, or how she got here. For your sake, I hope she brings you luck. And, for her sake, I hope you keep your friend in line."

Alrich chuckled. "Freudric would never hurt a child."

"Oh, I know. But, a woman is a different animal." Ondine wasn't a worrisome woman, but she was wary of a man's intentions. Especially those of Mendelson.

"She's just a little girl," Alrich said.

She stood from the bed. "For now she is." She opened the door. "I'll be back shortly to suture her injury." She left the room. Alrich was perplexed by the conversation. He never knew Ondine to be so enthralled with a patient, or seem so protective of one. After a second observation, Alrich left soon after. Hael slept in silence as stray locks tickled her nose.

****

Over hilltops and dense woods, miles away from the asylum, a manor lay in ruin. Mounds of ash and burnt brick littered the dead grass. The air was pregnant with the stench of scorched flesh and bone. A collection of crushed hands jutted out beneath bars of charred wood like weeds. Death left no quarter. Even the wind was on its last breath.

A smoldering finger was lodged in a wine bottle. A garnet ring was melted onto the skin. A man stood over it. Horrified, he scanned the ruins. Panicking, he ran to the far side of the rubble near the tree line.

In the ash, a strip of white lace covered a tiny severed

arm. He held the back of the hand. A dark figure loomed over him. "This wasn't supposed to happen." David wept. "This shouldn't have happened. Not like this."

A black boot heel cracked the arm in half. David launched at the shadowed figure. "You son of a bitch!"

Immediately, David was hoisted into the air. He was strangling. His lips turned blue. Dangling, his legs shook violently to break free.

The temperature dropped significantly. The cold was ungodly. The trees and surrounding flora wilted. Nature wasn't prepared for such change.

Red molten eyes sneered at David. "You idiot." The figure flung David like a used rag against a dilapidated wall. Loose bricks cut his brow. The man's shadow draped over him. "What use do I have of you flinching like a woman?" He struck David across the face. All that could be seen from the shadow was the metal end of a cane.

"That wasn't the girl," the man said. He walked over to the crushed hand. "This was her husband's child."

"How?" David asked. "Teresa's visit wasn't due till June."

This man's voice was deep, and it reverberated off the dead. "Was that a question?" David clutched his chest. His face blanched as his wound reopened underneath his vest. "I couldn't tell," the man said. "Was that a question?"

David wheezed. "No!"

"No?"

Blood spewed from David's mouth. He fell to his knees. He strained. "No, Sire!" The blood stopped.

The man's shadow covered David again. "That girl is not here. Nobody survives a blazing house fire like this, or flees very far from it. The arsonists were unknown. But, whoever started the fire took the girl as well."

David looked at the earth. "There are footprints running into the forest."

He snatched David by the hair. "Nobody steals my property."

David plummeted onto the sharp rubble. He held his throat. "Sire, may I ask a question?"

He turned towards David. He read David's thoughts. "If she was here, I would have smelled her body from the ashes," he replied.

The man walked towards the finger-corked wine bottle. He snapped the finger in half and pulled the melted ring from the bone. "My patience ran very thin with this household," he said. "Although the fire was a saving grace from that arrogant hussy, everyone here belongs to me."

The man examined Elizabeth's ring. Remembering his notes and the green flames within the fireplace, the man ached to return to its solitude. "Return the girl to me," he ordered. In the palm of his hand, shadows swallowed the ring. The man snapped his fingers. "David."

David hung his head in defeat and kneeled before him. "Yes Sire?"

"Hunt down the culprits. Search everywhere and bring them to me. I want them alive."

Chapter Four
Animals

Peacefully, Hael rested in the wings of sleep. Nurse Brimfield sutured her wounds. Unlike with her other patients, Ondine took great care not to botch the job. Steady and articulated, she handled the needle like repairing a bridal gown. She sealed and sterilized the wound, but time would need to heal it.

When Ondine finished suturing, Mendelson sketched the wound into his notes. Though his drawings were crude, they were never exaggerated nor censored. Freudric was a wonderful illustrator.

Throughout the following weeks, Mendelson made it his personal endeavor to find Hael's family. He took multiple photographs of Hael. He went into the city to visit the various orphanages and work houses. He showed her picture to every police department. The officers informed him that there were many missing girls, but none of them matched her description. The work house leaders and school matrons didn't recognize her either. There were no records of her at any orphanage. "Have you seen this child?" he asked them. No one knew who she was. He sat in his room at an inn. "How could no one know her?" he asked himself.

He exhausted every resource. At the end of his search, reality sank in. To London, Hael did not exist. Weary with disappointment, Mendelson packed his bags and left the city.

****

The sky was gray for days. London was a silhouette. It began to drizzle. Mendelson was happy to leave the city. He was a charismatic man as well as a grandeur linguist who could top the most gracious of hosts. But, he was only talkative when time called for it. He was not a socialite.

He grimaced at the smell of the city's common people. Mendelson possessed a very sensitive palate and nose. Whatever he smelled, he could taste to a certain degree. He could tolerate the countryside's smell, but city people were sour and foul. They were like animals. They reeked of open sewer and spoiled meat. As more of the city faded into the distance, the more content he became.

The rain draped over the carriage. Mendelson leaned his head against the cushioned seats, and looked at the clouds. Taking off his hat and glasses, he rubbed his temples. He watched the raindrops slide down the glass. They pooled and tumbled over the door. He listened to the sounds of the horses' hooves kicking up dirt as the carriage wheels smoothed the earth back down again. With his head pressed against the door, in minutes, he drifted to sleep.

****

Something slammed into the side of the coach, flipping it over. Mendelson's leg banged against the door's frame. The horses whinnied. They strained to break free of their harnesses. The coachman, Anthony, was thrown from his seat. Mendelson saw him plummet into a nearby ditch. Anthony's screams faded as he continued to tumble into the forest.

Steadying himself, Freudric flung open the coach door. Broken glass shattered onto his face. Holding his eye, he scanned the area. Nobody was there. He removed his hand. His eye wasn't cut, but his brow was bleeding.

He looked at the carriage. There was a large dent in the door. "Where are you?" Mendelson yelled. "You fucking coward! I know someone's out there!" He flicked his blood off his fingers. "Show yourself!"

Everything was silent. He didn't see anything, but, through experience, Mendelson knew when he was being watched.

He looked at the horses. With hooves deep into the ground, they were still in their harnesses. They were huddled together in fear.

"Anthony!" Mendelson called out to the coachman. "Anthony! Where are you?" His leg still ached from the impact. He ran towards the ditch. Anthony was gone. Freudric studied the ground. In deep grooves, the imprints from Anthony's body streaked into the forest.

Freudric crouched down. Removing his glove, he shoved his hand deep into the dirt. He closed his eyes. Gradually, the rain became muted. In the background, the horses grew more distraught as they distanced themselves from Mendelson. Freudric's fingers sank deeper into the earth. The feeling enticed him. Soft and wet, he smiled as the earth enveloped him like a woman's sex.

He could hear everything around him. From the insects scurrying underneath the wood's foliage to the panicking rhythms of the horses' hearts, nothing was out of earshot.

A scream echoed from the woods! "Help!" Anthony cried. "Help! Jesus Christ! Help me!"

Freudric slipped his hand out of the earth. Like an unstoppable force of nature, Mendelson burst into the thick of the woods. If it wasn't for the rushing wind in his path, he'd be impossible to detect. Freudric dodged his way through the trees. Anthony's scent grew stronger.

He stopped running. Anthony was against a tree trunk. The mangled coachman had his eyes rolled up towards God. His shredded arms and entrails were spread over the roots like margarine. The soil slurped his blood. From his jaw to his clavicle, deep claw marks stripped Anthony's bones.

Mendelson sat next to his friend. He took off his tie and gloves. Freudric seethed with rage as he clenched his fist. He couldn't detect the culprit. His eyes pulsed with an abnormal color. He tried to regain himself while closing Anthony's eyes.

The horses whinnied in the distance. Sprinting for its life, one of the horses dashed past Anthony's corpse. Splattered with blood, it fled into the woods. Freudric ran out to his toppled coach.

A headless horse dangled over the coach in shreds. Mendelson ran towards the whinnying. He stopped. Something snarled behind the trees. He picked up a severed hoof and crept closer.

With ravenous hunger, a large wolf attacked another horse. Mendelson threw the severed hoof at the wolf's head. The hit's impact resonated like a gunshot.

The beast snapped at him! With blood-drenched fangs, it growled as it sized him up. Its fur was dark and matted. Bare spots of peeled skin covered its back. The creature's paws were massive. One paw could easily collapse a rib cage. Its claws scraped the gravel down to nothing.

Mendelson stood his ground. Removing his shoes, he straightened his back and loosened his belt. He smiled. Tightly, he coiled his leather belt around his fist with the buckle hanging at the end. Observing his appearance, one would find it hard to believe that Freudric was a skilled woodsman. From wolves to bears, Mendelson survived many feral encounters.

However, this wolf was different. Locking onto his target, Freudric knew that there was something abnormal about his opponent. Besides Anthony and the horses' massacre, the wolf's gaze was too focused, too intentional.

With the snap of his belt, the wolf sprang at Freudric's neck. He whipped the buckle across its face. The force hit the beast like a stampede. The creature rolled to the ground. Freudric launched at the wolf and wrapped his belt around its neck. He beat its skull with the metal buckle.

The wolf gnashed its teeth into his wrist. Like a steam hammer, Freudric pounded the wolf's scalp to break its grip. The animal's eye was swollen shut, but it was still determined.

Freudric gnashed his teeth down onto the beast's ear, and ripped it off. It howled in pain. With his wrist freed, Mendelson threw the animal against a boulder. Whenever he tossed his enemies, Mendelson made sure to execute the move with the upmost brute force, making it a fatal blow. Sure of his victory,

Freudric tore his shirt to wrap his wound.

The wolf rebounded. It latched onto the back of his knee. The creature's maw nearly engulfed his entire leg. Mendelson dropped his full weight onto the wolf and pinned it to the rocks. It scrammed from underneath him with exact timing. The wolf bit off Mendelson's coat pocket and ran. Within a matter of seconds, the beast vanished into the woods.

Freudric's knees buckled as he rose from the ground. Foaming mad, he looked back at the dead horse and the broken skeleton of the coach. Anthony's trampled entrails reeked from the woods. Like hearing children's fingernails scrape against chalkboards, the sound of the crows' beaks nauseated Freudric as they stripped Anthony's meat from the bones.

Mendelson bled severely. He wiped the blood from his neck. Though it didn't go very far, one badly cut horse managed to get away. He found the horse and rode bareback to the asylum.

As he swayed on the horse along the dirt road, he boiled over the fight. "I should've wrung its neck." he said. He reached for his cigar case. He paused. Feeling his side, he realized that his pocket was ripped. He tightened his fist. "Damn it!"

Hael's photograph was gone.

****

Halfway down the path, the horse collapsed from blood loss. Freudric continued on foot into the night. The freezing wind bellowed down from the hill tops. As the wind moved through sharp branches, a weary traveler would fear that banshees were rampaging at his heels.

Damp, bloody, and horribly bitten, Freudric hauled himself to the asylum. Nurse Brimfield was in the lobby with a large ring of keys. She was about to lock up for the night. Freudric slammed his shoulder against the door. The edge nearly hit Ondine across her temple.

She screamed and jumped back. He propped himself against the door and pocketed his broken glasses. She gawked at him, for she'd never seen so much blood on him before. "What happened to you?"

Freudric said nothing as he limped to the couch.

"Where's your coach?" Ondine asked. "Where's Anthony?"

He spat blood onto the floor and told her to get his cigars.

"You're bleeding everywhere!"

He slammed his fist onto the table. "Go get my damn smokes!"

Ondine ran. His fist nearly cracked the table's veneer.

She reached Alrich's study. Frantically, she called for the doctor. "Dr. Strauss! Come quick!"

Alrich walked out from his study. Frowning, he spoke raggedly, "Do you know what time it is?"

"Your friend just came home. He's covered in blood!"

Alrich rubbed his eye. "Quiet."

She continued, "Antony's not with him!"

"I said quiet."

"The coach is missing!"

"Silence!" he ordered. His shout stunned her ears. Ondine sat down. Alrich put on his shoes. "Where is he?"

She wiped a tear from one eye. "He's in the lobby."

****

Alrich walked into the lobby. Freudric was on the couch with his leg crossed over his knee. He clasped his hands together in his lap. He sighed. "Bitch can't even fetch my smokes."

"Here." Alrich tossed Freudric his cigar case. "Have some of mine."

Freudric opened the case. He picked one out and bit off the end. He never needed to use a cigar clipper. He held the cigar. "I'm supposed to light this with my mouth?"

Alrich tossed him a match. "The way you are? Yes." Mendelson lit the cigar.

"What happened?" Alrich asked.

Freudric didn't respond.

He asked again, "What the hell happened to you?"

"That's not what happened first," Freudric said. Behind the smoke cloud, his blue eyes pierced through the gray.

"Okay. So, should I ask where Antony is first?"

"Yes. That's better." Mendelson blew another stream of smoke in the air. "He's dead."

"Dead?"

"Dead." Mendelson wasn't rattled by the wolf. Massacres never bothered him. He was angry because he didn't snap its neck. He limped towards the window. "It was horrid. The poor boy was ripped to pieces by a pack of wolves."

Alrich sat down. "Wolves attacked you?"

"Pack about seven. I got out. The horses were obviously going to run away." He took another puff of his cigar. "Anthony was the first to go. I tried to save him, but he was dragged off before I could get a good grip."

Alrich paused. "Good grip?" Alrich didn't believe him. "After all the experimentations you've had, you didn't get a good grip?"

"I have my off days, Alrich. You blame me for being human?"

Alrich snickered. "Human."

Mendelson cut his eyes at him. "Don't start." He walked towards the lobby entrance, and jiggled the doorknob. "You think you're so much better."

Alrich snatched the cigar case from him. "At least I don't relish in it." The two glared at each other.

"We'll have a memorial service for Anthony tomorrow. There's no use looking for the body," Freudric said.

Alrich walked away. "Go clean up. You're a mess."

"I always am." Freudric extinguished his cigar against the window. The ashes fell to the ground.

****

After washing away the dried blood, Freudric wrapped his wounds and went to his room. As he walked down the hall, he passed by Hael's room. The door was open.

Ondine sat on Hael's bedside. "She's still asleep," she said.

Mendelson observed Hael from the door. Ondine loathed him. Even though his injuries were alarming, she smiled at his cut flesh. "You should get to sleep, sir. You'll need the rest."

"Has she been asleep this whole time?" he inquired.

"Yes," she said. "She's had a peaceful day."

"Did she?" he asked. Ondine ignored him. He smirked. "I should know better. A witch knows how to brew her cauldron."

Ondine bit her tongue. "Not all witches have cauldrons, sir." She wrung the towel. "However, it's best not to cross one. One could end up getting cursed."

He chuckled in his throat. "I wish you'd fucking try." He closed the door.

Chapter Five
Difficult Discussions

As the months flew by, with no sign of a family, Mendelson decided to keep Hael at the asylum. He didn't want to put her into an orphanage. A sweet child with excellent manners, she carefully listened to her surroundings by either reading lips or having her ear to the door. When the doctors or patients talked to her, she wasn't scared. She was neither intimidated nor the least bit nervous. Being in that environment, it would be impossible to keep her away from all of the patients. But, both Mendelson and Ondine made sure she was placed far away from the loquacious and volatile inhabitants.

Hael was curious, but stealthy. She moved like a water snake. Rarely, staff members would see Hael's chocolate eyes peeping from behind doors and hall corners. She timed herself as she sneaked behind the doctors into the restricted areas.

However, she was never victorious. Mendelson always caught her. She was a pondering, adventurous child who grew easily bored by tedious activities. Mendelson understood this. He would let her get away with some mischief. Hael was fond of practical jokes. Occasionally, she either switched the doctors' pens with the nurses' eyeliner pencils, or emptied Alrich's flask to replace the contents with apple cider vinegar. Freudric chuckled at her games, but he stopped her when she'd done enough damage. Mendelson reprimanded her for her foolery in front of the staff. But, when the crowd dispersed and the rooms quieted down, Mendelson and Hael laughed at her various pranks.

Mendelson was vigilant. He'd always catch her sneaking around. But, he never lost his patience. He was a fun-loving man with children of his own. To keep her entertained, he gave her his drawing paper and assortments of ink to paint with when he was at work. Like the blue roses she wore around her neck, he was close to her. He was her friend. And, the more Mendelson came to know her, the more concerned he grew about having her reside in the asylum. Freudric guarded her from any hostilities and kept her happy. But, it was unhealthy to have such a young girl amidst such unsavory people.

Alrich wasn't surprised. When it came down to children, Freudric would either be nonchalant or completely fascinated. Occasionally, the asylum received children, but Freudric decided to create a different institution. He built and led the Halcyon Asylum for Orphaned Children. Unlike other youth institutions, Freudric gave them elocution classes, proper etiquette, and a superior education.

****

Alrich was asleep in his chair. His arms were wrapped around a book. Nurse Brimfield entered the room. "Any refreshments, Dr. Strauss?"

He jumped. "No. No thank you."

She placed the teapot back onto the tray. Alrich twiddled his fingers on top the book cover. Her beady eyes squinted at the book's spine. Alrich was reading about the female anatomy.

"What?" he asked.

"You still have that book?" She folded her arms, "I thought you said that book was obsolete. You must have studied it so much that you bent the spine."

Alrich yawned. "I needed it as a reference."

"For what?" she asked.

"I can't discard a book until I know every chapter from cover to cover." Alrich said. He kept old books in his study for the other doctors' references. Alrich had too much pride in his memory to reread something he already mastered. "I've encountered an anomaly." He looked out the window, "This girl, Hael, is about eight or nine years old. Correct?"

"She's nine, sir."

"How do you know?" he asked.

"I asked her how old she was."

The doctor adjusted his glasses. "Very well. Nine."

"What's so important about that?" Ondine asked.

"If she's nine years old, why is she menstruating?"

Ondine stared at the doctor. She was taken aback by that statement. With her injuries, Hael must've escaped from a horrible accident. Alrich's assumptions worried her. "She could be hemorrhaging from the inside."

Alrich disagreed. "No. I had the blood analyzed. She's menstruating. Besides, if she was hemorrhaging for this long, she would be dead by now."

"That's not right," Ondine said. She poured herself a cup of tea. "What's wrong with her?"

"I don't know," Alrich said. "The girl has no other symptoms of any hormonal imbalances or other reproductive abnormalities." He didn't know why she was menstruating at such a young age. He shrugged. "But, she seems alright for now. Whatever she endured isn't haunting her anymore. Besides, her head injury should be healing up nicely."

Ondine finished her tea. She rolled her fingers against the chair's arm. "Her head's healed."

"What?" he asked.

"It's nothing but a scar," she assured the doctor.

"There's no way a gash like that can fully heal in less than two months."

Ondine sighed. "Think what you want. Don't be surprised when you see it though." She took her tray and left the room.

Mendelson entered the hallway. The two stood side by

side. Mendelson glared at Ondine. She turned her nose up at him.

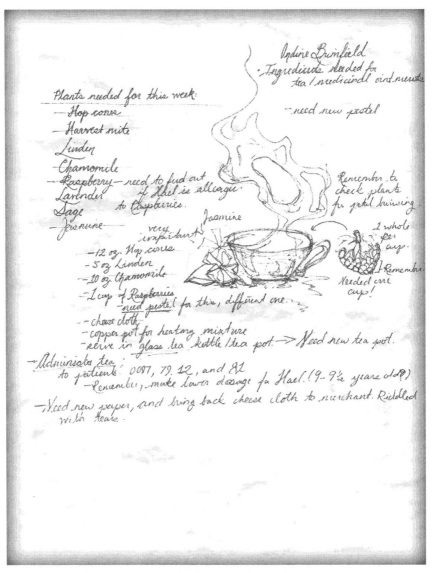

Mendelson wasn't disgusting to be around. He was well groomed, and he had a pleasant demeanor. But, there was something wrong about him, very wrong. There was nothing diminished about his features. He had a wealth of intelligence, and he was very eloquent. Some people commented that his color shifting eyes were unsettling. Others cringed at his Cheshire cat grin. No one could determine the source of their uneasiness. But, one thing held firm: prolonged exposure to him made one's skin crawl.

As the subordinate of the two, Ondine knew her place. She stepped aside to let him pass. He took one of the teacups before proceeding into Alrich's study. He glared at her. "What the hell are you looking at?"

"You're welcome, fat ass."

He shut the door behind him. Alrich snickered as Freudric sipped his tea.

"What's so damn funny?"

Alrich burst into laughter. "You two haven't stopped going at each other's necks since you met!"

Mendelson threw his clipboard at Alrich. The doctor laughed harder. It was funny how mad Ondine made him. "After all these years, she still pisses you off!"

Freudric cracked his fingers. "That woman's lucky she's of use to you. If it wasn't for that damn tea of hers, I would've ended her by now."

"Why so harsh? I thought you liked independent women?"

"I like independent women. Not insane."

"You don't like challenges?" Alrich asked.

"I love challenges. I don't like guilt-ridden hags who think they know everything."

Alrich crossed his feet on top his desk. He pushed away some of the papers. "So, if there was a woman with a mind as sharp as her tongue, you wouldn't complain?"

Mendelson finished his tea. "I would be happy!"

Alrich smirked. "You said it."

"That's not why I'm here," Mendelson said. Alrich gave him his full attention. "It's about Hael."

"Let me guess. It's her new condition?"

Freudric paused. "Her what?"

"Do you know what I'm talking about?" Alrich asked.

Mendelson shook his head.

"Never mind it. What did you want to tell me?" Alrich asked.

For the past months, Freudric kept a close eye on Hael. "I've noticed that Hael possesses a higher understanding, respect, and common sense than most young ladies her age." Mendelson said. "And, with her youth, I'm concerned about her residing in the asylum. Hael can't stay here anymore."

"Why not?" Alrich asked.

"It's an asylum, Alrich."

"So?"

"It's an asylum," he repeated. "She doesn't belong here."

"You've searched for any possible relations. There are none," Alrich said. "What do you propose?"

Freudric explained that it would be better if he housed Hael in his other institution.

"I thought that the orphanage was at maximum capacity?" Alrich asked.

"No. I don't want her to go in there. I want her in the Männlein Waisenhaus."

With a combination of land deeds, inheritance, and his father's military pension, Freudric Mendelson was an exceedingly wealthy man. Alrich remembered Mendelson's words before opening Halcyon Asylum. *The two things, Alrich, which the world will never run out of are: illegitimate children and mentally unstable people that nobody wants to exist.* Having this philosophy and wealth, Freudric built numerous orphanages and asylums throughout Germany, Austria, and England. Alongside Halcyon Asylum, Das Männlein Waisenhaus was one of the golden children of Mendelson's business affairs. Das Männlein Waisenhaus was famous for taking in unfortunate wards of the state and the abandoned while turning them into the highest pedigree of modeled citizens. Through his institution, Mendelson molded outstanding politicians, doctors, public speakers, and other institutional leaders. However, beyond the public eye, Mendelson's draconian methods and regulations danced infamously with cruelty and madness.

"Why don't you want her to stay here?" Alrich asked.

Alrich bit his tongue. "I have my reasons."

Seeing Hael as his little sister, Alrich was protective. "You saw what she's afflicted with," Alrich said. "Why do you want a recovering child to travel all the way to Germany?"

Freudric adjusted his neck. "Alrich, we're friends, right?"

Alrich nodded his head.

Freudric continued, "Did I not shovel out the money to build this asylum where you could be Head of Staff instead of working under a quack doctor?"

Alrich sat up in his chair. "True. But, I put a lot of my time into this place as well."

Freudric lifted his finger. "If it's true, then why are you questioning me?"

Alrich said nothing.

"I built these institutions. So, if I want Hael in Germany, it's going to happen." Alrich stared at him questionably. "Don't give me that look. I got mauled by wolves. Anthony's dead. Hael's picture is gone. And, no one on this godforsaken rock knows she exists!

"I have better connections over there anyway. She may have family elsewhere."

This discussion was difficult for Alrich. Freudric was great with kids. But, in his mind, something hollered at Alrich to keep her far away from him. But, Mendelson was his superior. He had no choice. Alrich agreed.

"Good," Freudric said. "I need to get my things ready. I'm supposed to return to Germany within the week. Have her ready by Friday."

"Why do you need to go back so soon?" Alrich asked. "Didn't you settle everything?"

"It never hurts to be safe."

****

Dr. Strauss was booked for the afternoon. His patients weren't as volatile as the months beforehand. But, nevertheless, his exhaustion lingered long after his shift was over.

In his study, opposite from his desk, Alrich's day bed stretched along the wall's bookshelf. The length was modified to ensure comfort for his legs. He plopped down onto the mattress. The springs squeaked under his shoulders. With a stiff neck and aching feet, Alrich fell asleep.

Moments later, his slumber was interrupted when Ondine came into the room. Irritated, he looked up at her. "What now, Ondine?"

Her face was stern. Her eyes were halfway open in hate. She could petrify a Gorgon. Alrich sat up. "What's wrong?"

She slammed the door.

"What's wrong?" he repeated.

She stormed up to him. "You're letting that bastard take that sweet girl to Germany."

"He's not a bastard," he interjected.

"He's a no good son of a bitch! I swear, if he takes her, I'll ruin you."

Alrich tightened his fist. "Who the hell do you think you're talking to?"

She slapped him across his face. Throughout her stay, Ondine kept Hael away from the poisoned words and leers of the manic inhabitants. "That little girl is important to me, Alrich! You know what happens in that orphanage!"

Alrich made no response.

"Do you really want her to become one of *them*?"

Alrich peered out the window. "Keep your voice down."

"*Seine kinder?*" She wiped her face. Ondine and Alrich knew Hael wasn't normal. Biologically, there was something peculiar about the girl. Ondine closed the curtains. "He can't take her."

He placed his hand against the bed frame. "What the hell do you expect me to do? I'm already over my neck in debt to him."

"What about the women you gave to him?" she asked. "What about the trafficking? That wasn't enough?"

He ran his fingers through his hair. "It barely scratched the surface."

Alrich could fake a lot of expressions, but the way he looked when he brought Hael in from the storm was genuine. He thought of Hael as his sister. He cared for her, and he wanted her protected. Ondine bit her lip. "You'll never forgive yourself if you let her go with him."

He wiped his neck. "It's not wise to cheat him."

Ondine grinned. For years, she waited for an opportunity to beat Freudric at his own game. "Leave it to me," she said.

"What are you going to do?" Alrich asked.

She straightened her apron. "Just play along."

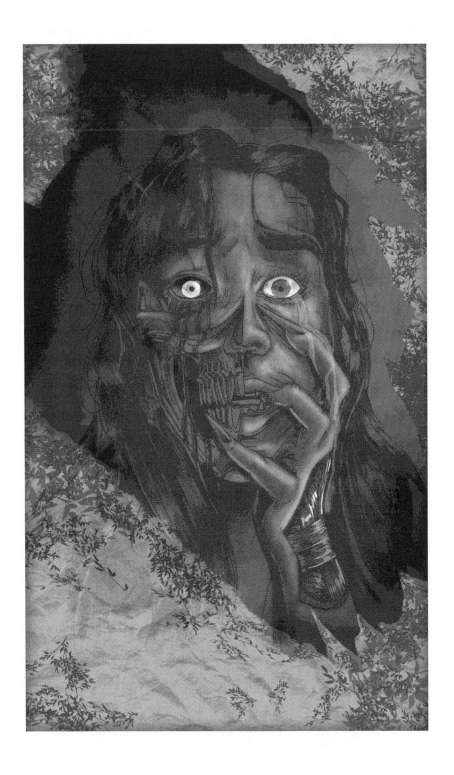

Chapter Six
Her Scullery Maid

Over the years, Alrich religiously documented his days in a journal. His study was too chaotic, and his mind was cluttered. His journal was the only space where he could think in private. He wrote:

June 12, 1884. I never thought I'd be grateful for rain. Everyone here is counting their blessings. Last year's heat wave has failed to repeat itself. The last thing anyone wants to do is to sedate a patient in an oven.

Freudric is still in Germany. For what, I don't know. That lying bastard. I have no idea what's happened to him. He wrote saying that the money for the asylum's repairs will be sent post haste, but nothing has been received.

Astounding as it is, Ondine was right. It was a terrible idea to let Hael go with Freudric. I'm thankful to Brimfield and her work. I'm glad I trusted her.

****

Alrich remembered the stage Ondine set years ago. Hael was very still. She was laid out across the bed. Nurse Brimfield stood over her. She shook Hael's shoulders, trying to wake her up. Hael's eyes were shut tight. Alarmed, Ondine called out her name. The child did not stir. Ondine ran out of the room, crying, "Dr. Strauss! Dr. Strauss! Come quick!"

Alrich rushed out of bed. "What's going on?"

She pounded her fist against the door. "Hael. Come quickly! She's not breathing!"

Wasting no time, Alrich ran to Hael's room barefoot and half-dressed. When he opened the door, Mendelson was already inside standing by her bedside. His hands were behind his back. The air around Mendelson was quiet and eerily still. Freudric's voice was dark. "She's not breathing, doctor."

Days ago, Hael came down with a terrible fever. Her sheets were drenched with sweat, and her appetite was severely diminished. Ondine closed the door. "I came in here to administer her medicine. I tried to wake her, but she won't move."

Mendelson ignored Ondine. Alrich walked up to Hael. He looked for a rise and fall in her chest as he checked her pulse. There was no heartbeat or breath, but her skin was still warm. Ondine had made her move. Wary of Mendelson's attitude, Alrich steadied his hands and calmed his breathing as he played along. "She must have hemorrhaged," he said.

"What?"

"Looks can be deceiving. All of the cuts, burns, and bruises must've taken a toll on her. She was only nine. Her body couldn't handle the trauma," Alrich said. "Judging by her pallor and temperature, she must've passed on no less than an hour ago."

Freudric sighed. He brushed the hair from his face. "It's a shame that science can't reverse such tragedies. A gem like her shouldn't be buried underground." He walked to the door. "I should've been in Germany a week ago. I have to leave tonight." He didn't want to leave Hael. Alrich never saw him like this before. Because he was a military man, Mendelson's posture was solid. However, as he looked at Hael's body, Mendelson's shaking chest was on the verge of collapsing. Freudric didn't weep. But, he couldn't mask his pain. "It hurts to do this, but I must leave tonight. Take whatever expenses you'll need to take care of her."

"Anything in specific?" Alrich asked.

Mendelson removed the necklace and gazed at the jeweled roses. He remembered how she used to play as the roses danced around her neck. For his closure and sanity, Mendelson pocketed the necklace to take with him to Germany. "Fill her casket with roses."

"What color?" Ondine asked.

"Every color you can find. She loved them all."

****

Alrich completed his journal entry. With Ondine's help, Alrich was able to keep Hael away from the asylum. Until she reached a suitable age, Ondine wanted dearly for Hael to live with her.

****

Alrich opened his journal. He entered his daily contemplations:

February 22, 1896. Ondine's health continues to diminish as of late. It may be a case of mild tuberculosis. She's been coughing up dark brown phlegm like clockwork. The tone of her face now complements the white of her eyes, and her hands are in a perpetual tremor. However, she works as perfectly as always. Although she performs her duties with the same speed and dexterity as before, I've decided to put her on paid leave until her condition turns for the better. She's pleased with the idea.

Ever since Ondine insisted upon more work, she decided that it would be wise to let Hael stay by her sister in Belfast. As promised, Hael's education has been upheld to my standards. Hael has been sending me letters about her journey and other activities. She seems happy.

I haven't heard from Freudric in twelve years. He told me that he had unfinished business to tend to back in Germany, and that he would return in six months. I sense the worst. Hopefully, he is not dead, but, knowing his nature, it wouldn't be a surprise.

****

Ondine lived in a small abode within the woods. It was a quaint little house with a large garden next to a shallow pond. Her house was far from the asylum, but Ondine had a private coach with excellent horses.

Ondine returned home, exhausted. She suffered from coughing fits. Her eyes rolled as she shook the water off her coat.

"Ms. Ondine!" a young woman called out. "You shouldn't have gone out today! I told you that the weather would be dreary." The young woman escorted Ondine inside.

"Oh, don't worry yourself about me, Hael." Ondine chuckled. "If I could withstand the asylum, I'll deal with this rain, dear."

Hael bit her lip as she studied Ondine's movements. "You've been so sick. I don't want you to get any worse." She helped Ondine take off her coat. She placed it near the stove to dry it out. She helped Ondine onto the couch and unlaced her shoes. "Supper is almost done. The potatoes are mashed, but the roast still has a little bit to go."

Ondine placed her hand on Hael's cheek. "Such a good girl."

Hael placed the shoes by the door. She checked the roast in the oven.

"How's your head, love?" Ondine asked.

"Better. The headaches are still bad. But they're better than before."

"I worry about your headaches." Ondine wrung the rain water from her hair. "Are you sure?"

"Don't worry yourself. I can manage," Hael replied.

Ondine rubbed her palms together.

Hael locked the door. "Are you ready for supper, ma'am?"

Ondine smiled. "Let's eat."

****

Hael was Ondine's treasure. She schooled Hael in everything she knew. She showed Hael how to read, write legibly, understand rhetoric arguments, and analyze assessments. She taught her the skill of inference while schooling her in botany and biology. From her mother's notes, Ondine taught Hael astrology, calculations, horticulture, and the superstitions of the world. To Hael, Ondine was a blessing. Ondine thought the same of her as well.

Many women at Ondine's age didn't have the heart to raise a young girl as her own. Hael constantly thought of new ways to show her gratitude. With Ondine in her present illness, Hael was at Ondine's beck and call. Hael wanted dearly to see Ondine's eyes smiling again.

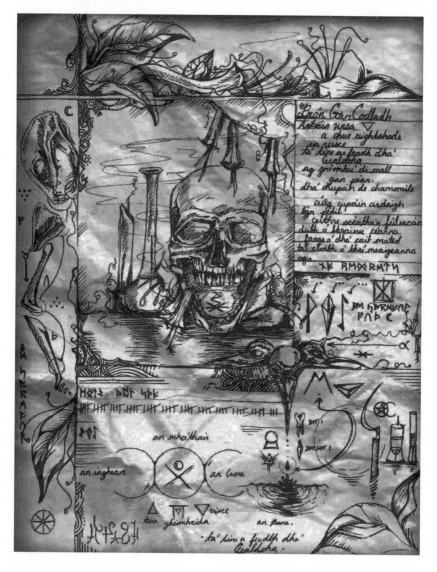

However, living with Ondine came with its quirks. Ondine came from a superstitious household. Her sister, Eveline, and she knew the secret world as well as their birthdays. As Hael cleaned the dishes, she remembered Ondine teaching her nature's symbols. Ondine was a soft spoken elder. *Remember, if you see a butterfly fly at day, it's good luck. Two butterflies sitting together on a branch, bad luck. If you see a butterfly fly at night, death is near.*

In the morning and before bed, Ondine instructed Hael to brew a concoction of herbs from her mother's personal journal. Hael couldn't understand the language. It was written in an old Gaelic script. But, Ondine's mother's drawings were easy to decipher. Ondine was very strict about her tea. Even though she had a kind smile, Ondine's glare petrified Hael when she served her tea late.

Before she went to bed, Hael was ordered to place both her and Ondine's shoes at the end of the bed with the toes pointed towards the door. Behind closed doors, Hael cracked her knuckles and wrung her hands together in agitation. But, Hael never fussed about anything to Ondine. Usually, when Ondine became too demanding in her orders, Hael went outside for a breather. She would always carry matches with her outside, and strike them against the stones. One by one, she gazed deep into the fire as she watched them burn and die out. She didn't know why, but there was something about fire that soothed her.

The only things that Hael lied about were her own problems. Hael always went to bed at night, but she could never sleep. She desperately wanted to sleep, but she was plagued with horrible nightmares. In her slumbers, she was entangled in visions of fire. It was a blazing fire with broken mirrors and shattered glass. She saw smoldering eyes, red-drenched fabric, and cracked bottles with melting skin. They were so vivid that the wood's scorching surface burned the soles of her feet when she dreamt. Distorted faces crackle and burn amidst the howling flames, except for one. Behind the shadows of the hellfire, a small girl with tanned skin desperately reached out for her with tearful gray eyes that screamed, "Take my hand!" No matter how hard she tried, Hael could never grasp her hand. Every night, Hael wished the Sandman would whisper sweet nothings in her ear. But, all she heard was screams.

In her dreams, only the sound of a broken music box kept her from waking up screeching. Its song entertained her. It amused her as she twirled about the floor. It was so enlightening that, even after the terrors stopped, she found happiness within its broken tune. That song belonged to her. But, she didn't know where it came from. How could she possess something that she never knew?

In her head, the music box tune played on repeat throughout the day. During her chores, Hael's fingers danced in precise synchronization with the box's harmony. Watching Hael on her invisible piano, Ondine regretted not teaching Hael music.

****

Weeks went by. Ondine's health waned. Dr. Strauss wrote to her saying that he had medicine to give her, but there were no replies. Her scullery maid, Hael, religiously brought him the same letter. Sometimes, Ondine wrote, "This is all a phase." Or, she wrote, "I'll be as right as rain soon enough." Alrich didn't recognize Hael's face when she delivered the letters. The years made Hael unrecognizable from the sickly girl she was before. Hael didn't attempt to remind him.

Spending her days as a caretaker, Hael read through Ondine's notations about Dr. Strauss's treatments for hysteria. Even though Hael recalled Alrich being quiet and diligent at his work, the scraps of notes and recorded documents Ondine had on Alrich were fiendish. When she came of age, Ondine showed Hael the numerous papers she collected about the doctor. Hael remembered Ondine whispering, "With secrets like these, it's no wonder why he was so quiet." With great detail, Alrich enjoyed inventing new tools for proper insertion and lubrication as well as hand positions he used to investigate a woman's sex to cure their hysteria. The most vulgar of his trials Hael read about dealt with a young woman named Mary Geneva. In those annotations, Hael read the depravity of his obsession through his hastily jotted down notes. Alrich happily recorded his newfound oral and finger fixations as he fondled Mary's curves and curls. Alrich's methods abhorred Hael. After reading the papers, in her current age, Hael enjoyed being unrecognized by him.

****

It was a long night. Alrich was worn to bits. On the job, he worked from daylight until midnight. When he slumped back into his office, it was only one hour till dawn.

From neighboring countries and provinces, waves of conferences swamped every time slot of his day. From England through France, more and more women between the ages of seventeen to thirty years old were diagnosed with severe hysteria. As he drifted to sleep in his armchair, Alrich remembered the echoes of squabbling medical professionals from England to Hungary. The voice of the assembly's host gobbled in his head, "Gentlemen, followers of the Hippocratic Oath, the many leaders among you and I have assembled this meeting tonight to approach a grievous situation in our midst. Lately, within the respective communities from London to Eastern France, young, vivacious women have been put under the cloud of hysteria. As you all know, this condition is new to our profession, and our methods are not yet perfected in the means of a long term treatment. However, just because the lot of you in this assembly are still experimenting with improving your treatments, it does not give you an excuse to not help out your fellow brethren in solving this crisis. Young ladies, in both the noble aspect and unfortunate habitats, are succumbing to this mental epidemic. None of my colleagues nor I have discovered the source of these episodes. But, we strongly urge all of you to turn no face away that calls for assistance. You never know whether the next one you meet may be the key to our resolution." Alrich fell asleep.

****

A crash jarred Alrich out of his sleep. He grabbed the back of his head. A terrible crick burned in his neck like lightning. He adjusted his shoulders and looked over towards the ruckus. Alrich's medical certificate lay shattered on the ground. He walked over to it. Broken glass spread over the rug. He slid his certificate from beneath the glass. A smear of blood streaked across the frame.

"Nice night, isn't it brother?" a voice sounded. Alrich dropped the frame. He whirled around. Mendelson stood behind him as he sucked the blood off his thumb.

"Freudric?"

Mendelson put his glove back on. "Surprised?" He walked over to a rum bottle near the window.

"Where were you?" Alrich asked. He walked over to the lamps. "I thought you were dead!" Alrich froze after the flame ignited. Like an oil slick, Mendelson's irises swirled with amber and an eerie pale blue hue. Alrich shuddered.

Freudric poured himself a drink. He capped the bottle. "It's been twelve years, my friend."

"What the hell is wrong with you?" Alrich asked.

Mendelson shrugged. "What's wrong with what?"

"Your eyes, man! What's wrong with your eyes?"

Freudric took another swig of rum. "Startling, isn't it?"

Alrich moved swiftly to the side. "Your eyes never looked like this before! What did you do?"

Mendelson laughed. "You're actually frightened." He finished his drink. "It's working perfectly."

"What's working?" Alrich asked.

Mendelson sat in the chair near the door. He tapped his glass. "Do you remember the longevity research?"

Alrich grimaced at his vaulted past. "I remember. But, that was years ago. What the hell is with all this?" he exclaimed, pointing at Mendelson's eyes. Alrich and Freudric conducted many experiments together during their medical career, but nothing was as heinous or rotten in Alrich's mouth like their longevity operations. Alrich's hands trembled at his memories, "All those women. All those dead women. Oh, the children! We vowed never to dabble in that research again. You made a promise, Freudric!"

Freudric laughed. "I knew you'd remember. You always had the best memory between the two of us."

"Did you hear me? What else did you do to yourself? What's the meaning of this?"

"I've made so many discoveries, Alrich. Marvelous discoveries." He poured himself some more rum. "Tell me, have you heard the Austrian mathematician named Mendel?"

"The monk?" Alrich asked.

"Yes, the monk," Freudric replied.

Alrich poured himself a drink. "What do peapods have to do with our research?"

"Everything." Freudric looked out the window. "Mendel's genetic experiments have helped me greatly."

Alrich blanched. "You told me you wouldn't start this again."

"I tell people a lot of things." Mendelson opened the window and poured out his drink. "No one believed that I could do it. They said that I'd fail. They'll all regret it deeply."

Alrich tightened his fist. "What are you planning this time?"

"You'll see soon enough. A master never shows his work until it's complete." Freudric looked around the study. "Now, for the matter at hand. Where is Ondine?"

The air was still around Mendelson as he looked at Freudric's stare and wide-toothed grin, Alrich's knees locked in fear. Dread hung within him like an ethereal hand waiting steadily to strangle his lungs. Alrich choked, "Why do you ask?"

"Because, brother, I know she poisoned Hael." He snatched Alrich by the throat. "That witch knew that girl was unique. She was more than just a child!"

Alrich gasped. "What the hell are you talking about?"

"Don't play dumb!" Freudric shouted. The fire in his eyes could've set the whole room ablaze. He shook Alrich's throat. "You saw the way Hael's wounds healed. You saw the how fast she adapted to her surroundings."

The oil slick glow of his eyes turned more dangerous the more he raged. Mendelson tightened his grip. "Her lungs were halfway filled with mud when you lifted her out of the ground. After all of that, you let that Celtic beldam do her in!" He paused. The glow in his eyes subsided as he cooled his temper. "I shouldn't blame you."

He let Alrich go. "When it comes to his patients, a good doctor abides by a steady contract with Death." He grinned. "But, Ondine's no patient."

Alrich swayed. His mind was blurry. He looked at the bottom of his glass. A thin residue coated the sides. Alrich struggled to speak. His legs wobbled and staggered as he walked. He fell flat on the floor.

Freudric kicked the glass to the side. He looked down at him. "Of all people, Alrich, you should be wary of what you drink." He rubbed his forehead. "I shouldn't drink so early."

Mendelson walked over to the desk. Dr. Strauss stored all of his employee files inside of the top drawer. Freudric jiggled the handle. It was locked. He tightened his grip around the lock, and cracked it open.

****

Ondine was very quiet. The rare time she would speak is when she told Hael to brew more herbal tea. Hael stayed up late into the night at Ondine's bedside as her faithful assistant.

Ondine had a high fever. Hael wiped the sides of her face and arms with a cool towel. As much as she hated Alrich, Hael implored Ondine to contact the doctor for help. Ondine refused. The old woman was the closest thing to a mother that Hael ever knew. Although Hael understood the severity of Ondine's illness, she tried to convince herself that Death would never beckon her beloved guardian.

As the week drew to an end, Ondine's condition worsened. Her face became like yellow wax. Her cloudy, bloodshot eyes turned more and more glazed as her temperature dropped. What were once sweaty hands and arms were now blocks of ice. Hael slept in the chair near her bed. She never strayed. Ondine couldn't talk. She barely had enough energy to lift her head, or reach with her lank and emaciated arms to pat Hael's hair. As much as she despised the doctor's methods, Hael begged Ondine to see Dr. Strauss. Ondine still refused, though she knew Hael was looking out for her wellbeing. In her own dying whispers, Ondine mumbled Hael's name affectionately.

****

Hael stayed up later than usual one night to clean up the kitchen. She prepared Ondine's tea for the next morning. She strained to keep her eyes open as she dried the dishes.

A cup fell from her hand and shattered. Exhausted, Hael plummeted to the floor, landing dangerously close to the glass.

The kitchen chilled as a dry wisp of air drifted past her legs. The floorboards were coarse and unleveled. Even though the moon shone through the windows, the darkness of the house was insatiable. A shadow loomed in the doorway.

Hael woke up. She rubbed her head. Tiny pieces of glass clung to her hair. Hael was accustomed to silence, but the quiet hush of the room riddled her with caution. Grabbing onto the side of the sink, she lifted herself up. She looked out the window. A butterfly fluttered over the rose bush, and landed on the windowsill. Superstition swamped her. Running into the bedroom, Hael gasped. "Ondine!"

Enveloped in the moonlight, Ondine's arm hung from the side of the bed. Hael stepped closer. "Ondine?" she asked.

Ondine's eyes were closed, and her jaw was shut tight.

"Miss Ondine?" Hael placed her fingers on Ondine's wrist. There was no pulse. "Lovely, it's time to wake up." Her voice was sweet, but it cracked with dread.

Hael placed her fingers against her neck. She felt nothing.

Her heart froze in her chest. Ondine was dead.

Hael's weeping turned frantic. She wrapped her arms around Ondine's head and held her close. Ondine looked so calm. Her guardian's skin was clammy and hard against hers. She felt the stiffened muscles of her torso as she hugged Ondine closer. Hael ran her hand through Ondine's alabaster curls. The hair was thinned and chilled.

"Please. Please, come back to me." Her tears beaded down Ondine's face like water on a candle.

She did not know how long she held her beloved guardian. But, she knew she couldn't stay there forever. She dried her tears. Struggling to regain her composure, Hael gently placed Ondine down onto the bed and covered her with the sheet.

She didn't know what to do. Ondine left no specific directions as to what should be done for this event. She didn't know if Ondine wanted to be embalmed, cremated, or sent home to Ireland. In her last years, Ondine became careless. If Ondine had written down her final wishes, Hael had no indication on where to find it. All she knew was that Ondine didn't want Dr. Strauss anywhere near her body. Hael needed to cool down. She needed something to drink. She went to the kitchen.

She stumbled. Looking down, Hael nearly tripped over the ceramic cup she served the tea in. The cup was chipped on the ground. Hours ago, before she washed the dishes, she remembered placing the cup on top of the vanity, and leaving it there. There was a loud thud in the kitchen. Hael crawled towards the door. She peered across the frame. There was a man in the room. He was examining the kettle and the grinding stones. His hand was in a tight fist on top of the counter. Something had gone severely wrong. She couldn't say exactly what it was, but there was a dense déjà vu about him.

Her vision became fuzzy. She closed her eyes and shook her head to focus. She looked back at the counter. He was gone.

Hael grabbed the ceramic cup and tiptoed into the kitchen. She held the cup at the ready as she surveyed the area. He had disappeared. This man was husky, and the kitchen had no large objects that could conceal him. Perplexed, Hael scratched the back of her head as she continued to look around.

The fuzziness in her head returned. Her eyes went blurry. She stumbled over a loose floor board. The ceramic cup slipped out of her hand. "What's happening to me?" she whispered.

Her condition worsened. Her neck, her eye lids, and her limbs stiffened and froze. She couldn't move. The room was spinning. Shadows twisted and spun in the darkness. Sweat covered her brow. Her breathing turned painful. Inhaling air was like swallowing woodchips. Something arched her back. There was a presence behind her.

Thick hands wrapped around her waist. Her body fell limp. Her eyes flew open. She stared at the floor. She tried to call out for help, but only a faint wisp of air seeped out. She couldn't speak. She hung in the hands of the shadowy figure like a warm marionette. Its fingers strayed all over her body. Around her sides, her back, and hips, its hands groped her. She jerked away from them.

A hand snatched her throat and tilted her head up. Hot breath blew in her ear. It reeked of hard liquor. "You smell nice, *fräulein.*"

Hael shuddered. That voice. She recognized that voice. *It can't be,* she thought. She dismissed the idea. She told herself that this whole ordeal was a bad dream. *No, it's a lie!* It couldn't be real.

Mendelson stroked her cheek. "You're soft, too."

She twitched remembering his face. She hadn't seen him in years. She thought he was dead. Mendelson put his hand underneath her gown and traced his finger against her stomach. He turned her face towards him. "Very soft." He gave no sign of recognizing her. This was the same man who taught her nursery rhymes. The same man who bandaged her cuts when she fell over tree roots, and caught her when she was mischievous. This was her childhood cohort. Why was he there? Why was he doing this? How did he get in the house?

Mendelson continued his observations. "You must be the scullery maid?" he asked. She nodded her head. He chuckled. "Aww, come now. A witch always teaches her familiars how to talk."

Hael continued to pull away. He stroked her skin. "Now, tell me something sweet." He slid his hand between her legs.

"Stop!" she screamed. She panicked and tried to pry away.

He licked his teeth. "I knew you had a lovely voice."

She banged her leg against his shin. Without missing a beat, she elbowed him in the throat and slammed her knee into his chest. She launched her foot into his groin. He caught her ankle and flipped her on her back. She turned over and ran. He pounced on top of her and crashed her against the floor. He laughed. "I never would've guessed that kind of power in your legs!"

His smile broadened as he spun her around.

Fury built up in her chest. This could not be real! This was not the Mendelson she knew. Her vision blurred. Her heart thrashed in her ears. She plunged her fist into his cheekbone. His glasses flew across the room and cracked against the cabinet.

With a slacked jaw and a wide-eyed leer, Mendelson froze. The last time Freudric endured that much force was when an ex-marine smashed a bar stool over his face. She faced him and rammed her heel into his diaphragm. The wind flew from his lungs. He went into a coughing fit. She stomped her foot into his gut like a battering ram, and kicked him over. While he was on his stomach, she grabbed the carving knife from the sink.

"*Nein!*" He pushed her against the sink, bending her neck backwards. He forced his weight against her as he snatched the knife from her grasp. "That's quite enough, *fräulein.*"

Something wet trickled down his neck. He touched his face. He wiped his blood from his cheek. He snickered. "You cut me."

He wiped his fingers against her apron. "You drew first blood," he said. "I'm proud to give you your first victory scar." He pushed his hand over her mouth and lifted her garment. The knife's tip was frigid. The cold blade shocked her as the tip traced a line through her sweat.

A sharp pain accumulated in the back of his neck and traveled upward. Adjusting his neck, he gazed at her glistening skin in the moonlight. He crouched down. "It's been a long time since I saw a virgin, much less her skin."

He grinned as he threw the knife aside. Mendelson could tell if a woman was a virgin by her scent. Sometimes, he could tell by the way a woman walked, but the scent usually gave it away. Unlike a virgin, a deflowered woman had the scent of her mate or other lovers embedded with her natural smell. After the brawl with Hael, he could smell that she was untouched. He kissed her stomach. "Softer still." He continued to think out loud. Hael cringed and tried to pull away. He leaned his face against her cheek. "Keep smelling sweet. I'll see you for round two."

With that, he bashed a glass cup over her head. Darkness took over.

****

Her face was numb when she awoke. The wooden patterns of the floorboards were imprinted on her cheek. The hair on her skin rose from the cold. The air was still. Something was awry. As Hael recalled the episode, a vicious nature consumed her. All of her thoughts turned rabid as the sounds of gnashing teeth and scraping nails swamped her mind. After she regained her full consciousness, she searched through Ondine's personal items. The arguments that Mendelson and Ondine chewed through came to mind. Hael raided the dressers in the bedroom until she found one of Ondine's journals. She remembered how much Ondine detested that man. But, Ondine never told her why. Hael had to know.

Ondine's journal was a trench of evidence. In shock, Hael

read pages upon pages of testimonies and charges against Mendelson. Hael could never tell why Nurse Brimfield or the female patients loathed him until now. She read all of the stories about Mendelson. All of the things Ondine said about him being a womanizer, a pervert, a lecher, an advantage taker, and monster were all documented from numbers of women. The journal was an ocean of tortured lives.

Hael had to know if there was any more evidence. Hael remembered that Ondine kept her most personal journals in the vanity dresser. Then her eyes fell upon Ondine's corpse lying stiff in the bed. Even after death, Hael could hear Ondine's stern voice as she approached the vanity, *Keep to your own business, Hael. A girl that searches for things that don't belong to her will soon find things that don't belong anywhere searching for her in return.* The vanity drawer was locked. She walked over to the end dresser near the bed.

"Forgive me, Ms. Ondine." She took the key and opened it.

The drawer was filled with drawings of plants, dried insects, and mandrake roots. A small pack of thin candles was placed to the side. In the back, a blue leather bound journal was wrapped with twine. It was stuffed. Envelopes and crumpled papers were bursting out of its sides.

There were letters from Belfast. She read the signature on the front of the envelope. "Jane Brimfield." She paused. "Jane Brimfield?" She looked back at Ondine. "I didn't know you had living relatives." The letter was written in small print:

> *My dear sister,*
>
> *Only God knows why you keep your employment at that institution. I understand that Alrich pays well, but, seriously, I have no idea how you can stomach the man. Erratic behavior? Unstable hormones? Hysteria? It's all bullocks, and you know it. Honestly, you saw what the likes of them did to Ma, and yet you watch the same kind do it over and over again, and for what? Money? Alrich couldn't pay me enough*

to sit there and watch while Mendelson and the rest have their way. Good Lord, I can't believe that you haven't done him off yet. I cringe just thinking about him and that smile. How many women has he cured with hysteria? Seven? Twelve? Or was that last month? And, just last month, you sent me a letter saying how Alrich took in an injured girl? For her own good, get her out of there.

I hope you're feeling well. I'm always waiting for your visits. — Love, Jane

****

Into the night, Hael continued sifting through the letters. A strange sensation ached and nauseated Hael from inside her chest. She dismissed the pain since she believed it stemmed from the fight before.

Some of the journals contained pictures of Ondine's sister and Jane's husband. Ondine's daily writings were unruly. The books had writings and sketches, but they didn't resemble the normal entries of an elderly woman. As she read deeper into the letters, horrible secrets came into light. From the readings, Hael learned that Ondine and Jane Brimfield were the daughters of Elsa O'Curry.

Elsa O'Curry was trialed for witchcraft and corruption of the town's doctor. The same doctor that pleaded being a victim to Elsa's O'Curry was a close associate to Dr. Alrich Strauss. Dr. Strauss helped his colleagues form the trial against Elsa. After the hanging, Ondine and Jane changed the name O'Curry to Brimfield. They wanted a clean slate. The new surname gave Jane access to more of Ireland and it showed Ondine a gateway into the medical world. When she earned her license as a nurse, Ondine played the woman in distress. She tracked down Dr. Strauss, claimed that she escaped from a famine, and pleaded to him for help. Once in his favor, she kept a close eye on Strauss and his work as she waited for the opportune moment. Then Mendelson came.

Alongside Strauss, Ondine expected to work with many

oddities and hassles in the asylum. What she didn't expect was Mendelson. Ondine quarreled with men of all statures on a buffet of subjects. But, Mendelson was the only man who clung in her insides like a tapeworm.

****

In the past, Ondine visited her sister to calm her nerves. Her sister tried to give encouragement. "Ondine, stop being so wired over him, love," Jane said. "It's not doing you any good."

"No. Jane, I swear on Ma's grave, that man is on to me," Ondine replied. "He has it in for me. I've tried everything that I could think of, but still he gets under my skin. No! He digs his way under, fucking stays there, and eats at it. I'm not holding my tongue anymore."

****

Hael continued to read. The sisters had planned to exterminate both the doctor and his friend, but they could never find the right opportunity. And, due to old age, they didn't have the strength necessary to fend for each other if anything went wrong. Then, Hael came along.

Hael was the daughter Ondine never had. Hael brought her joy. But, what was even more enticing was the golden ticket Ondine thought she'd never possess. From correlating her mother's stories, Ondine knew there was something different about Hael. There was something powerful. Maybe she was a changeling that the Fae inside the wood sent out to extract their vengeance. Maybe she was part nixie that was abandoned in the mud by her conjurers. Who knew? When evidence proved that no one in the city knew she existed, it was the perfect time to take Hael for her own. These thoughts and ideas were exchanged between the letters.

Hael stood like a grave marker. She took everything in. She couldn't believe it. Every pen scratch in the letters was like throwing match after lit match into a vat of oil. It hit her hard. "So, this is why she was so nice to me? I was her meal ticket?"

She reviewed the letters again. She talked to herself.

"That's the only reason she was nice to me." A dark void devoured her. "That's the only reason she ever loved me."

The pain in her chest accumulated. Her right eye started to burn. She placed her hand over it and applied pressure. The burning increased. It was a mild sensation at first, but it exploded into a fiery agony that burrowed deep into her skull. She clutched her eye, and yanked her hair to make it stop. Her efforts were futile. Tears pooled into her open mouth. She fell to her knees and made her way towards the mirror. She could hardly lift her head. The pressure behind her eye was unbearable. She looked into the mirror.

Her whole eye was solid black. Panicking, she grabbed the wash bowl and splashed her face. "What the hell is this?"

Black fluid streamed down her face from the inside of her eye. Her heart rattled with fear. She thought her ribcage was going to collapse. Her eye bewailed black blood. As the fluid drained, she could see the white of her sclera return. The fluid was viscous and foul as it covered her cheek. It stopped. From the edge of her iris towards her pupil, the color smoldered from brown to a brilliant dark red. The pain faded after the color settled. Soon, the red disappeared altogether. Her chocolate iris shined once more.

Hael wiped the substance off her face. She whimpered in confusion and fear. She didn't know what just happened, but she hoped that it would cease to repeat. Her prayers were useless. Her torment continued in waves.

****

That night, Hael went through a feral transformation that began with her eye. Within minutes, the same searing pain appeared in her fingertips, nose, ears, and teeth. She thrashed on the floor with her face and arms covered in a viscous black fluid. It felt like old blood between her fingers. From the letters, Alrich was revealed as a womanizing malfeasance. And, with her memories tainted by Mendelson, loads of betrayal descended upon her. From everyone that she held dear, everything she loved was a lie.

She touched her teeth and nails. A powerful primal compulsion vexed her. Rage surged through her veins. Her nails morphed from their smooth edges into lethal daggers. Like hot iron cooled in heartbroken tears, they glistened in the light and shredded the floor boards like paper. Her canines lengthened into sharp fangs, gleaming of sheer wrath. Any creature that was brave enough to overcome her failed when seeing her eyes. The reflection of all who looked burned alive into the blood fire of her iris.

She could smell everything. From the grasshoppers underneath the cold wooden floors to Ondine's decaying insides, there was nothing she couldn't identify. Her ears ripped through everything private. No secret could evade her hearing.

Her mind fogged. Her limbs and body panged in distress as she hoisted herself from the ground. Her gums and teeth pulsed in agony. She tried to comfort herself. Her words were incoherent. She couldn't understand what she was telling herself. When she talked, drool pooled out of her mouth. The pain in her chest spread to her mouth and stomach. She needed fresh air. Her body was covered in the black fluid. Its stench polluted her nose. She walked towards the door.

She stopped. Multiple heartbeats pounded in her ears. She placed her ear against the door and listened. In the distance, she heard a carriage ride up to the house. The horses began to whinny fretfully. There were men talking outside. "What the hell's gotten into Norman?" one of them asked the coachman.

"I don't know!" the coachman answered. "Norman's usually the most docile. All the horses are acting up."

"Just keep them over there!" the leader of the group ordered. The coachman kept the horses at a distance and took a sip from his flask. Hael listened intently to their conversation. "You!" he shouted to the footman. "Go get the woman!"

"Which one?" the footman asked.

"The scullery maid with the black hair," the leader answered. Hael heard the footman approach the door. She locked the door and backed away swiftly.

The doorknob jiggled angrily. "It's locked," the footman said.

"Here," the man said, handing the footman a crowbar. "Get on with it. I'm freezing out here." The footman rammed the crowbar into the wood.

Hael trembled with pain and anxiety. Who were these men? The crowbar banged furiously in her eardrum. They were coming for her. She had to hide. Hael dashed into her bedroom. With aching arms, she lifted a loose board and hid underneath the floor.

The wooden door splintered and the lock fell to the floor. The door flew open. The footman stormed inside, brandishing the crowbar. "Miss?" he called out. "Oh, Miss? Where are you, love?"

He saw Ondine's dead body in the bedroom through the open door. He closed the door and continued searching. "We heard you had a frightful night, my dear. We just want to see how you're doing. You must be awfully scared."

"Barry, stop talking!" the man outside shouted. "Just find the bitch, and let's go."

The footman rolled his eyes. "This is a delicate situation. These crazies always run off when you're not nice to them."

Hael scurried underneath the floorboards towards the outside. The footman heard low fumbling movements. He ran into Hael's bedroom and slammed the crowbar into the floorboards. The floorboard splintered and cut into Hael's calf. She screamed. The footman flung the loose boards to the side and heaved her to the surface. She kicked and swung her claws at him. He pelted the crowbar against her wounded leg and dragged her outside.

"I got her!" the footman said.

"What the hell is all that?" the man said, pointing to the black fluid on Hael's body.

The footman shrugged. "No idea."

"Never mind it," the man said. "Strap her down and put her in the back."

The footman signaled the coachman to bring the carriage. "Come on, love," he said, jerking Hael's arms.

Hael relentlessly yanked her body away from him. But, she was too weak to fully escape his grasp.

The footman laughed. "He said this would be difficult."

"The job's not done yet," the man said. "Mendelson specifically instructed us to bind her legs."

Hael's mind came to a grinding halt. "Mendelson," she said quietly.

"What?" the footman asked her.

"Mendelson." That name fumed in her brain. Mendelson! Mendelson! Oh, how those three syllables cursed the letter "M!" She repeated the name. Her words foamed in her mouth.

The footman yanked her arm. "Come on!"

"No!" she roared. She elongated her nails and plunged her fingers into the footman's shoulder. The man howled with agony. She ripped his arm from his socket and beat the footman with his own severed limb.

The leader of the group yelled and charged at Hael with a dagger. He stabbed her in the back. She fell to the ground. Over and over again, he stabbed his blade deep into her torso. Hael roared in fury. She grabbed the severed limb and brained the leader. When the severed arm gave way, Hael buried her claws into his skull, and gouged his head wide open. Brain matter and blood splattered across her face. Her entire body became a walking nightmare of black and red.

She heard the horses go wild in the distance. The coachman desperately tried to mount one of the horses, but the beast was too frightened to stand still. Hael walked over to the coachman. The front horse saw Hael from the corner of its eye, and reared its back legs frantically. The horse's hoof clocked the coachman in the chest and sent him plummeting to the ground.

His flask flew out of his pocket.

The coachman held his beaten torso and coughed violently. A twig snapped in front of him. He looked up. Hael looked down upon him. Her body was still, but the red of her iris swirled like hellfire. The coachman sobbed and pleaded for his life. Hael looked at the carriage. "Where were you going to bring me?" she asked him.

"Please, don't kill me," he cried.

Hael rammed her heel down onto his hand. His bones broke through his skin upon impact. She repeated herself. "Where were you going to bring me?" Her voice was calm and authoritative.

"To the docks," he answered.

"Why the docks?" she asked.

"We were supposed to bring you and some others to the docks, and place you all on a boat bound for France."

"Why France?"

"I don't know," he answered. "That's all Mendelson wrote to us. I swear it!"

"Do you have the instructions?" she asked. The coachman nodded. He reached into his back pocket and handed her an envelope. She read postage marks. The letter came from Germany. "What others?" she asked. The coachman said that there were other women that they collected during the week to bring to the docks. Hael was a surprise adjustment to the original list. He stated that after the delivery was made, they were instructed to burn the letter.

She gave the letter back to him. "Thank you." She walked over to the flask and unscrewed the top.

The coachman shuddered. "What are you doing?"

"Following instructions." She poured the liquor over his body.

"Stop! I told you what you wanted to know."

"Yes, you did." Hael picked up a stone from the grass. She held it firmly in her hand. "And, I said, 'Thank you.'" She struck her nails against the stone. Sparks flew off her claws and ignited the liquor. The coachman screamed as his body writhed within the flames.

Hael dropped the stone. Walking back to the house, she gathered all of Ondine's journals and other notes, and placed them in a satchel. With the satchel secured around her torso, she walked over to the horses, and cut the reigns. She grabbed the strongest steed out of the selection, and mounted it. With Ondine's body left to rot, two dead men, and a burning corpse, Hael rode deep into the night.

Chapter Seven
The Never-ending Hunt

War was rampant. Hael was unleashed. For over forty years, she tracked down hordes of women and children that were abducted by Mendelson and his affiliates. She didn't know if Mendelson was still alive, or if someone was taking his place as the lead. However, in every shipment she busted, the instructions and the henchmen swore loyalty to him. Why were these people being stolen? And, why so many? In the awakening of the new era, Hael didn't care if the world was conquered by the Nazis, the Japanese, the Americans, or if everybody was blown to hell. As far as she was concerned, finding Mendelson, sabotaging his plans, and discovering her origin were crucial. Ever since the night of betrayal, Hael did not age, and her abilities grew more refined.

On her hunt, the information she gathered captained her deep into the underground. Since Ondine's death, Hael kept all the journals with the botanical notes and other jotted-down concoctions. In the pages, as well as other blank journals she accumulated, Hael recorded any evidence or other suspicious news she came across in both notes and drawings. As she moved through the slums and shadows from London to München, she teamed up with Josef Faust Ludmila. Josef was an ex-auxiliary

man and gunsmith from Czechoslovakia. Due to illegal experi-
mentation with ammunition and tampering with weapon supplies, Josef was banned from the military.

Josef met Hael at a small tavern in Oeventrop called "The
Nachzeher." Hael operated via a male persona. Hiding feminine
attributes proved convenient while traveling from country to
country. Josef wasn't fooled. When he followed her out of the
tavern, she attacked him for spying. They scuffled.

Hael broke Josef's jaw, and fractured his ankle. She
stepped on his chest, and grilled him for information. Josef
chuckled as he felt his jaw. Underneath his fingers, his bones
started to shift. Hael stepped back. She watched him laugh to
himself as his bones mended. She readied herself for his re-
bound.

Shaking his head, Josef stood up. "Wait! Wait. Hold on,
girl! Hear me out." Josef explained that he posed no threat. He
was just interested.

Hael lowered her fists. "What makes you say I'm a girl?"

He snickered. "Your feminine scent's potent, and being a
dhampir didn't help your camouflage."

"What's a dhampir?" Hael asked.

"A dhampir is a person who is half-vampire by blood
due to influences in their DNA," Josef said. "Normally, because
of our heightened abilities and reflexes, we make good hunters
as well as psychics."

"Is that why you're in the underground?" she asked him.

"There's plenty of work here," he replied. "Although,
since the majority of our origins come from Slavic gypsy lore,
our reputation is becoming less necessary and more nonsense."

"But, you're not Romanian," Hael said.

"What does that have to do with anything?" Josef asked.

"The Nosferatu is from Romania. It's the only vampire
that can impregnate a human. You're a dhampir, and you're not
Romanian."

Josef told her that the first trace of the vampire came from Mesopotamia. However, as it migrated over time, the gene stabilized in Romania where it became the Nosferatu, the Plague Bringer. The gene spread like wildfire across the eastern and western hemisphere. It changed within each country it touched. "There are more species than just the Nosferatu," he said.

"What kind of dhampir are you?" she asked.

"An Alp," Josef replied, folding his arms . "Why are you pretending to be a man?"

At the time, she gave no reply about her attire. Her eyes shifted downward. "I'm just looking for somebody."

"A liar knows a liar when he sees one," Josef said. "The only women in that tavern were a part of the family who built it." The rest of the bar was populated with rouge dhampirs and traveling vampires. Before she could support her case, Josef interjected, "Listen, whatever your reason is for secrets, it must be good. Just tell me, is this your first time visiting a place like this?"

"No," she replied.

"Good. You're used to this crowd." He looked her up and down. "How's about I come with you?"

She shook her head. "I can't pay you."

"I suspected you didn't have any money, but I don't have anything better to do," he replied. "If you get into any trouble on the way, I'll have some fun dealing with it."

"Why do you want to help me?" she asked. "You don't even know who I'm looking for."

"I never met a woman strong enough to even pin down my hand. You fractured my bones. Whoever you're looking for, I don't want to miss the moment when you catch them." He handed her a cigarette. "What's your name anyway?"

Hael wasn't very partial to cigarette smoke. However, during her years of hunting Mendelson, she picked up a taste for cigars. Unlike cigars, something about cigarette smoke made her uncomfortable. But, to dull suspicion, or in this case, being out of cigars, she took him up on his gesture. She tossed him her lighter. "I'll tell you later."

****

Three months passed. After the First World War, Berlin was a warren in Eastern Europe. In the midst of WWII, the city molted into a new ruin: the capital of the Nazi regime.

A meeting took place between the Luftwaffe leader Herman Goering and the head of the SS, Heinrich Himmler. Himmler and Goering agreed to meet on a mutual understanding that involved the incidences around the perimeters of Berchtesgaden and the Kanzlei des Führers.

The meeting was held at the Kanzlei des Führers. Goering entered the room. Himmler was waiting for him. He sat in the chair, and examined documents. He stood up. "Heil Hitler."

Goering saluted, "Heil Hitler."

"The weather's been bad lately," Himmler said. "I thought that you wouldn't be able to make it."

Goering sat opposite from him. "I just got in before the thick of it." For the entire week, Goering dreaded this meeting. He removed his hat. "I know what you're going to ask. So, don't say it."

Himmler removed his glasses. "Is there any new information regarding the killings?"

Goering clenched his fist. "I told you I don't know." He scratched his head. "There are no fingerprints on any of the victims. No leads. It's as if whoever's doing this is burrowing under their feet."

"Do you know how they're dying? Is there a pattern?" Himmler asked.

"It's all a mess," Goering replied. He rubbed his temples, and poured himself some water. "The medical examiners claimed that every victim died of an abnormal hemorrhaging."

"Hemorrhaging?"

"I don't believe them," Goering said.

"Why not?" Himmler asked.

"The majority of them didn't suffer from a severe enough wound from previous battles. There's no way that they could've hemorrhaged."

Himmler fidgeted as he read the case files. "Is it really as bad as they say?"

"The men were practically marinated in their own blood. Half of it is still clinging to the carpet." Goering shook his head.

"We're at a standstill."

Himmler sighed. "That's all you have?"

"Yes."

Himmler put the documents back into his suitcase. He shook hands with Goering. "Thank you for coming here. I know there are many concerns, and these questions are redundant. However, this situation is exceedingly dense. The evidence is gruesome, but these are the only leads we have. We have to move forward. Remember, these aren't just your men, they're the Füehrer's investment."

"Is there anything that you want us to do?" Goering asked.

"We'll discuss the other matters later. If the evidence on the bodies goes dry, do whatever you deem necessary to seize the culprit."

"Where will you be, sir?" Goering asked.

"I'm going away for a short time. I'll be back before the month is out." Then Himmler saluted, "Heil Hitler."

Goering clicked his heels together and saluted, "Heil Hitler."

****

The weather was monstrous. Rain dropped like boulders. The horizon and buildings of Berlin vanished behind a dank cloud of gray. From the steps of the Kanzlei des Führers, Himmler raced to the car. The driver opened the door.

"Where to, sir?" he asked.

"Take me home," Himmler ordered. The driver closed the door as he wiped the rain drops from his glasses.

The streets became onyx streams as the rain continued to pour. Once at the house, the driver opened his door. "Is there anything else, sir?"

"Wait here. I'll be back out. Keep the car warm." It was half past two in the morning. Himmler's wife had already left home. Himmler grabbed two packed suitcases and returned to the car.

"Where to?" the driver asked.

"Schneewinkellehen," he replied. Schneewinkellehen was Himmler's villa in Schönau. His wife awaited him at the villa. It had been a long time since they had a weekend to themselves.

****

Inside Himmler's villa, Hael studied the road from behind the curtains. "Is she tied up?" she asked.

Josef crouched down in front of Frau Himmler. He tugged on the gag in her mouth. "It's tied."

Hael closed the curtains. "Good. Knock her out."

Josef bashed the woman across the temples.

"Put her in the basement," Hael ordered. She arranged the furniture back in place. "Get to your post. Be ready."

"I know what to do," Josef said, closing the door.

She straightened the couches. Car headlights shone in the distance. Himmler's car pulled up into the driveway.

Josef crept alongside the house as he watched the driver step out of the car. The driver opened the door. "Anything else I can do for you, sir?"

Himmler straightened his jacket. "Come in and grab a drink before you go."

"*Danke,* sir. I'll be right in." The driver thanked him.

Hael took a deep breath. She opened the door. She took the guise of Himmler's wife. Once she gathered a sufficient amount of blood, Hael easily created an illusion of anyone she tasted. The amount of time the illusion stayed up depended on how much blood she drank. Alongside this, via skin to skin contact, Hael could briefly infiltrate a person's mind in order to cloud or lead thoughts astray. Though severely exhausting, this skill proved useful when ducking in and out of unsavory close quarters, or avoiding conflict. Ingesting bodily fluids nauseated Hael. She couldn't wait to vomit it out. The taste of blood abhorred her. In the form of Himmler's wife, she opened the door. "Nice to see you, Heinrich."

Heinrich smiled. "How are you?"

"Good, good," Hael replied. "Did the weather hold you up?"

"A little bit. I need to sit down."

"Take your time, dear," she said.

Josef had successfully disguised himself as the driver. He entered the house. Hael looked at his hand. A long gash ran across his palm. "What the hell happened to your hand?" she whispered.

"The fucker pulled out a knife!"

"Shh! Keep it down." She peeked into the hall. "He's in the back getting a drink. Did you hide the body?"

Josef looked at his hand. "Yep."

"Go sit down. I'll be back shortly." Hael went into the wine cellar and grabbed a bottle of Riesling. She took out a small white envelope from her pocket and emptied its contents into the wine. "I found it!" she said, walking into the den. "Grab a glass."

"*Danke,*" Josef said. He poured Himmler a drink.

Himmler raised his glass. "*Prost,* to the new world order."

They all raised their glass. "New world order!"

After his first swig of wine, Himmler dropped head first to the floor. Josef set down his drink. "Damn! How much did you put in that? You were supposed to make him semiconscious!"

She threw out her drink. "I've been practicing apothecary way before you learned what a fucking tree was. Don't tell me how to make my drugs." She looked at the wine bottle and shrugged. "He'll wake up in a few minutes. Go and search the villa for any safes."

Josef searched the villa's kitchen, den, and living room. Nothing was there. He searched the bedroom. Under a crease in the floorboards by the foot of the bed, an iron safe was snug inside layers of straw. Josef pushed the straw aside. "I found it! Bring him in here."

Hael dragged Himmler into the master bathroom, and

strapped him backwards over the tub's rim. She put his face underneath the faucet.

"You said you weren't going to kill him," Josef said.

"I'm not. But, one can never have too much information."

"So, he'll be near death," Josef said.

She cuffed Himmler's wrists. "If you want to go and break your arm trying to crack another safe, be my guest."

Moments later, Himmler regained consciousness. He strained to get out of his restraints. "Who the hell are you people? What are you doing here?" Hael turned on the faucet. Hot water flooded Himmler's mouth and eyes. "Stop! Stop!" he shouted.

She pushed his head back. "Not until you tell us the safe combination!"

"Safe combination? Who are you?"

"Talk, bitch!" She turned the rest of the cold water off. Steam piled the room. Himmler's face reddened. Thin layers of skin started to blister. She shook his hair. "I said talk!"

Heinrich yelled, "There is no money in the safe!"

"Did I ask for money?" She forced his mouth open. "Did I ask for money?"

Scalding hot water ran down his throat. Himmler coughed. "*Nein! Nein!*"

She shook his face. "The codes!"

Heinrich pleaded, "There's nothing valuable in the safe!"

Hael turned off the water. She dried her hands. "Josef, go outside. Whatever you hear, don't come in. I got this." She closed the door. She turned back to the tub. She paused. Himmler had a Walter pistol aimed at her chest.

Heinrich's arms shook with fury. "Untie the ropes, or — "

"Or, you'll shoot?" she interjected. "Kill me?" She shrugged. "I've heard it before."

Heinrich froze. She smiled at him. "Let me help you." She leaned herself against the pistol and squeezed the trigger. The bullet dug through her chest. Blood splattered against the door.

Josef opened the door. "Is this going to be another clean up job?"

She pushed the door closed. "Didn't I say to keep your ass outside?"

Himmler's hands shook. "What the hell was that?"

"It wasn't a magic trick. But, I can show you how I make things disappear." She aimed his gun at his head. "Being Hitler's future replacement gives you access to a lot of lives, especially those that the Nazi regime doesn't want to exist."

Heinrich shuddered. "If you kill me, you won't get anything."

"You're right. I won't get anything from a corpse." She aimed the gun at his groin. "The reason why I'm not going to kill you is because I don't want that man outside to have to break his arm again cracking a safe. She pulled the pistol's hammer back. "But, that doesn't stop me from neutering you."

He screamed, "7-21-19! 7-21-19!"

"Good boy." She twisted her fingers around the muzzle and bent the pistol like a wooden skewer. "Josef, you can come in now."

Josef chuckled. "I take it he didn't want his nuts blown off."

"I told you the code," Himmler said. "Let me go!"

She threw the gun across the room. "Josef, I think Herr Heinrich doesn't want to be here anymore. Oblige him." Josef pinned Himmler's torso down. He took out a syringe from the inside of his coat pocket, and stuck it deep into his chest. Hael opened Himmler's eye. "Forget our faces."

Heinrich passed out. Josef unlocked the cuffs and carried him out into the front room. He plopped Heinrich down next to his wife. Hael lifted the safe from the straw. She dragged it across the floorboards. The metal scuffed the wood. "Here," she said pushing Josef the safe. "Put this in the car outside."

"Why are we taking the whole safe? We have the combinations."

"The Nazi's have forensic technology that can analyze crime scenes. My hands and yours have been on this. I'm not in the system, but you are. The last thing we need is a bunch of detectives riding our ass." Nobody knew about Himmler's iron safe. But, Hael wasn't taking any chances.

"We're taking the Mercedes?" Josef asked.

"Yes," she replied.

"Himmler's Mercedes?"

She cleaned her blood up from the bathroom. "Himmler was dropped off here by his driver. Therefore, if *somebody* hid the body properly, it would look like the driver hijacked the car." She wrung out the towel. "Didn't you tell me that you wanted a Mercedes once?"

Josef nodded. "True."

"Let's go."

****

Hael and Josef smuggled survivors out of the country. Cloaked in secrecy, their operation was neither against nor for the Nazi regime or any other capital. Their efforts aided people who were sick of their country dragging their families into war. Most of these people were gypsies, farmers, and tradesmen. They wanted to survive without being detected by the nations so they could start over. Everything they had was gone.

Their operation lay within the ruins of Dresden. Dresden, a once a thriving German city, was razed by bombs and invaders. Markets that were filled with fresh food sat stuffed with decaying flesh. Bustling streets were buried in ash and coagulated blood. And, homes, once overflowing with children's laughter, were now hazardous snares which the vilest of rats wouldn't enter.

Josef decided that one of the still standing apartments would be their refuge. The hospitals had plenty of room for the families, but the amount of medical waste made it too dangerous for camp. The locks on the entrance to the apartment complex were melted shut. Hael, Josef, and the families had to crawl through a blasted out basement window. Hael hid the hole with a large piece of concrete to keep patrols unaware.

Josef moved the concrete slab. "I'm serious. We should make another entrance. This one is too snug."

"We can't risk that kind of noise right now. Help me get this safe through." Pushing the safe in first, they entered the basement.

"I've heard that Nazis have been rummaging through the dead for gold possessions and fillings," Hael said.

"Why?"

"They want gold bricks as backup for the economy," she said calmly.

Josef quirked his head. "There's one thing that I just don't get about you."

"What now?" she asked.

"I don't know what you are."

"I don't either."

"Still," he said, "I don't know what you are, but I know what you can do."

Hael shrugged. "I'm still learning."

"Yes, but your skills are crucial."

She paused. "What are you getting at?"

Josef closed the entrance. "Why don't you kill Hitler?"

"Because Hitler has a lot guards with a lot of guns," she replied.

He dusted his coat. "Bullets can't kill you."

"They still hurt! Besides, Hitler already has enough Grim Reapers at his throat. Let them have him. I have my own priorities." She lifted the safe onto a stack of cinder blocks. She lit some candles, then sat on the floor. "Go see if anyone's hungry. If so, tell them to give me twenty minutes, and I'll go searching." Josef left closing the door behind him. She turned the safe's dial, reciting, "7-21-19." It opened.

The safe was packed to all sides with loose papers, a gold bar, German Marks, and folders bursting with documents. There was a brown accordion folder shoved all the way to the back with a small lock on it. She scoffed. "No key." She took off her gloves. "I should've guessed." She bit the lock in half. "Found you." Flicking her lighter, she read the case file. "Classified. Case sensitive material. Freudric Sigmund Mendelson."

Freudric Sigmund Mendelson was wanted by the Third Reich for human trafficking, prostitution, illegal experimentations, malpractice, operation of a clinic without proper license, the operation of military equipment without permission or proper license, rape, theft, abduction, treason against the German public, false advertisement, witchcraft, tampering with illegal substances, and crimes against nature towards the fairer sex.

Mendelson's appearance and other definitive attributes were unknown to the military. Mendelson ranked second on the German Third Reich's most wanted list concerning affairs in the occult. Recently, Mendelson was placed beneath Alastar Crowley, but he was elevated due to discoveries of his new offenses. Hael continued to read, "Mendelson has made no attempts of attack or threat against the Führer. However, the German peoples have suffered the loss of their women and children by Mendelson's hand for over seventeen years."

The majority of the women held captive by Mendelson were between the ages of eighteen to thirty-nine years old, and labeled missing to the general public. The victims' bodies were found during scattered times of the year. The bodies were either discreetly hidden, or placed directly in the center of the *stadt* from where they came. All of the women were reported to be sexually assaulted, battered, or starved. The numbers of men who were taken from their families by Mendelson were never seen or heard from again.

Hael turned the page. "Abducted children and infants were brought back at separate times, unharmed, to either their families or the nearest local officials. As a whole, the children neither recall where they were held captive, nor can they give details about Mendelson's appearance. None of the children were sexually assaulted in any matter or form. However, all of the returned children experienced seizures and night terrors at random."

Mendelson's family once held a highly decorated position in the German military during the early 1800s. After the fire of their family mansion in Frankfurt, the residence was converted to the orphanage Das Männlein Waisenhaus in 1823. Das Männlein Waisenhaus was currently shut down.

No photographs or sketches of Mendelson were documented. A few traces of fingerprints, semen, saliva, and skin particles were found on the corpses of eighteen-year-old women and older. The total numbers of people kidnapped by Mendelson over a seventeen year period were: one hundred and seven women between the ages of eighteen to thirty-nine years old, fifty-eight men above the age of eighteen, twenty-nine female children, and twelve male children.

Hael dropped her lighter. The flame extinguished on the rocky floor. The horrendous sights Hael witnessed were inexhaustible, but the photographs and descriptions of Mendelson's victims made her vomit. Their bodies were bruised and broken. The women found in the woods had their pelvic bones crushed, and their legs permanently bent. Their necks and wrists were badly discolored from rope burn, and their breasts were purpled with bruises. Their backs were either concaved or arched with their stomachs split open.

Hael turned her face to the ground, and retched everywhere. From the pictures, she heard the groaning victims. Their bloodshot eyes, broken bones, and gray skin were nothing compared to the way their bodies lay open like stockpots holding their mangled organs.

Josef opened the door to the basement. "Hael, they're ready to eat." He stopped. "What happened?"

Hael wiped the vomit from her mouth. "What?"

"Why did you throw up?" he asked. He looked at the documents. "What's this?"

She closed the folder. "Nothing. Come on."

"Hold on a second. It takes a lot for you to puke. What was in the safe?"

"I said it was nothing. We need to get food. Come on."

****

Up and down the streets, Nazi patrol officers scoured the area for anything they deemed suspicious. The soldiers pulled all-nighters. For these jobs, they kept their trucks stocked with a nice supply of canteens and canned food. The soldiers were a wolf pack. If any supplies were taken by ransack, the patrol would lash back and swarm the entire area. When they slept, the soldiers rotated shifts to watch over the trucks. Hael and Josef were veterans of stealth.

For stealth jobs, Hael crafted a thin syringe with an even thinner acupuncture needle tip. These syringes were designed to be shot from an arrow. Bows and arrows can be easily made and repaired. And, in the current area, loose wood, wire, and string were in good supply. Hael's narcotics would black out targets for over five hours. "Do you see him?" Hael asked.

Josef steadied his arms, "If I didn't see him, I wouldn't be a marksman."

"Just take the shot. The kids are hungry."

He chuckled. "You ever think about settling down?" She cut her eyes at him. "Okay! Okay! I'll take the shot."

He snickered and released the arrow. The guard never got the chance to clutch his neck. He fell to the ground like a sawed tree. Josef put down the bow. "They fall harder and harder every time. Are you sure you're not changing the formula?"

"No. That just means that Hitler's working them to trash." She tied back her hair. "Let's move."

From the truck, they stole bags of canned meat, vegetables, dried milk, water, and booze. Luckily, they found a jar of caramels. The children always wanted something sweet to eat when they couldn't sleep at night.

Some of the children and their parents were asleep when

they returned. Hael extinguished some of the candles. If it was muggy outside, the rooms were freezing. If it was freezing, every room was like a bog. Hael did whatever she could to make sure that the families were comfortable and safe. "You did well, Hael," Josef said. He patted her on the shoulder. "Get some sleep."

"I will. I just need to secure the entrance before I do."

"I secured it," he said.

"I'll double-check. It'll be really quick." Josef scratched the back of his neck. Hael looked at him. "What's wrong?"

He stumbled. "Huh?"

"You okay?" she asked.

"I'm just tired," he said. "It's been a long day."

Hael smiled and left the room. "Night, Josef."

"Good night, Hael."

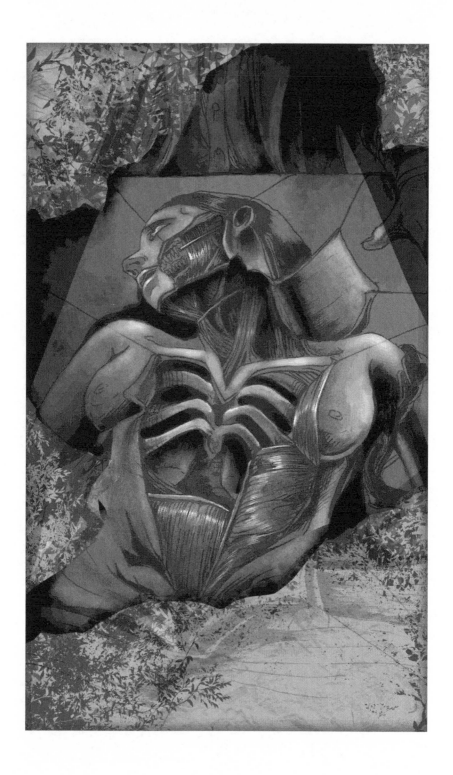

Chapter Eight
Maintaining Leads

A blinding light flickered, illuminating stained and scuffed floor tiles. A young woman convulsed on top of an autopsy table. A man loomed over her, holding a clipboard. A loose mask covered his mouth. He checked his watch every three minutes and documented how long the convulsions lasted. She stopped moving.

The man removed his mask. "Finally," he said. He picked up his watch from the table. "Seven minutes."

An assistant walked into the room. "How did the procedure go, sir?" he asked.

"Pitiful," the man replied. He took off his gloves and threw them on the dead girl's face. "Every time we get a new one, they're weaker than the last."

"What was the time on this one, sir?" the assistant asked.

"Seven minutes exactly," he replied.

The assistant laughed. "At least she was punctual."

He swung around and snatched his assistant by the throat. "You find this amusing?"

"No! Sir, I thought that the new shipment would suffice!"

He tightened his grip. "The next shipment had better be satisfactory, boy, or you'll be shipped out in a box."

The assistant choked. "Herr Mendelson, I'm sorry! I'll make sure, I swear!"

Mendelson pulled him closer. He tightened his grip. "You don't try. You do."

He let go of his throat. The man fell backwards onto the floor.

"I only have so much to work with until it's all gone," Freudric said, throwing away the gauze. "There is no room for failure." He looked down at the man rubbing his throat. "Get out of my sight."

The man jolted from the floor, leaving more scuff marks on the tile. Mendelson looked at the girl on the table. "You seemed so promising." He pulled the white sheet over her head. He walked to the door and picked up the phone.

A nurse answered the phone. "Yes, sir?"

"There's one for the freezer," he said.

"Yes, sir. We're on our way."

Before the evening came, the girl was tagged and placed into a steel case in the main freezer. Mendelson glared at the corpse, severely disappointed. Within that month alone, the girl was the twelfth to die. Freudric's success rates dropped dramatically as his experiments continued. Even though he did not age, his darkened eyelids and bloodshot gaze projected his exhaustion. The women he gathered over the past months either became sickly from his procedure or died. Concerning his procedures, no one knew what Mendelson wanted to achieve. He kept the heart of his medical aspirations private. He grabbed a milk pitcher from the kitchen and headed back to his study.

****

Mendelson's study was a whirlwind of files. On top of dressers, chairs, area rugs, and counter tops, thick folders and loose papers dominated the surface. He plopped down on the couch next to the fireplace. He took off his lab coat and searched his pockets. He pulled out his cigar case and lighter. Breathing deeply, he walked over to the dresser. A trail of smoke followed behind him. He twiddled the cigar in his mouth, whisking the smoke back and forth. When Mendelson knew that an experi-

ment was bound to fail, he insisted on pushing on until the end.
He was not known to quit. After the subject's death, he recorded
his observations and thought nothing else on the matter. He did
not dwell on things that were out of his reach. However, his appetite to own was insatiable. No matter how long or hard he
worked, he was determined to get whatever he coveted.

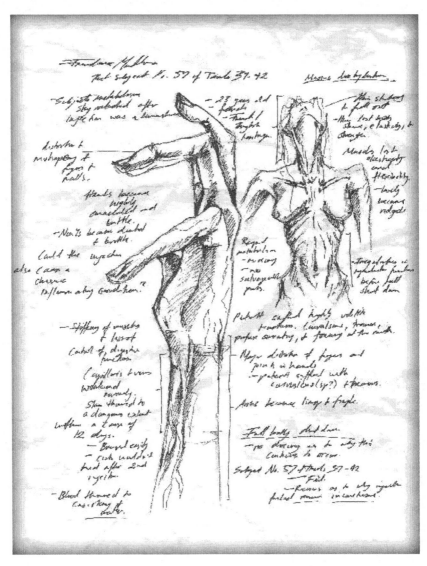

At his dresser, he opened the bottom cabinet and took out a blood filled jar. He held the container in front of him. "You're almost gone, precious." He swished the blood around in the jar. He admired the blood's brilliant red hue. "I've had you for this long and you've held up perfectly. But, you're nearly gone."

The clock chimed in his office. He lowered his glasses and watched the pendulum swing. He lifted the jar to his face. "Keep on holding on for me, beautiful. I'll find a way to replenish you soon enough." He kissed the jar and placed it carefully back into the cabinet. There was a knock at the door. "Who is it?" he asked.

"Kirk," a man replied.

"Come in," he said, locking the cabinet. Kirk was Mendelson's right hand man. Daily, Kirk filed papers and kept Mendelson's appointments in line. "What is it?" Freudric asked.

"Everything has been sterilized for future procedures," Kirk said.

Mendelson nodded his head. "Good job."

"Should we expect any new arrivals?" Kirk asked.

Mendelson put out his cigar. "Which ones?"

"Will you need any new women, sir?" Kirk questioned.

"No. I'll retrieve them myself."

"Will you need any other assistance, sir?"

Mendelson buttoned his cuffs. He chuckled. "No, boy. I won't need any help where I'm heading."

****

Dense fog layered the air. The damp cobblestones reeked with fermented beer and vomit. A dim flame flickered in a gas lamp above a narrow door. The door's wood was splintered and carved with different initials. Mendelson approached the entrance. A man with two silver teeth opened the eye slit in the door. "Who is it?"

"Open the door, Emil," Freudric ordered.

"Yes, Mr. Mendelson."

Mendelson was a regular in every known brothel, gentlemen's club, and tavern in the area. He was infamous, but generous. The entire brothel smelled of hard liquor and scented powder. The smell was so pungent that it stung the sinuses of any man who stepped through the door. Embroidered throw pillows and water pipes were grouped against the walls on low circular tables. Tapestries depicting orgies and gardens hung from the ceilings as dividers for the tables. The courtesans were dressed in transparent robes and gowns with veils draped over their mouths. Their coin anklets and bracelets jingled as they drifted across the floor. Every call girl and client stayed away from Mendelson's path as he strolled to the Madame's office. Fear hung in their eyes.

He tapped lightly on the door. He lit a cigar. "Madame Levinia?"

Quick footprints tapped from behind the door. "Who is it?" a woman asked.

"You forgot me already, *liebchen?*"

Levinia sighed dishearteningly. "No, I haven't." She unhooked the door chain. "What brings you here this evening?"

"I think you know," he replied.

Levinia strained to keep a smile. "A hot soak? Warm oil massage? An Old Fashion, perhaps?"

"I'm looking to browse your selection."

"You know every girl I've got," she said.

He leaned forward. "Your *special* selection." He blew a cloud of smoke above her head. "Ring any bells?"

Madame Levinia ran one of the best hidden brothels in Germany as well as the most notorious trafficking checkpoint for any vampire species living in the eastern hemisphere. If any vampire was caught, Levinia paid the coin for its bail and brought it under her wing. From a young age, as a Dhampir, Levinia sold out members of both her vampire and human relations for money, status, and land. And, with Nosferatu blood running through her veins, Levinia couldn't be swayed or easily tricked by dark influences. If the vampire was male, she either kept him for her own amusement, or had him cremated for her cosmetic ointments. With female vampires, her decision depended on two things: how recent the transformation was and how steep the maintenance would be. If the female vampire was recently turned, that means that she was still naïve as to what she could do. Therefore, Levinia could sell her to the highest bidder as a house maid or sex slave. If the vampire was older than five years transformed, Levinia kept her as one of her new girls. A vampire's maintenance depended on the requirement of blood necessary to uphold its youth and vitality. The maintenance equaled the price. Levinia accepted no national currency. She was paid strictly in gold. Mendelson had no qualms.

Mendelson was a wealthy patron. The amount of women he wanted never bothered Levinia. The majority of the women he paid for never returned. Levinia paid no mind. She was a cold woman. A newborn could be bludgeoned against the drywall, and her eyes would still remain at ease. However, Mendelson's recent endeavors with her employees began to eat away at her conscience. Plenty of Levinia's clients were battered and bruised by him before. But, now, slews of her girls returned with bite marks littering their bodies, or not at all. Mendelson always reimbursed her for the missing women. However, seeing the gaping wounds on their bodies and how they festered ate away at Levinia's thoughts. "We haven't received any new ones this month," Levinia informed him.

"Madame," he said placing his hand on her shoulder. "You must have something tucked away for me."

She brushed his hand off her shoulder. "I've got no new sweets. You've had the lot."

He finished his cigar and flicked the end into the corner. He sighed. "If you say so." He adjusted his cuffs in the mirror. "I guess I'll just have to do some picking."

"The best of luck to you," she said.

"Oh," he said, grinning. "I don't need luck."

"Really?" Levinia asked as she stocked her shelves.

"I've already got my next flower in sight," he replied proudly. "This won't be difficult."

"What's she like?" she asked.

He combed his fingers through his hair. "She's a small little thing."

"Is she?"

"She has a Fae resemblance," he said, watching her organize the shelves.

"Yeah?"

"She reminds me of one when I think about her. Her limbs are tiny as well as her feet. A person can see the stitching in her clothes. I think she works in a tailor shop." Levinia paused. She watched him through her peripherals. "Her face is small with a thin nose. She has auburn hair." He laughed. "Her name even reminds me of a fairy. What was that girl's name? Rose? Lilly? Or, was it Marigold?"

Levinia took out her shiv from her dress pocket, and lunged at him.

Mendelson caught her wrist and bent it backwards onto the desk. Her face blanched as her bones splintered. She shrieked in pain. He pinned Levinia in an arch. "Gardenia."

"You pig! Leave her alone!" she demanded.

"Ooh. Mama's angry, isn't she?"

"Leave her alone!" Levinia yelled.

"Listen to me, you raggedy tramp. I've heard the rumors circulating about my business and women. And, that's exactly what they are: my business and my women." He shook the shiv from her hand. "I pay you well. Without my patronage, this cesspool would be festering right now like it should have been a long time ago."

He unpinned her and threw her across the room against a bookcase. Her head slammed against the lower shelf. The books from the top shelf fell hard onto her temple, nearly hitting her eye. He cornered her. "I like meeting new family members, Levinia. So, if you want to keep this place, and not have your daughter know that her mama's sucking my cock to support her sewing career, send your entire shipment my way when it comes in. Am I clear?"

"Yes, Freudric," she said. He grabbed the back of her head, and yanked her hair. She thrashed. "What? I told you I understand!"

"No, no, no, no, no. I know you understand. Trust me. But, you, my dear, lied to me. Therefore, you've lost the privilege of using my first name." He tightened his grip, "You have to earn it back."

Levinia's scalp started to tear. The pain wouldn't cease. Blood trickled down her neck. She pleaded, "Please! Please, stop! What is it?"

He let go of her hair. Madame Levinia hit the floor face first. He took off his hat. "I've had every piece of ass this place has to offer. And, let me tell you, sweetness, I've been very patient."

"Do you want them to work overtime?" she asked.

He laughed. "Gardenia is a lovely woman. By the looks of her, I'd say you've worked hard to make the child as beautiful as she is." He sat in the armchair and smiled. He took off his belt. "Show me how hard you've worked."

****

Several hours passed. Before dawn came, Mendelson made his way through every woman in the brothel five times. Both Madame Levinia and her selection were bruised, battered, and broken. They lay panting where he finished. On top of pillows, mattresses, and tables, they lay on their backs in sweat with slack jaws. Their hair stuck to the sides of their faces as their limbs twitched wrenchingly at every attempt of movement. Blood trickled down their thighs. They wept, holding their torsos. Six women had their ribs cracked.

Levinia struggled to stand up. Mendelson buttoned his shirt. "Well done," he said. "I suspect that the shipment should be arriving soon."

Levinia sat herself up. She choked. "It's going to take another three months."

He stopped buttoning his collar. He looked over his shoulder. "Pardon?"

"Three months!" she repeated. "I can't make the shipment go any faster."

"And, why not?" he asked.

"We've had problems on the roads," she replied.

"What kind of problems?"

She wrapped a scarf around her torn bodice. "I thought you said you took care of the SS?"

Mendelson's eyebrows furrowed. "I paid them off over eleven months ago. I pay the same price once every year."

"The shipments have been delayed more and more," she informed him. "The last one almost didn't come in at all." She scoffed. "They must be greedier than I thought."

"If they demand more money, it'll be for their coffins."

"If tracked, the new ones can get here in two months."

"That's better," he said. He put on his coat. "Well, Madame, thank you for the evening."

"Whatever. Just have the money ready."

He put on his hat. "You know I always take care of you."

****

Smuggling the survivors from Dresden proved more treacherous than Hael suspected. The people she harbored this time around had family members deep within Eastern Europe. Hael and Josef smuggled six people from the ruins of Dresden, through eight Nazi perimeters, three surveillances, and one bird's nest. The roads were littered with patrol cars. Traveling on foot was the best way to stay hidden. However, when the children or elders couldn't walk any further, Hael commandeered a passing patrol car.

"When the kids see blood on your gloves, they're going to freak," Josef said.

Hael dragged the dead driver behind her. "Just shut up

and put the bastard in the ditch!"

When she took a car, Hael kept driving until the gas ran out. If the car she took had an extra tank, she burned the car to eliminate any evidence that they were there. Hael stripped the soldiers of any weapons, gas masks, or food they had.

At the end of the road, before they approached a border-line, Hael told Josef to watch over the families. She'd cause a commotion to distract the guards. When the soldiers left to investigate the noise, Josef ran the family across the border. If she was driving a car, and there were only two to five soldiers at the border, she would let the families out at the safest distance. Once out of sight, Hael barreled through the border, crushing any soldier she saw underneath the car.

Josef remembered when one of the elders in the group witnessed Hael's methods. He remembered the old woman questioning him as she clasped her hand over her mouth while tugging his shirt sleeve, *How can she bring herself to do these things?*

Josef put his hand on the woman's shoulder. *Her methods are ruthless, but she's never lost anybody on these trips.* The look on her face was impossible to forget, but he kept reassuring her that they were going to be okay.

One trip to bring the survivors to their destinations lasted an average of three weeks to two months. When the smuggling's urgency increased due to pregnant women or children younger than five, Hael made the trip last from two weeks to a month at most. Josef recalled every job he pulled with Hael, but the two-week memories were a blur.

****

After they finished another job, Josef and Hael set up camp in the woods. Josef leaned back against a tree and wiped his brow. "So, how many do we have left back in Dresden?"

"Zero," Hael said. "We're pretty much done for now."

"How many provisions did these guys have?" he asked, pointing to a slaughtered regiment.

"A good bit," she replied. She struck a match. "I found a couple of cans of beans and meat. There are some water canteens and seven packs of cigarettes." She dumped the rest out of the bag. "And, four decks of cards."

"Can I see?" he asked, pointing to the cards.

"Here," she said, tossing him the decks.

He counted the decks. "You said there were four."

She tossed the two decks onto the burning wood. "There's two for you and two for the fire." Josef scoffed sitting next to the flame. He poked at the wood. Hael stirred the fire in deep thought.

"What's the matter?" he asked.

Hael sighed. "Nothing."

"No," he said, scooting closer. "Something's up."

She tossed the stick into the fire. "I can't believe how many kids there are. We've smuggled over twenty orphans to their new havens within the last month alone."

"I'd thought you'd be surprised at the amount of pregnant women who have been asking us for help," he said. "There's been what? At least a six percent increase from the usual?"

She shrugged. "People are just trying to escape it all." She opened her flask.

He searched through the bag. "It's gotten too risky."

"Smuggling is risky."

"But, smuggling a pregnant woman is even more dangerous. Anyone of them could've dropped at any time."

Hael choked on her flask. "Thanks for that image."

Josef laughed. "I'm just saying."

"I know you are."

"I'm just saying that it is a real danger," he clarified. "If that would've happened, we'd be helping a woman in dire need for medical assistance, and a crying newborn across dicey turf."

"I need to get them to safety. There are no exceptions."

Josef smiled. "I swear."

She took another swig from her flask. "What?"

"It's easier to tame a wolf than to convince you."

She took a big swig of her drink. "You've never tamed a wolf in your life!"

"Yes, I have."

"When?" she asked.

"Well," he said, looking at the flask. "Pass the bottle, and I'll tell you."

She handed him the flask. "Go on."

Josef snatched her drink out of her hand, and ran off.

"Come back!" she shouted. "That's the only spiced wine I've found in years around here!"

The two chased each other through the trees until they were ragged. Whether they passed out because of the wine or tired feet remained a mystery.

****

Josef had connections in every *stadt* from Oeventrop to the edge of Berlin. But, he always stayed away from the Black Forest. When they reached the nearest *stadt*, Josef was able to get a room in the best inn with the least amount of soldiers occupying it. "Think this is a good place?" he asked, locking the door behind him.

The room was spacious. Hael peeked behind the curtain. Groups of soldiers trotted across the streets. "You don't want that answer, Jo," she said.

Josef examined the bathroom. "This is the best I can do for right now."

"No! No. I'm not saying that this isn't good. I'm saying that this place is no safer than the next. As long as they're around," Hael said, pointing to the soldiers, "it really doesn't matter where we stay."

"We won't stay here for long," he assured her.

"Why are we even here?" she asked.

"I need to catch up with a friend," he replied.

She kept watching the soldiers. "Yeah?"

"My friend may have some new supplies for us."

She looked to the other street. "Good! Good. We need that."

"I'll be back in a few hours."

"Wait!" she said. "Before you go, how much cash did we bring?" she asked.

"Why?"

"I need my fix. This place has a good bar."

He straightened his sleeves. "I know the people here. They owe me. The bar and dining room are free."

"How much do they owe you?" she asked.

"You're covered. Trust me."

"Remember, you said that. Not me."

He rolled his eyes. "Keep the door locked."

****

The hallways were packed. The owners were hosting a reopening party after the renovations. Josef kept his head down and made his way towards the wine cellars. A woman stood by the door. "Kirk is waiting for you," she said. "He's in the back."

Josef opened the door. "*Danke.*"

In the back of the cellar, a man with wide framed glasses stood against one of the shelves. Kirk blew smoke. "It's about time you got here. How long were you expecting me to wait?"

Josef closed the door. "I'm here. Where's my stuff?" Josef kept his composure, but this entire scenario left him bleak and irate.

"Over there," Kirk said, pointing toward the wine barrels.

Josef walked behind one and found a brown package tucked into the corner. He untied the string.

Kirk tapped Josef on the shoulder. "Hold on."

Josef turned around. Kirk aimed a pistol at Josef's face and held out his hand.

Josef's teeth sharpened. "What the fuck, Kirk?"

"You know hand gestures. If you want the goods, pay up."

Josef glowered. "I paid you already."

Kirk snickered. "You paid the package price, but not mine."

Josef pressed himself against the nozzle. "I paid you enough." His eyes were fixed on Kirk's throat.

Kirk looked at Josef's teeth and the nozzle then put his gun down. He stepped back.

Josef put the package down. "Do you really want to play games?"

"No. But, how would she feel if she knew you played on our team?" Kirk asked, pointing the gun towards the ceiling.

"I'm not on your team!" Josef shouted.

"Bullshit! If you hadn't paid me, you would have never known Himmler's location. The Reich would've had their boot so far up your ass you couldn't swallow anything without tonguing their heel!" Kirk hissed. "You're a fucking collaborator. So, unless you want my friends finding out about that gypsy upstairs, cough it up!"

Josef's fist was clenched so tight that his nails broke the skin.

"Well?" Kirk asked.

Josef flicked the blood off his hand. "How much is it?"

Kirk grinned. "Forty percent increase."

Josef clenched his fist again.

Kirk turned towards the door. "Eva!" The woman by the door entered the room. "Can you tell Rudolph and the rest to —?"

"Here!" Josef emptied his wallet. He threw Kirk the money. "You'll get the rest after tonight."

Kirk smiled and picked up the money. "Forget it, Eva. You can go back to the bar." He rolled up the money and placed it in his back pocket. "Go put your uniform on," Kirk said. "We're already late."

****

The rendezvous was a two-hour drive away from the inn.

The car ride was bumpy, but traveling with Kirk would make anyone nauseous, Josef concluded. For the entire ride, he stomached the odor of greasy hair, cheap aftershave, and tobacco chew coming off Kirk. They arrived at a warehouse. Josef got out the car. "When did warehouses become the ideal place for meetings? Or, did fucking in cemeteries get boring to you people?"

"Keep your hands behind your back and your mouth shut, Czech," Kirk said. "I'm doing you a favor bringing you here."

"What favor?" Josef scoffed. "It's just more files with the same shit. When are you going to get something new?"

"How's this for new?" Kirk opened the doors. The lights turned on. "Choose your poison."

Josef cringed. "What the hell am I looking at?"

"You, good sir, are looking at the storage for one of the biggest trafficking sites in the Eastern hemisphere."

Josef looked at the cages. The room was a menagerie of anguish. The shackles around the women's waists kept them attached to the bars. The coagulated blood and soiled clothes suffocated the senses. Josef touched one of their hands. It was ashy and scarred. "Why is there no uproar about them?" Josef asked.

"Simple." Kirk walked over to the cages. "You see, Josef, there's no reason for an uproar for something that one would gladly throw away."

He grabbed a woman's face and pried opened her mouth. Very slowly, the woman's canines began to elongate until her whole mouth resembled anything but human. "The females here were willfully divulged by their cities. Or, they were running loose in the countryside."

The women looked like dogs awaiting euthanasia. "Why the hell would someone want all these vampires?" Josef asked.

"You mean why would *he* want them?"

Josef stopped walking. "Mendelson's in this?" For years, Josef wandered the whole of Germany and Austria looking for Mendelson. No one knew why Josef needed to find Mendelson.

And, no one dared to ask. Josef spent countless hours tracking down every lead he had on Mendelson's imports and exports. Alas, nothing took him directly to the source of the operation. By swindling, bribing, and bartering, Josef spent everything he had for information in hopes of finally catching this elusive madman.

Kirk released the woman's mouth. "You're shocked, Josef?"

"Mendelson has always trafficked women, human women. Why the sudden change?" Josef asked.

Kirk laughed. "My God. You must be dumber than I thought." He lit another cigarette. "One human woman to Mendelson is equal to three female vampires."

"Why?" Josef asked.

"I've heard that one is better than the three."

"That's stupid. A vampire is three times stronger than a human could ever be."

Kirk blew smoke. "I didn't say it. The others did." He finished his cigarette, and tossed the end into one of the cages. "Besides, what the hell are you getting so riled up for? Aren't you one of these things, too?"

Josef launched at Kirk. He slammed Kirk's head against the bars. The caged women jumped back in fear. He choked him. "Half vampire! Half!"

Kirk coughed. "What's the difference? You're still a monster!"

"Life and humanity, Kirk. It's a huge fucking difference. Unless you want to lose the first one, *never* say that again!" He dropped him. "I've seen enough of this place. Any new information you get, you bring it to me first." Josef grabbed Kirk's truck keys, and stormed off.

Kirk sat on the ground and watched Josef leave the warehouse. He rubbed his throat. "You brought this on yourself."

****

Josef returned to the inn within the wee hours of the morning. Eva was cleaning behind the bar when he came in.

"Where's Kirk?" Eva asked.

"He said he was catching a ride back with some friends," Josef replied.

She nodded. "Of course he is."

He walked up the stairs to the room. On the ride back, he changed into his original attire. Hael was asleep on her bed. He dropped his clothes bag on the chair, took off his shirt, and went to wash off. The pipes groaned and creaked behind the tiled wall. The noise traveled down through the room.

Hael woke up. She grabbed her pistol from underneath her pillow. "Josef?"

"It's me! It's me. Don't pop anything off," he said from the bathroom.

She looked at the clock. "It's a quarter past three! Where were you?"

"Out," he replied.

"That must've been a damn good shipment. Where did you put the supplies?"

The faucets squeaked behind the bathroom door. He put his hand under the water. "Oh, the shipment isn't going to be brought here. They'll bring the supplies to us in Dresden."

"Why? Who's going to look after it?" she asked.

"A friend of mine is," Josef replied.

Hael walked around the room and stretched her legs. She did not sleep well. Once she woke up, it took at least thirty minutes for her to fall back asleep. If it weren't for the street lamps, the room would be in total darkness. She plopped herself onto the chair.

She sat on something, and stood up. She brushed her hand over the cushion, and picked up Josef's bag. The handle slipped from her fingers. The bag's contents emptied out over the carpet. She rubbed her eyes. Her foot pushed the objects into the light.

****

Fifteen or so minutes flew by. Josef walked out of the

bathroom, towel-drying his hair. Steam billowed out behind him. "Hey, do me a favor," he said holding a towel around his waist. "I got a shirt and pants somewhere around the dresser. Toss it over, please."

Hael tossed him his clothes. He felt them drop by his feet. He bent down to pick them up. He paused at the texture. He removed the towel from his head. Looking down, he was holding the SS uniform.

"I'm pretty sure that's the wrong one," Hael said. "What do you say, Josef?"

He saw Hael sitting in the chair. She sat in a lax position, but her stare could melt a diamond. "Is it the wrong one?" she asked. "Or, are you more comfortable in that?"

He put the towel down. "I know what you're thinking."

"Liar? Collaborator? No. Nothing like that."

He threw the clothes on the ground. "I am not a collaborator!"

"Really?" she asked. "So, how'd that get here? I don't see any bloodstains on it."

He stood in front of her. "You're talking to me like you never once put on that uniform!"

"No. For two weeks, I did put on that uniform. Then, I made sure everybody who wore that uniform was on a gurney. I didn't make friends with them!"

"They're not my friends," he said.

"How am I supposed to believe that?" she asked.

He stood over her. "What did you say?"

She repeated herself. "How am I supposed to believe you?"

He wiped his face. "After everything I helped you with, you're grilling me for this?"

"Josef, you betrayed the army you worked for by selling weapons to the black market, and you experimented with the artillery. I think I can be a little suspicious when that same person is working for me without pay."

His face reddened. "I don't want you to pay me!"

"Why not? Why in God's name would you take on any of this shit without benefits?"

Josef stared at her. He sat himself on the bed, rubbing his temples.

Hael clenched her fist. "Why?"

"We're going after the same guy."

She paused. "What guy?"

He sighed. "Come, sit down."

She stepped away from him, "No. What guy are you talking about?"

"Please!" He cleared his throat. He placed his hand on the space beside him, "Please, just sit down. I'll explain."

She raised her eyebrow. "Even the Nazi suit?"

"Yes, even the Nazi suit." He patted the bed. "Please."

"Wait." she said. She walked behind the chair, and picked up his clothes. She handed him his shirt. "Here."

He thanked her. She sat beside him. He put his shirt on. He tossed the pillows onto the chair for more space. "I will admit that the first few weeks I started work with you, I was about to ask you for money. But, things changed." Josef explained that when Hael told him about the different places they would travel to, he realized that the places she mapped out were the same destinations he marked to discover his leads. And, when he learned about the main cities she targeted, such as Berlin, he didn't bring up payment. While transporting survivors and stragglers to their new safe havens, he started to doubt his decision. But, before he could ask for payment, Hael told him about her new target: Himmler. He remembered Hael describing her target, *If anything happens to the leader, Heinrich is ready to take his place. Any information we need about the grit that the Reich's hiding, he's sure to know something.* For as long as he's conducted business in the underground, Josef saw plenty of people try to scar Hitler's army. But, nobody he knew went for the kill like Hael did. Spying on meetings between the Gestapo, breaking into

Himmler's villa, beating the hell out of him and his wife, stealing his safe, and hijacking his car was the best operation he's pulled in decades.

"I was pumped," Josef continued. "The timing and style were through the roof. I never wanted to stop."

He told her how hard his heart beat every time he went on another mission. "But, something went awry when we brought the safe home." he said. "You were so tired. After taking that hit and hauling the safe back, I thought you were going to collapse. You told me not to worry, but something was off. I don't know what got to you. Whatever it was, it must've been really messed up." He walked over to his briefcase. "I looked through the files on the table."

"Josef, I don't care if you looked at my things," she said.

He sat his case on his lap. "I know who Mendelson is."

The air in the room went still. A crimson tint flickered in Hael's eyes. "Josef, don't play with me."

"I'm not."

An eerie smirk appeared on her face. "You sure?"

"Hael," he said, placing his briefcase in her lap, "I never play with madmen." The tint faded from her gaze. Josef quirked his head at her. From what she could do, Josef's was certain that she was a dhampir. But, when things like this occurred, the chills she shot up a person's spine rivaled winter's grip. "As much as I hate doing it, you're right. I collaborated with the Nazis. To get this kind of access, I had to do it."

She opened the briefcase, and picked up the files. The weight of papers was equal to a newborn. She was amazed as she bounced the stack in her hands. "How much do they have on him?"

Josef lowered his head. "Not enough."

"Then, what the hell is this?" she asked, holding the papers.

"Those," he said flipping the pages, "are all his victims' descriptions."

"That's it?" she asked.

"The paper you had was the only description of Mendelson," Josef said, lying back on the bed. "All of these are his victims' personal details."

She flipped through the stack. "How can a man bring himself to do these things?"

"Simple, he's not a man. He's an animal." Josef laughed. "An animal in a well fitted suit." Josef sneered at the files and pushed the case on the floor. He stretched out his legs.

She plopped the stack onto the floor. "How do you know so much about him?"

He pushed himself further onto the bed. "I told you. I get more information about enemies to the public by involving myself with the Reich." He flipped over on his stomach. "I can't say if I'm going to continue."

She glared at him. "You're continuing?"

"Okay, I'm not continuing it."

"I bet they're asking a fortune from you to keep your whereabouts a secret," she said. "That money is needed for ammo and food. We can't afford to give up anymore." She placed the stack of papers back into the case. "Besides," she said, adjusting herself on the side of the bed, "the best insurance is to keep hidden. The army has too many files on you for you to keep doing this."

"True." He rolled closer to her. "So," he said, placing his arm around her back, "what do we do now?"

She moved his hand back on top of his stomach. "Simple, you tell me everything you know, I tell you everything I know, and we catch him."

"Simple?"

"It's not like we have a better choice. Why make things seem more depressing?"

"Right." he said sliding down the side. He grumbled, getting back on the bed. "You know, I could've avoided this life."

She smiled at him.

"Seriously, I could've," he said. "I could've owned my mother's bakery, bought a nice house, got a wife, and all that stuff."

"Why didn't you?" she asked. "What made you choose this?"

He put his hands behind his head, and stared at the ceiling. He shrugged. "In this life, I know what I'm doing."

Chapter Nine
Eight Balled

A ruckus shook the inn from the downstairs lobby. Hael sprang from the bed and ran towards the door. Josef awoke from the couch. He looked out the window. The clanking of fallen silverware and shouting echoed from the bottom of the staircase. Doors opened throughout the hallway as frightened guests peeked from their rooms. Like a stampede, the crashing sounds of jackboots and the smell of gunpowder filled the narrow stairway. The guests scurried back into their rooms. Just as quick as they receded, the soldiers bombarded their rooms, and dragged them out one by one.

Hael grabbed her weapons. "Josef."

"Yes?" he said, arming himself.

"When this is over, pay up," she said.

He took the safety off his Lugar. "Why?"

She pulled back the hammer and unlocked the door. "Because, after this, you owe me a new coat." She kicked open the door.

Like target practice, Hael's bullets burrowed between the soldier's eyes. She picked up the dead soldier and used him as a shield. She shouted at the guests in the hallway. "Stop staring! Get in your rooms. Now!" Doors locked behind her in a chain reaction. Fingers and chunks of skin spattered off the dead soldier from the bullet barrage. Hael dug her hand farther into the soldier, and carried him like a Spartan shield. When she drew close enough, she hurled the body against the regiment with brute force. They collapsed like dominos down the narrow staircase. Underneath the mound of fallen bodies, she heard their bones snap under the weight. She turned around. "Some help would be nice, Jo!"

Josef ran down the hall to the back staircase.

"Where are you going?" she yelled. "They're over here!"

"Follow me," Josef said, leading Hael down the hallway. The worn floorboards creaked and groaned under their feet. A soldier with a broken leg managed to hoist himself over the rest. Josef broke the latch to the back door and headed down the staircase. "There are more of them outside blocking the front of the inn along with every surrounding street."

Hael kept shooting. "I thought you paid them for secrecy?"

"A rat will always want more cheese." Josef led Hael down the staircase to the back door of the wine cellar. Eva was in the room when they entered. Before she pulled the trigger, Josef fired three rounds into Eva's chest. "Do you see what I mean? I paid that bitch a huge lump sum of money, and she still tried to shoot me."

"Is there an exit from here?" Hael asked.

"The sewers are one, but that's not why we're here." He unsheathed his dagger, and stabbed the kegs against the walls. "If we go out that door, we can force our way out the inn. But there are three times more soldiers waiting outside. It's only a matter of time before they find this back entrance." He grabbed a wine bottle from the shelf and bashed it against the wall. "There's enough liquor here to douse every wall in this cellar. When you're done dousing, get into the sewer and head down the west tunnel. Keep going west until you hit a dead end. An exit will bring you to the farthest edge of town near the forest line. I'll meet you there."

"What are you going to do?" she asked.

He lifted two beer kegs onto his shoulders. He ran up the back staircase. "You have four minutes."

Hael tore off Eva's clothes, and doused them with wine. She stuffed the drenched apparel into the air vents and tossed a cracked wine bottle to the back of the air shaft. Within two minutes, every wall in the cellar was saturated. Hael stood with her feet five inches deep in wine. Hael ran up the staircase towards Josef. At the end of the hallway, Josef stood with the beer kegs in front of him shooting the last remaining soldiers. "Josef!" Hael called out to him. "Josef, it's done! There's no more wine!"

"Well done!" he said. "I'll meet you near the forest! Go!" Hael ran back down the steps and busted open the sewer grate. She ran towards the west.

The west tunnel underneath the inn was closed due to native superstition. The residents believed that since the west tunnel beneath the *stadt* led to the edge of the forest, the darkness of the sewer gave malevolent forces unlimited access to the *stadt's* inhabitants. The last thing Hael wanted to deal with was raw sewage.

Boom! The tunnel vibrated. Hael ducked. Debris of chipped brick, compacted dirt, and plaster fell from the ceiling. Rats scampered away from the east and trailed over Hael's arms and legs. She stood up. "Josef?" She looked behind her. The echoes of the explosion receded, but the rumbling in the tunnels continued. She removed a match from her pocket, and struck it against the wall. The rumbling continued. Rats screeched and continued to pour in from the east as they tripped over one another. *Boom!* "Was that the sign?" she asked, looking into the darkness.

A light sparked at the end of the tunnel. In a hard gust of wind, dust flooded the pathway and clouded her vision. She dropped her match. The tunnel heat became unbearable. As she staggered backwards through the hordes of rats, more and more hot debris clung to her skin. The smell of the sewer vermin, stagnant water, and scat polluted her senses.

Something burned her ankle. She scraped the remaining dust from her eyes, and looked down. The scattering rats had ignited into orbs of fire. The stagnant water steamed as a violent surge of char and embers billowed into the tunnel.

She ran to the west. A storm of fire and vermin chased

her through the tunnels. She tore through the swarms of rats crowding the escape hatch. They bit and scratched her hands and face as she pried loose the rusted manhole cover. From below, she could feel splashes of boiling rancid water and fiery char eating at the soles of her feet. Furious, she focused her energy in her fist and punched the lid open. As she clawed her way to the surface, a torrent of fire and rubble blasted out of the ground.

For a few moments, she was dazed and confused. On her back, she thought that the superstitions were true and that she had awakened a sleeping dragon. But, the falling rat carcasses brought her back to reality.

The ground above the tunnels buckled and caved in from the collapse. Hael scurried backwards so her leg wouldn't be sucked in. She looked above the tree line. The eastern sky burned red. A cloud of black smoke floated in the air.

Hael looked at the ground and the burning skyline. She shook her head. "Josef! Josef! You son of a bitch! Don't you die out there." She watched the smoke billow higher. "Please, don't die out there."

A tear ran down her cheek. She wiped her face. "Why couldn't you just go down the damn sewer with me?" She sat on the ground and watched the smoke climb further into the night. She sat there covered in dust and debris. The wind whistled past the brittle tree branches. She heard the forest sigh as the leaves shook in the cold air. The surviving rats scampered around her, searching the debris for food. She watched their tiny paws imprint the dirt. She watched how their dusty little noses twitched and wiggled. They looked like fluffy puffs of ash. The rats ran around in circles, and chased each other. Hael studied them. It stunned her that, even after a near death experience, these rodents easily went back to playing. She wiped another tear from her eye. "I envy you animals. Half of your friends just died; yet you still find solace amidst the ashes."

A tiny scream sounded from underneath the piles of

overturned earth. Hael stood up and pushed away the loosened rubble with her fingers. A rat was caught under the dirt. It was solid black, and smaller than the rest. It wriggled and scraped at the rock that caught his paw. "Poor thing," she said lifting up the rock. The rat jumped from the dirt and ran to the top of the pile. With its nimble fingers, it wiped the dust from its face. Its eyes were so shiny, but they were hardly noticeable since they blended well with the rest of its glossy fur. From nose to tail, the rat was blacker than the smoke cloud and twice as fluffy.

"You're welcome," Hael said.

It squeaked. She looked at it. It squeaked again. She crouched down and stared at it. "Why are you still here?" she asked.

It sat there. She watched its little body puff up and down with every breath. It sneezed. "Bless you," she said.

It wiped its face again and ran down the rubble. The other rats moved out of the way as it fled into the forest. "Curious little thing, aren't you?"

The ground quivered beneath her feet. The piles of rubble and bricks shifted as it the earth broke apart. Hael picked up a dead branch and readied herself. A hand burst through the dust and clutched the grass. A large blackened ash body pulled itself to the surface. She didn't know what it was, and her nerves were too shot to question it. Hael bashed the creature across the head.

"Damn it!"

She paused, but she still held the branch. The creature continued to pull itself up to the surface. It plopped on the ground and rolled over on its back. She bent over to look at its face. "Josef?"

Josef wiped the char and grime off his face. He rolled over. His knees buckled as he stood. "What the hell was that for?" He spat out a wad of dirt. "I had," he said, hawking up another gob of dirt, "I had to charbroil a whole Nazis regiment, go down a sewer, and burrow through mounds of broken tunnel to get smacked by a dusty nut with a branch?"

Hael dropped the branch and hugged him. "You had me scared out of my wits!"

He was stunned. "Wait. I scared you?"

She caught herself. She stopped hugging him. "No," she said, straightening her sleeves. "Well, no. I was worried that you got caught up, or that something may have gone awry. I mean, you've never planned something like this before, and I was just—" As she looked at him, a calmness came to her eyes. Though riddled with filth and surrounded by death, Josef's visage eased her apprehension.

"I was concerned." She dusted her hair. "You're the best partner any outcast could ask for. I'm glad—"

"You're glad I'm here?" He grinned.

She exhaled deeply. "Yeah. I'm glad you're here." A strange feeling came over her. Amidst the scenery, the hellfire skyline, dead rodent carcasses, and ashy rats, Hael was overwhelmed by a vast breath of peace in knowing that Josef was alive.

Josef sensed the silence between them and broke it. "Look, I don't know about you, but I need a bath." He laughed and wrapped his arm around her. "I got a friend in Berlin."

"Not another Nazi," she said.

He laughed and rubbed her back. "No. Remember when I told you about those experiments I did a while back?"

"Yes."

"I had a friend who helped me get connections," he said. "The guy I met here was a poor connection I made after I got out. I never would've suspected that he was this much of a bastard. But, don't worry. None of my associates know each other. So, this," he said pointing at the fire, "never existed."

She smiled in relief. The fastest road to the nearest city passed through the forest. The little black rat was near the tree line. Hael quirked her head at it. "What are you still doing here?"

It squeaked. When Josef looked at it, it scurried away.

"You scared it away," she said.

"It's a rat, Hael. It's their nature to be scared."

"Well, that one wasn't. I saved it from the rubble. It thanked me."

He raised his eyebrow. "It what?"

She shrugged her shoulders. "It squeaked."

"They all squeak." He laughed, then added with a smile, "I never thought you had a soft spot, Hael."

She tripped him, and walked ahead.

He shook his head. He laughed harder. "That was cute! That was really cute." He cracked his knuckles. "You don't know where you're going!"

She shook the dust from her hair. "So, come on!"

****

Back at the inn, the stench of scorched flesh and melted glass hung in the air. Thick layers of gunk and burned wood suffocated the ground. This was a small town. With the combination of shattered wine bottles, busted beer kegs, gun powder, rotten wood, and close housing placement, the entire town was torched to the bedrock within the hour. A few survivors sifted the rubble for dead relatives and valuables.

A dark shrouded man stepped into the town. With her two children, a woman tried to pull her husband out from under smoldering wood. The shrouded man raised the plank and helped the woman free her husband. She fell to her knees. She held her hand over her mouth, screaming. The man looked at the husband. "He's not dead."

The woman looked up at him in shock and disbelief.

"Trust me," he said. "He's not dead. Feel his neck."

Trembling, the woman gazed at him with weary eyes. He pressed the woman's fingers hard against her husband's neck. "See? He's weak, but he's still alive."

"Karl! Karl!" the woman shouted. "Wake up. Please! Please, wake up, Karl!" Behind her, her two children stood huddled together in tears.

"He's out cold. And, by the looks of him," the man said, opening Karl's eye, "without immediate tending, he'll never wake up again."

"Please," she cried, grabbing his hand, "help him!"

Beneath the shadow of his shroud, his smile leered at her. "My dear, you're talking to me like I'm a friend."

Her voice cracked as she wept, "I don't care who you are. All I know is that you're not a corpse. My neighbors are dead. My brother is dead. Now, my husband is dying. I have no one around to help me except you. Please, help me."

He smiled. "With pleasure. However, I have a request."

"What?" she asked. "I'll do anything."

"Let's help your husband first, shall we?" His voice was so calm and nonchalant. The entire *stadt* was in chaos, yet he stood there in his shroud unfazed. He hoisted Karl up, and dragged him to his two children. The shrouded man towered over the two. They cried over their unconscious father. "Behave yourselves, children, and help your father. He's in great pain," the man said. "Your mother has business to attend to." He approached the woman. "Now, about my request."

"I don't have much, but whatever's left is yours."

He extended his arm, and placed a finger over the woman's mouth.

She shuddered under the cloth of his black glove.

"I have no need for material possessions," he said. "I request input."

"I don't know what good that'll do you. The majority of the people who lived here are dead."

He smiled. "I can see." His long, black hair covered half his face. "Tell me, did the town receive any guests as of late?"

"Yes," she said. She pointed to the inn. "Just a few days ago, a man and his gypsy walked into town. They stayed at that inn just before it went up in flames." She straightened her sweater. "You don't think they started the fire, do you?"

"That's not my concern," he replied. "Other than the man

and his gypsy, did any other people come through?"

"Not that I recall." She thought hard. "Wait. There was a soldier who stayed at the inn. I think he was friends with the owner. But, I don't think he was here when the fire started. He left before that."

"Which way did he go?" the shrouded man asked.

"He went northwest to Berlin."

"Berlin?" He bowed his head. "Thank you, my dear." He walked off.

"Wait! Please!" she said, walking after him. "You said you would help my husband."

He stopped. "Of course, dear lady. However, I sense that this is more of a family matter. Besides, you have very clever children. They know their place."

"What?"

He grinned. "They're ridding their father's pain."

The woman turned towards her children and screamed. An ungodly hue lingered in their eyes. Her son sat on top of his father and jabbed a mirror shard into Karl's neck. "No! No!" she shouted. "Dear God! What are you doing?"

"Are you hurt, my dear?" he asked. "I'm sure your children can help you, too." He beckoned the twins. "Oh, children?"

The twins launched themselves at their mother's legs. They pinned her down. The woman shrieked, "Margret! Jan! Stop!" She cried as they anchored her to the ground. She struggled, but she couldn't bring herself to hurt her own children. "Please!" she cried. "Please! It's your mommy! It's Mommy! Don't you recognize me?"

The boy grabbed the mirror shard from his back pocket.

She looked at her son with tears flooding her face. Something bewitched him. His chipper hazel irises were dulled and foreboding. Holding the shard in his hand, he butchered his mother's jugular. Blood splattered across the man's leg. While his sister held down her limbs, the woman bled to death. With her last ounce of strength, she grabbed her children's wrists.

Blood filled her mouth. She couldn't speak. The pain was too great. She kissed their hands. She wept silently. *"Meine lieblinge."*

The twins snapped out of the trance. Jan looked down at his hands and mother. "Mommy?" he said, tapping her shoulder. He placed his hands on his mother's shoulders and shook her desperately. "Mommy, Mommy, wake up! What happened to you?"

He shrieked. "Margret!"

Margret shook her head. "Huh?"

"Something's wrong with Mama! Look!"

"Mama!" Margret patted her mother's cheek. "Wake up!"

The man shook the blood off his shroud and proceeded west.

Chapter Ten
Herr Drosselmeier's *Puppe*

Mendelson sat in front of the fire, his eyes closed. He straightened his back and crossed his legs as he meditated on the current events. He clasped his hands together with the jar of blood clenched between them.

There was a knock at the door. "Herr Mendelson?"

"*Einkommen*," Freudric said calmly.

Kirk walked through the door. His throat quivered as he straightened his shirt collar. "Good evening. Are you well?"

"I'm breathing, aren't I?"

"That was a silly question for me to ask," Kirk said. "Of course you're doing well."

Mendelson rubbed the side of the jar. "What did you come here for, boy?"

Kirk straightened his posture. Mendelson tilted his head back. Kirk read his report. "The eastern Dresden shipment has unfortunately been delayed."

A dense silence filled the room. Mendelson leaned his head forward and placed the jar snugly into the corner of the couch. He faced Kirk. His eyes were still shut. "Why?" he asked.

"Our shipment was compromised," Kirk said. "However, I have managed to get a secure rerouting for half the time."

Mendelson patted Kirk's shoulder. He grabbed the jar and placed it back into the cabinet. "Let me guess," he said, locking the cabinet. "This secure rerouting is half the time, but double the cost, right?"

"No, sir," Kirk replied. "The rerouting is the same amount as the original was."

The air was still. Mendelson balled his fist. Kirk's body stiffened from his heels upward. Kirk grunted as he struggled to jerk his legs loose. "Sir, I understand that this is frustrating, but, if it pleases you, I can see if the price can be dropped."

"No." Mendelson chuckled. Standing behind Kirk, he grabbed his shoulder. He placed his head in the crick of Kirk's neck. "Kirk, I have no problem paying the price."

Kirk choked. "Sir?" His arms became like stone. Panting, Kirk's face reddened as he strained to lift his arms. From his wrists to his shoulder cuffs, Kirk felt his muscles tighten like piano wire. His eyes welled up as his blood vessels popped in his wrists and forearms.

"Besides, a young man like you could do a lot of things with that money," Mendelson said.

Kirk clenched his teeth and wheezed. His throat muscles tightened.

"Having trouble?" Mendelson asked. "Are you tense?" Mendelson yanked Kirk's arm above his head. Veins and muscles tore through Kirk's skin. Blood coated Kirk's entire left side and spattered into Mendelson's clothes. The entirety of Kirk's throat clapped shut as he choked on his own vomit. His bloodshot eyes streamed with tears as he whimpered and pleaded for mercy. Mendelson seized Kirk's arm behind his back. He spun Kirk around and grabbed his face. "You've been having fun with my money."

"I swear I can repay you every mark! I swear it! Just don't hurt me anymore!" Kirk begged.

"You're lying," Mendelson said. "The second I let you go, you'll disappear."

"No! No! I won't! Anywhere I go, you'll know where I am."

"You swear this?" Mendelson asked.

"Yes!" Kirk replied, sobbing.

"Good." Mendelson let go of him.

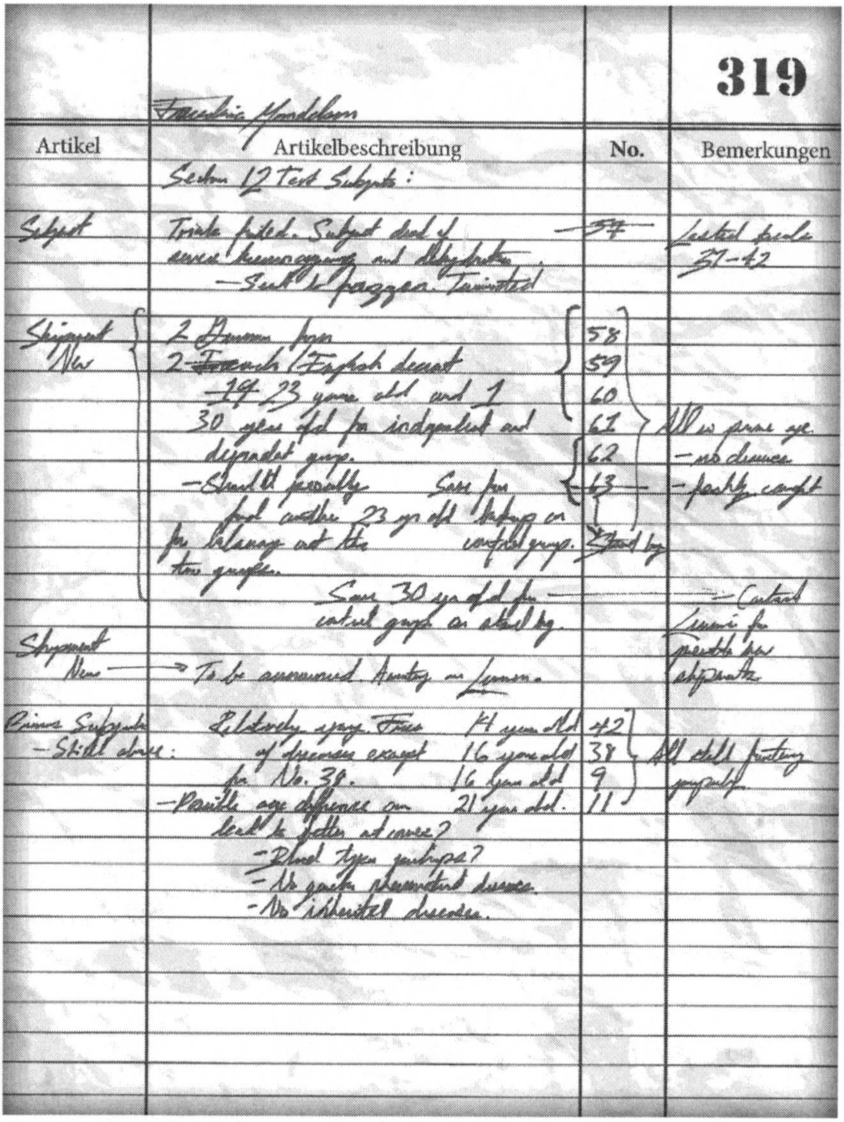

			319
	[illegible]		
Artikel	Artikelbeschreibung	No.	Bemerkungen
	Section 12 Test Subjects:		
Subject	[illegible] Subject [illegible]	~~57~~	[illegible] 37–42
	[illegible]		
	— [illegible]		
Shipment New	2 [illegible]	58	
	2 ~~[illegible]~~ / [illegible]	59	
	~~19~~ 23 years old and 1	60	
	30 years old for independent and	61	All in prime age.
	dependent group.	62	— no disease
	— [illegible] Save for	63	— [illegible]
	[illegible] another 23 yr old [illegible]		
	for [illegible] control group.	Stand by	
	[illegible]		
	Save 30 yr old for		— Contact
	control group as stand by.		[illegible] for
Shipment			[illegible]
New →	To be announced [illegible]		[illegible]
Prime Subjects	[illegible] Free	14 years old 42	
— [illegible]:	of diseases except	16 years old 38	All [illegible]
	for No. 38.	16 years old 9	[illegible]
	— Possible age difference [illegible]	21 years old. 11	
	[illegible]		
	— Blood types perhaps?		
	— No [illegible] disease.		
	— No inherited diseases.		

Kirk fell limp to the floor. He cried and vomited onto the rug. He stabilized himself on his knees. Half of his body turned numb. On his knees, Kirk watched his blood leech into the carpet. His eyes fluttered wildly in the fight to remain conscious. "I promise, sir, everywhere I go, you'll know where I am."

"That's a good boy." Mendelson straightened Kirk's back and patted him on the head. "I knew I could trust you again." He placed his hands on Kirk's neck.

"Anywhere I go, you'll know where I am."

"Go to hell."

Snap! Kirk's body fell hard and loud like a stunt dummy. His head rolled from side to side against Mendelson's heel.

Light footsteps traveled down the hall. A nurse called out, "Herr Mendelson! Are you okay? I heard a thud." She gasped. She stopped at the doorway and clasped her hands over her mouth. "What happened, sir?"

"Elsa, I'm fine."

Elsa looked down at the body and shuddered. She looked back at Mendelson. He was standing two feet in front of her. She flinched.

"Is something wrong?" he asked, picking the dried blood from his thumbnail.

Elsa made no eye contact with him. "Nothing's wrong, sir. I was just startled."

"Startled at what?" Smiling, he lifted her head. "Hmm?"

"The noise startled me, Herr Mendelson." Elsa's voice trembled. "I was startled by the loud thud. I thought you may have been hurt."

"I'm fine. But, my good friend here," he said, pointing to Kirk's corpse, "seems rather ill."

Her jaw quivered. "Will he need assistance, sir?"

"Oh, yes. He will," he said. "He nurses the bottle too often. He fell and hit his head. I hope he's okay."

"I see what you mean. That's a terrible situation, him clinging to that bottle." She stared at Kirk's broken neck.

"Bring him to Alrich," Mendelson instructed. "He'll take care of him."

"*Jawohl.*" she said.

"Oh. Before you go," Mendelson said, removing a small folder from his desk, "can you make copies of these? I need them done right away."

"Is there an emergency, sir?"

"Yes, there is. I'm out of an assistant."

"What about Kirk?" she asked.

"Kirk's a drunk," Mendelson said sharply. He sat down on his chair. "You see what he brought upon himself. He's been my assistant for too long now. I need someone fresh and alert. I need someone dependable."

The nurse nodded her head and dragged Kirk's body out the room as quickly as she could.

He frowned as he watched her leave. "She's so stupid." He sneered at the doorway. "Alrich, you need to take more pride in your employment," he said to himself. "They all have to be better than just a decent squeeze."

****

Josef and Hael traveled through the woods to avoid the major *stadts* on the way to Berlin. Due to their plan's urgency, Josef contacted some friends around Dresden to help them smuggle the people through the borders. As they drew closer to Berlin, Josef received a message saying that his contact had an emergency of his own. Josef read the letter:

> "*Josef,*
>
> *I'm sorry, but I won't be able to meet you direct-ly in Berlin. Something came up with the family, and I have to go see what's wrong. I will be back as soon as I can. – Kale.*"

Hael was suspicious about the news, but she used the opportunity to scout the place for wire taps.

"Hael, just don't wreck the place," Josef said.

"You're one to talk. Didn't your last friend try to kill us?" she asked.

The farther they traveled, the more uncomfortable Hael

became. She possessed a keen and sensitive nose. When they traveled through the countryside, the air was filled with the stench of sweat, burned rubber, gunpowder, dirty clothes, and filth, but it was tolerable due to the wide open space. The same couldn't be said for the *stadts*. When Hael came in contact with the compacted buildings, tight alleyways, and sewers, the stench gagged her. She tried breathing through her mouth to lessen the impact. But, the odor still made her retch.

****

Kale was Josef's most trusted contact. Being an Alp himself, Kale worked with Josef for decades on numerous jobs in the underground while supplying him with information about Mendelson. Kale resided in an expensive hotel less than ten minutes from the central business district. It was risky being close to that much activity. But, the information gathered was worth it. Josef and Hael were dressed up in their best attire. Kale wrote down specific instructions upon their arrival. Josef read the instructions:

> *"Josef,*
>
> *When you get to the hotel, tell the concierge that you are visiting Herr Hans Krebs in the pent house suite. Your names will be Mr. and Mrs. Klaus and Lillian Zimmerman. If the man brings up any small talk, tell him that you are visiting from Frankfurt. Nothing more. – Kale"*

They followed Kale's instructions, and made their way to the penthouse suite. The bus boy carried up their luggage. "Is there anything else I can do for you, sir?" the bus boy asked Josef.

"No." Josef thanked him, and paid him handsomely to cease any further interruptions. After he left, Josef put his ear against the door. He waited until there were no footsteps in the hallway.

"He's gone," Josef said, turning around. "What's wrong?"

Hael looked up at the windows. "They're humongous."

Josef took off his tie. "They're just windows."

"But, they're huge! Look how big the curtains are."

"You're easily entertained, aren't you?" he asked.

"Sorry, if I like grandeur. I wasn't raised around a lot of windows." She removed her shoes from the couch. "I hate heels."

"Poise and grace," Josef teased her. "Poise and grace."

She chuckled. "Like you know so much."

"I took etiquette classes when I was a boy."

Hael stared blankly at him.

Josef continued, "My mother always told me, 'Sweetie, if you don't remember anything important in life, at least make sure that you get a nice girl to help you remember them all over again.' She made me take etiquette classes to reassure me that I would get a nice girl."

Hael shook her head, laughing to herself. "I don't believe you."

"Alright," Josef said, standing up, "come on." He held out his hand.

"What?" Hael giggled.

"I'll show you."

"You don't have to prove anything," she said.

"Obviously, I do."

"No, no. I believe you," she snickered. "I believe that you're proper."

He gently held her hand. Hael hesitated, shocked at how easily he led her into a dance. His thumb glided across the top of her hand as he lifted her up. "Let me show you," he said kindly.

He wrapped his arm around her waist as he placed her hand on his shoulder. He led her into a small box step.

She glanced at her feet. "Are you putting me in a trance?"

He winked. "Just a little."

She smirked. "Okay. Okay. You've proven yourself once again. You took etiquette classes."

"But?" he asked.

"But, why are you so eager to prove it?"

Josef twirled her around. "Because, I'm not like my father."

"Come again?" she asked.

"I was remembering my mother."

"Ah. I see," she said. They ended the dance, and bowed to each other. "That was nice. I needed a mental break. Thank you."

"Any time, my lady."

"Just don't go soft on me when I need you," she said. He agreed. Hael unpacked her bags and took out a leather-bound notebook. She reviewed her notes.

"What's that?" he asked.

She flipped the pages. "Every piece of evidence I receive on Mendelson is recorded in this notebook. There are so many rumors about him. It would be insane to try to remember the details without writing them down."

"I'm confused," Josef said, looking at the notes. "None of the case files know what he looks like. How can you have that much detail about him?"

"I just do." She chewed on her pen. "Is there any more stuff you have of him other than what you told me?" she asked.

Josef paused.

She turned to him. "Jo?"

"There's nothing else. That's all I had."

She sighed. "Well, that was more than anybody else could give me." She tapped her pen against the side of her head as she scanned her notes.

"Is something wrong?" he asked.

"I've had these notes for so long. I haven't found one common factor to any of his crimes. Not one." She marked the corner on a page.

"Maybe you're thinking too hard," he said.

She bit her pen. "Maybe I'm not thinking hard enough."

He sat next to her.

"What?" she asked.

He snatched her notebook from her hand.

"Hey! I need that!"

"What you need, my dear, is anything but this."

She raised her eyebrow at him. "So, you know what I need?"

"*Pojd' sem.*" He told her to come close. He felt her neck and limbs. "Let's see. Tired muscles? A tense neck? Sore feet and legs?"

"You're really pushing it, Jo."

"You need a treatment," he said.

"You have the treatment?" she asked.

"No," he replied. "But, the spa does."

She snickered. "I'm not fond of people touching me."

"You seemed to like it just now."

She grabbed his fingers and placed them to the side. "That's because I know you. But, you're still pushing it."

He chuckled and rubbed her back. "You win. I'll leave you be." He draped his coat over his shoulders.

"Where are you going?" she asked.

"I'm meeting Kale."

"This isn't going to end up like last time, is it?" she asked sternly.

"No! No," he said turning back around. "I'm going to meet him at his job."

"Oh. Where is it?"

"Why are you asking so many questions?" he asked.

"Well," Hael replied as she removed her socks, "a good partner always knows where the other one is when they're on a job. I don't want to search for you around Berlin if you need help."

He tied his laces. "What's wrong with searching?"

She rolled her eyes. "You're right. Nothing's wrong with searching. Nothing's suspicious about a black haired gypsy looking around Berlin for her fugitive partner."

Josef bit his tongue.

She closed her bag. "Where is it?"

"He owns a private recreational center," he said.

"For who?"

"For those with an exceptional cultured taste."

"Be safe," she said, waving goodbye. "Wait."

"What? I have to go."

"Does this spa have a sauna?" she asked.

"They do. Do you want me to look into it?"

"That won't be necessary. Tell your friend I said, 'Hi'."

"I will."

Hael browsed through the pamphlet of services the hotel offered. She sneered at the wig she wore. Every blonde curl sent her eye twitching. She decided to stay in the room. The bathroom had a deep porcelain tub.

****

Hael relished the privacy of her afternoon. She filled the bathtub and undressed. It was a long time since she had a hot bath. The water swallowed her from her feet up to the top of her head. She resurfaced, leaned back inside the tub, and tapped the faucet with her toe. Tiny ripples appeared and vanished on the water's surface. No lights were on in the bathroom. The amber sunlight shining through the window made the rippling water appear as melted gold. As she lifted her hand, she watched the steam float up across the golden rays and dissipate into the air. In this moment, she was serene. She was unwound. She was sleepy.

A shadow passed across her face. She lifted her head from the water and looked around the bathroom. The golden rays illuminated the room. The water became tepid. She passed her hand over the water to calm the ripples. The shadow passed her again. Alarmed, she stood up in the bathtub and grabbed the marble soap dish. She wrapped the towel around her and scanned the room. "Who is it?" she asked aloud.

There was no response. Something stroked her back. She

swung around and flung the soap dish against the wall. The dish broke into pieces. "Where are you?" she shouted furiously,

Still, no answer. Minutes ticked by. With nails sharpened and teeth bared, Hael's guard was unwavering in the tub as she stood prepared for the phantom trespasser.

The sun's golden rays shifted into a rust colored gaze. The water around Hael's legs grew cold. She was still alert of her surroundings, but she remembered her previous serene moment. She ran the hot water again. Within a few minutes, the tub returned to warmth. She leaned forward in the tub and watched the ripples. Like autumn leaves, the sunlight changed from its golden shine into a deep copper.

She was sleepy. The water hugged her sides and ran between her fingers. Lying back, she rubbed her legs and arms. Underneath the surface, she felt the hot water from the faucet breathe bubbles around her toes. Her eyes fluttered. She reached towards the faucet to turn it off.

Something whispered in her ear, "Relax."

"What?" she shouted, alarmed. Her eyes flickered tiredly as her fingers fiddled in the air. Her left arm reached for the faucet with half closed eyes.

"Relax," the voice spoke again. "I'll take care of it."

The water stopped running. Silence filled the room. The absence of sound put her on edge. She did not move. The water seemed like it was rising. But, when she looked down, the water level remained the same. A warm sensation submerged her up to her neck. Perplexed, she glanced into the bedroom, and saw one of Josef's jackets folded over the bed. "Josef," she said reaching for the jacket. She thought that he may have stored a copy of his friend's phone number in the pocket.

She stopped. As she reached towards the jacket, she realized that her left arm was suspended in midair. She couldn't move her arm. She pulled herself backwards to loosen the invisible grip, but her efforts made her slide forward.

The whispering breath filled her ears. "Relax."

"What are you?" she asked demandingly. She felt her body succumbed to a warm, heavy pressure. She looked at her arm. Massaging her limb, deep synchronized fingerprints appeared on and off her skin. She elongated her claws and attacked the space above her.

"Save your energy," it said.

Something caught her wrist and suspended her right arm in midair. Both of her limbs were locked. Against her hand, a slimy sensation wrapped and glided down her fingertips and palm. As it traveled downwards, she saw a series of sharp indents trace her wrist. Her heart raced. Despite the warm water, her hair stood on end. The pressure increased. A wave of pain and pleasure coursed through her body.

"Stop," she begged. "Please, stop." Hael was not one to beg, but this was entirely out of her realm.

It laughed softly. "If you insist, my dear."

The pressure lifted from her wrists. Her arms were still suspended, but the grip on them steadily released. She tried to sit up. The pressure on her chest and neck held her down firmly. Involuntarily, her arms moved to the sides of the tub. Her head was pushed back. She looked forward as much as she could and kicked her legs under the water.

Two hands subdued her ankles. She called for help, but her head was plunged beneath the water. She lifted her head back up. She coughed violently. "Get off me!"

The hands that pinned her ankles traced and swirled around her calves. She jolted. They groped her faster and faster as they kneaded her flesh. They traveled between her thighs, and onto her sides. "Stop!" she demanded.

It ceased.

She jumped up to feel her legs and sides. She regained control of her limbs. She felt violated. But, she realized that she was alone in the bathroom. Her paranoia slowly faded. She rubbed her shoulders. "It was nothing," she reassured herself. "You've been out of sorts as of late. Your mind was venting its anguish. It was a nightmare."

She collected her thoughts. "You almost fell asleep in the tub, and you were shifting through a nightmare," she continued. She flinched as she rubbed her sides. She looked at herself, and rubbed her skin again. Carefully, she traveled her hands across her thighs onto her sides. She flinched again. Beneath the water, there were deep scratches across her skin.

The voice returned. "*Mea culpa.*"

Shadowed hands sprang out from behind the shower curtain. They dragged her under the water. She fought for air. The hands squeezed her. She jerked her head above the water and gasped for breath. She looked towards the ceiling. They yanked her back under and pinned her at the bottom of the tub. The invisible hands finished tracing her sides. She struggled to hold her breath. The pressure building in her lungs was painful. Her diaphragm weakened.

Something licked her from her stomach to her neck. "This was fun," the voice said. Soft lips kissed the nape of her neck. It rammed its hand against her stomach. The air was forced out of her body.

****

Hael jutted from the bottom of the tub. She flung her arms over the tub's rim. The water was ice cold. By the window, the pale white street lamps lit a small portion of the room. Water spewed from her mouth onto the floor.

"Agh! Ahh!" she coughed. Hael grabbed her chest as she spewed drool and water. She was freezing. She grabbed her towel and crawled limply over the side of the tub.

"Jo?" she called. Her coughs rattled her body. "Josef!"

Josef hadn't returned. Wary from the previous incident, Hael darted her eyes towards every corner of the room. On the floor, she could still feel the horrid fingertips that groped her skin. But, nothing was in the room with her. She was alone.

She slapped herself across the head. She came to her senses and shook off whatever paranoia was left. She remembered the conversation she had with Josef before he left. He was meeting his friend Kale at the recreational center. She hoisted herself onto the door frame and turned on a lamp. Her feet drenched the carpet. She dropped onto the bed and rubbed her throat.

"Where the hell is he?" she pondered out loud. Her throat was raw. She searched the jacket's pockets. They were bare. She threw the jacket onto the floor, angered.

There were voices in the hallway. Drunken voices. Hael pressed her ear against the door. It was the bus boy and another man. The bus boy slurred his words. "And, this is the suite."

"Wow!" his friend said. "People have money for this shit?"

"Yeah!" the bus boy said stumbling over his feet. "In fact, we got a couple staying in there right now."

"Who?" he asked.

"Fuck, I don't know." The bus boy jingled his keys. "Whatever. Hey, you wanna see what it looks like?"

"You can't get in there," his friend said.

"Uh, yeah, I can. My girlfriend's one of the maids here. I can snag a key to any room I want. Come on." Lethargically, the bus boy fiddled with the lock, and tried to aim the key into the slot. "I fucking hate doors," he said, chortling.

Hael flung open the doors, and bashed the two in the head, rendering them unconscious. "I do, too," Hael said. "You never know who's behind them."

She rummaged through their pockets, and took any extra keys or money they had. Dragging them by their ankles, she stuffed the two boys in the hallway's janitorial closet. She went back inside to grab her trench coat before heading out.

She stopped. Josef's scent was on the two men. She searched their coats again. In one of the pockets, there was a piece of folded paper. It was a welcoming flyer to a grand opening:

"Willkommen, Herren! Willkommen bei Herr Drosselmeier's Haus! Herr Kale Drosselmeier has traveled far into the Land of the Ris-

ing Sun to bring you an extravagant feast for your luxury and loins a like! Indulge yourself in the celestial glow of the toy maker's newest doll: The Geisha! The mysteries of the Far East await you with their silken touch!"

Hael's eye twitched. Josef's scent coated the entire flyer. *Recreational center*, she thought.

After locking the room, Hael exited through the worker's entrance. She read the finely printed address as she followed Josef's scent.

****

The coordinates and Josef's scent led Hael into a high class neighborhood. Tall metal fences encased manicured lawns of this large suburb. Children's toys were on the front porches. Stuffed bears leaned against the panes of slightly opened windows. A soft wind whistled past thick tree branches. Green leaves shook and fluttered in the breeze. Rose bushes of pink, red, and white lined mailboxes, curbs, and driveways. Even the trash cans at the front of the houses were clean. In a two story window, Hael saw a mother sing her baby to sleep in a rocking chair. This was a wealthy neighborhood.

Josef's scent grew stronger. She sprinted ten blocks into the neighborhood, keeping her head low. She arrived at a little toy shop. She read the sign, "Der Nussknacker." Hael peered inside. The shop was empty. She grabbed the door handle. It was unlocked. She looked around the block. There was nobody there. She entered the shop.

Wooden marionettes of sparrows and hummingbirds hung from the ceiling. Tin soldiers lined the windowsills as they protected their ballerina princesses. Fluffy teddy bears sat with their families on the floor and on top couches. An elaborate carving of a treasure map was engraved into the floor with footprints leading to a giant "X" underneath a mammoth treasure chest. Trimmed with gold and silver, the treasure chest was made of pure mahogany. Its contents spilled over the sides. Jeweled play necklaces, rings, bracelets, amulets, and tiaras drooped over its hull. Amongst the jewelry, stuffed giraffes, tigers, panthers, elephants, boas, lions, and more teddy bears slept between glistening entanglements of gems. Train tracks rode alongside a vast painting of hills and mountains that covered the background of the shop. Blank marionettes hung on multicolored strings with their assortments of clothes folded neatly beneath. Carved magical dragons soared from corner to corner of the shop.

A sweet yet potent musk filled the room. It reminded her of warm wood, fresh bread, and good schnapps. Josef's scent was everywhere. Hael walked towards the register's counter. Saw dust surrounded the counter's base and the back wall. Josef's shoes had a special sickle design engraved into the bottom of his boots. His and other boot prints traced through the saw dust and behind a large carving of a nutcracker. The nutcracker wore a patch over his left eye; he was armed with a long bayonet that he held in his right hand, and a shield in his left hand. There was a crease behind the carving. Hael pushed the carving aside.

The shield moved and blocked Hael from continuing. Traced in gleaming silver, a question was carved onto the shield. Hael read the inscription, "I am the guardian of this shop. Foul play or trespassing is my duty to stop. I, the Nutcracker, have caught you in one of these deeds. If you answer correctly, then you may proceed. If thou think you are worthy enough to pry, tell me who caused the tragedy of my eye?"

Recalling the old story, Hael remembered the villain of the tale. She stepped back, replying, "The Rat King." Once she answered, the nutcracker's shield returned to its original position.

An old man's voice emitted from the carving: "Well said."

A clicking sound resonated behind the nutcracker. When it stopped, the nutcracker's mouth dropped to the floor, and revealed a dimly lit staircase behind it. There was a small door at the bottom with a sign above it. It read, "Herr Drosselmeier's Haus." Hael walked down the steps and grabbed the doorknob.

It was an old bronze doorknob with an uneven tint of color. Behind the door, Hael saw another room at the end of a long corridor. The corridor was decorated with pastry-designed, striped wallpaper with dangling keys tied to the ceiling. Each key had its own specific symbol engraved into it.

At the end of the hall, a circular room contained five doors. Each door was differently embellished, but all of them resembled the front porch of a dollhouse. Hael read the doormats in front of each door: "Baby Dolls. Glass Figurines. Ballerinas. Marionettes." She turned to the last door, the one that said, "The Geishas."

Noise erupted loudly from behind the doors. The Japanese themed door had the most ruckuses. The Japanese door was made out of bamboo wood. It was decorated with carvings of cherry blossom trees, Japanese characters, and fans painted with mountains. A sunrise draped the background. Paper lanterns hung on both sides of the door. The doorknob was fashioned as a parasol. She slid the door open. On the other side of the door, there was another floor mat that read, "Shoes off." Hael took off her boots and placed them at the end of a row of shined leather shoes.

Kotos, kotsuzumis, shakuhachis, an *odaiko, biwas, shamisens, sokans*, a *takebue*, and *shinobues* played in different arrangements. Plum blossoms covered the floor. The scents of plum wine, sushi, sake, *donburi, onigiri* with sesame chicken, *sashimi* with pickled ginger, and *udon* noodles filled the air as it mixed with invisible layers of light perfume. Nothing was of cheap quality. The octagon-shaped room was large. Men ate off of low tables. Soft pillows surrounded an elevated black glass walkway. Beneath the walkway, a lavish bonsai and stone garden was well maintained. The walls were made of glass with waterfalls behind them. Behind the waterfalls, soft lights of red, orange, pink, and lavender blended from one color to another. Mist covered the ground.

Avoiding the indulging patrons, Hael snuck her way towards the back. There was another sliding door hidden behind a mist waterfall. The plaque on it read, "Danna." Josef's scent wafted from behind the door. She walked in.

There was nobody there. A heavily pungent smell hung in the air. It was different from the other room. Peculiar and sweet, the odor was highly intoxicating. A long desk was placed opposite from the door. Picture frames and documents covered the desk. Hael picked up one of the frames. It was a picture of Josef and another man. They seemed to be fixing cannons. The man in the picture wore an eye patch just like the nutcracker carving in the shop.

Laughing burst from behind the door. Hael put the picture down, and hid in a storage cabinet. Josef stumbled out of a dark room with the man wearing the eye patch. White smoke followed them out of the room. Josef laughed. "Kale, it's really good to catch up."

"I know! You were away for so long," Kale said. "Where've you been?"

"I told you. I've been with Hael," Josef replied.

"That's right." Kale scratched his ear. "So, what's the deal with you two? You--"

"No!" Josef shook his head. "She'd murder me."

"She's not the touchy feely type, huh?"

Josef shook his head. "Far from it. But, I can't lie. She's one hell of a partner."

"I bet she is," Kale ogled.

"Nothing's going on like that!" Josef shouted.

"So, you're in the dog house?" Kale asked.

"I'm her friend. I'm not in any house."

Hael stood behind Josef. "Well, you're in his house."

"Fuck!" Josef jumped backwards. He almost tripped over Kale. He didn't expect Hael to be there. "Don't scare me like that!"

"Oh, you're scared? Can't imagine why."

Kale adjusted his eye patch. "Hello, *fräulein*. I don't believe we've met."

"You're Herr Drosselmeier?" she asked.

"Kale," Kale replied. "But, yes. I am Herr Drosselmeier. Welcome to my house." He bowed. "Any friend of this guy is a friend of mine."

She bowed back. "Very nice to meet you, Kale. Would you mind if I have a small word with Josef?"

"Not at all, good lady," Kale said. "Take all the time you need. Are you hungry? Can I get you something to eat? Drink?"

"I'll get something in a little bit, thanks," she said.

"Just let me know when you're done." He leaned towards Josef. "You're in the dog house."

Josef cracked his knuckles. After Kale left the room, Josef turned toward Hael. "So, you made it!" He smiled. Hael smirked back.

"Kale's a really neat guy," Josef continued. "He supplies the best ammo."

"I'm sure he does," she said.

Josef rubbed his hands. "He invited me to come over."

She nodded her head. "To his brothel."

"He's the contact who supplies--"

"Ammunition from a brothel under a toy shop," she interpolated.

Josef chewed his tongue. "We were discussing the new arrangements."

She laughed. "And, smoking opium. Josef, my day has gone from Nazis to hookers. Please, tell me that this guy has some fucking incredible info on Mendelson."

"Whoa!" Josef cried. "Why did you track me down anyway? And, what's with your voice? You're not getting sick, are you?"

She coughed. "I was reading some of the files, and a folder had some dust in it. It blew straight into my face. Don't worry about it," she replied, her voice a tad hoarse. "I fell asleep in the tub, I woke up, and it was night. You weren't there."

The incident she endured before was still plagued her

memory. To herself, she labeled the scenario a nightmare. In truth, she didn't know what to call it. But, nightmare was the closest word that made sense to her. However, in the present moment, she refrained from speaking about it. "I thought you were in trouble."

He chuckled. "What could possibly happen to me?"

"You're serious?" she asked. "The SS is constantly marching around with their angry fucking boots looking for fugitives like you! I do not want to spend any more time here than I have to. They could catch you. I don't want you to wind up on death row!"

"Okay! Okay! You're right," Josef said. "I should've told you I was going to a brothel."

"I don't give a damn if you are in a brothel!" she shouted. She pushed his shoulder. "We watch each other's backs. That's our job!"

Josef nodded his head. He looked at Hael's face. Her eyes were unmoving and fixed into a hard stare. Her mouth was shut tight, but Josef could tell by her jaw movements that she was grinding her teeth together. She was genuinely worried.

He sighed. "I'm sorry," he said, hugging her.

She hugged him back. "Just tell me where you're going. That's how these things work."

He smiled. "Can do."

She sighed. "Great." She scratched her head. "Let's get something to eat. I want to talk to your friend."

"He's been waiting to talk to you."

****

Shaking hands and directing the servers, Kale attended to his guests around his bordello. His employees sashayed around the blossom and mist covered floor. They were dressed in pastel kimonos with painted faces. "Come, sit down," Kale said, waving from his seat in the back corner of the room on grand pillows. The table in front of him was filled with hot plates of his menu choices. "So, how long have you been in Germany?" he asked Hael.

Hael leaned back on the pillows. "Too long."

"I see." Kale laughed. "Same old scenery?" He sipped his sake. "That's why I travel. I suggest you see Japan."

"I wonder why," Hael said, pouring herself a drink.

"I'm serious," Kale said. "Japan is beautiful."

"Scenery isn't why I'm sick of Germany," she said.

Kale swirled his drink around in his cup. "Oh?"

She lowered her glass. "I'm sick of looking through it."

Josef stretched his legs. "Hael, for the majority of her life, has been searching for Mendelson. I've given her as much advice as I can on his possible dwellings and where he may strike next. She wants to learn more about him from you."

Kale stared at Josef. He put his drink down. "I know about him. But, Josef, you're--"

"Fresh out of ideas!" Josef interjected. "I'm fresh out of ideas, advice, and all sorts of things."

Kale rolled his eyes. "Whatever." He looked at Hael. "So, you got a beef with Big Eyes, hmm?"

"Who's Big Eyes?" she asked.

Kale chuckled. "Big Eyes! My dolls personally gave Mendelson that nickname."

"He comes here?" she asked.

"He's a patron," Kale replied. "He comes here every other month when the girls change roles."

"Why do they call him Big Eyes?" Hael asked.

"Do you see that big pillow you're sitting on?" Kale said, indicating a large white embroidered pillow. "That's his seat. He always sits in this corner."

"Why?" Josef asked.

"This corner is the darkest spot in the entire room. On top of that, this spot has the best view of everything." Kale picked his teeth with his fingernail. He explained that Mendelson watched both the girls and the guests. He studied their behavior. When he sat in his corner, the only thing distinguishable about

Mendelson was his shoes. He always crossed his feet on top of the table. Nobody saw his face unless they were close to him. "You wouldn't want to be close," Kale said.

"So, how do you know it's him?" she asked.

"Aside from his shoes, his eyes give him away. Nobody can miss those big amber circles."

"That's the source of the nickname," Josef said.

"And, you're not worried?" Hael inquired.

"Well, yes. I am. But, I can't do anything to him. He's the best paying client I've ever had," Kale said.

Hael downed her drink and leaned forward.

"What?" Kale asked.

She filled her cup. "You can guess what I'm about to say."

Kale grinned. "You want me to get rid of him?"

"Or, you can let me tear him to pieces," she replied.

Kale disagreed. "I can't do that."

"Why?" Josef asked.

Kale's neck muscles tightened. "Because Mendelson knows where I live." Studying how Kale rolled his shoulders, Josef and Hael sensed Kale hid details about his affiliation with Mendelson. Kale handed an employee his empty plate. "He knows everything about me. I wouldn't cross him."

"I don't want to cross him," Hael said. "I want to kill him." She stood up. "Thank you for the information."

"Where are you going?" Josef asked.

"Back to the hotel," she replied. "If this is what Kale has to offer, I'll wait until Mendelson returns."

"Hold on," Josef said. He walked after her. "We've already discussed an option."

Kale stood up. "I can't lay a finger on him."

"Because, he's rich?" she asked.

"He's filthy rich," Kale replied. "But, I can get you close to him."

"What do you have in mind?" she asked.

Kale took another swig from his drink. "I'm not saying

anything until you give me a good reason."

"Stop toying with us," Josef said. "Are you going to help or not?"

"Easy! I just want a good reason." Kale pushed his empty glass toward the end of the table. "As I said before, this guy is my best client. His wallet paid for my new dolls. I know his reason for wanting Mendelson dead." He pointed toward Josef. "But, I want to hear yours. Your reasons aren't my concern. But, if things turn sour, I'd at least die knowing it was for something solid."

Josef scoffed. "How much more do you need to know?"

"Don't act like you don't know me," Kale told Josef. He turned towards Hael. "If you really want to get close to him, just tell me your reason. It doesn't have to be long."

"One reason?" she asked.

"That's it."

Hael went silent for a few moments. She took out her lighter. Leaning back into the pillow, she slowly cracked her fingers one by one. In full clarity, her struggle with Mendelson replayed in her mind as she stared at the bordello's floorboards. Her body was still, but as she flicked her lighter, Josef heard a low continuous growl emit from her throat. Her eyes turned darker and darker as the visage of Mendelson's wide-toothed grin burned her memory.

Josef placed his hand on her shoulder. "You okay?"

Hael didn't answer. A tiny smirk appeared on her face as she imagined disemboweling Mendelson with a broken sake bottle.

Josef nudged her arm. "Hael?"

"I'm okay," she told Josef. Still smiling at the thought of eviscerating Mendelson, she leaned forward. She closed her lighter. "He tried to rape me." With her calm voice and ironclad stare, Hael sent chills through Kale's body.

"When he failed, he tried to steal me," she continued. "When that failed, his henchmen tried to kill me."

The two men were silent.

"Why so hush? I gave you my reason. What happens now?"

Josef turned to Hael. "When did this happen?"

"Kale, I gave my reason," she said. "Now, what's the plan?"

There was a moment of silence. Kale smiled. He clasped his hands together. "Good enough for me!" He crossed his legs. "First off, you must remember that Mendelson is fastidious."

****

In the following hour, Kale told them everything he'd observed about Mendelson. Whenever he visited the brothel, Mendelson always sat in the corner of the room with the widest view of the guests. He religiously drank glass after glass of mead, milk, and the darkest lager Kale had to offer. "He's exceptionally punctual," Kale told his companions. "My place opens at nine to let guests get situated. The girls start their first walk on stage fifteen minutes after opening. When their curtains open and the lights turn red, Mendelson's already in the corner ordering his first drink. Nobody hears him come in." Mendelson would never pick right away. He watched each geisha's act and stance three times before he made his choice. "Nobody sits with him," Kale said. "He's always alone. Whichever girl he picks is the one that sits with him for the entire night."

"What else does he do?" Hael asked.

"If nobody strikes his fancy, he picks his first choice, and goes through the geishas until last call."

Hael nodded her head. "Does he do anything else?"

"Nope. He comes here every weekend."

"How many girls, on average, does he go through in one night?" Josef asked.

"The whole twelve shows unless he sees something special," Kale said, smiling at Hael.

Laughing, Hael smirked back at him. "I see where you're going."

"Then, that saves me a mouthful of pitching," Kale said.

She gave Kale her full attention. "Tell me the details."

To get close to Mendelson, Hael had to convince Kale and the rest of his employees that she wouldn't crack under pressure of time and perversion. The clients were too drunk and too forward for their own good.

"I can deal with that," Hael said. "What's next?"

Kale informed her that due to the war and word of mouth about his bordello, his employees were fluent in German, Japanese, French, and English.

"How good are you with Japanese?" Kale asked.

"I'm fluent," she replied.

"French?"

"Fluent."

"What about English?"

"Fluent."

Kale informed her of the daily routine, and time length of the girls' acts. "I know that you're savvy," he said. "Your decision is unwavering. However, Mendelson is very good in spotting a setup."

"What do you propose?" Josef asked.

"I propose that for the next week, starting tonight, she stays here at the brothel," Kale replied.

"Why?" Hael asked. "I know that Mendelson is ruthless, but he's still old." Throughout her travels, Hael had to reside in many hazardous and unsavory venues. Therefore, the proposal of residing in a bordello didn't bother her. She wanted to go back to the hotel with Josef to finish in detail their future plans. However, the nightmare of her hotel incident still lingered. The whispering voice and phantom limbs of her faceless attacker made her insides contort.

"Mendelson? Old? No. He looks barely out of his thirties."

"How?" she asked.

"Nobody knows," Kale said. He signaled one of his employees. "Fuki."

A petite woman with purple and green eye shadow strolled up to the table.

"Take a seat," Kale said. He wrapped his arms around the woman. "I visited Okinawa thirty years ago. I like traveling to small villages, and there was one right outside of Okinawa. The residents there were plagued by a ghastly nuisance called a *gaki*." In Japan, the Gaki was a terrifying vampire that had the appearance of an emaciated woman. It would float around in the night air, and search for victims with its hollow eyes. "The gaki," Kale continued, "when fed to satisfaction, can look like a voluptuous woman."

Hael looked at Fuki. "So, you're a gaki?"

Fuki smiled. "I was infected by the blood of one." She curled up against Kale. "When I'm sick, I start to look emaciated, and I gain a deathly pallor. However, when I eat to my fill, I can change my appearance into any kind of woman my John wants."

"What's your blood source?" Hael asked.

Kale ran his fingers through Fuki's hair. "She keeps the stray animal to resident ratio at an excellent level."

Hael scratched her head. "You're okay with eating strays?"

"We all have to do things at one point or another that we're not accustomed to," Fuki said. She smiled at Hael. "You'll have your turn soon enough." She adjusted her slipper and turned her gaze toward Kale. "Have you told her everything about Mendelson?"

"She'll know everything before the weekend," Kale said, chuckling.

Hael cleared her throat. "Who am I bunking with tonight?"

"You'll room with Fuki," Kale replied. "She'll give you everything you'll need. You'll have your attire, time schedule, and stage name. Three days before the weekend, you'll tell me how you're going to kill him."

"Don't worry yourself. I already know what to do," Hael

assured him. "It'll be clean."

"Make sure it's silent," Kale said. "The last thing I need is my best sector getting a bad reputation."

Josef put his hand on Hael's shoulder. "Are you going to be okay? Do you need anything from the hotel?"

"No. I'm good," she said.

Josef walked over to Kale. "Don't do anything stupid."

Kale snickered, patting him on the back. Josef turned towards Hael. "I'll be back tomorrow night."

Hael waved bye to Josef. She followed Fuki into the backroom.

****

In the following days, Fuki introduced Hael to the rest of the employees. All the women had vampirism influences. Kale thought it enhanced their shows. Since their influences dealt with illusions, the women used their abilities to keep customers at a never ending climax, and win themselves a devoted patron. "We really hope that your plan works," Fuki said.

"What do you think about Mendelson?" Hael asked.

"We hate that guy!" Fuki cried. "That pig! He's the reason Kale's hooked on opium!"

"He's an opium addict?" Hael asked. Other than the tension Kale had displayed when speaking about Mendelson, he'd first impressed her as a levelheaded and calm person.

"Yes!" Fuki shouted. "Ever since Mendelson became a client here, he's been shaky. Kale's had years of practice to cover up how strung out he is. This place looks great, but Kale is a wreck!"

"What did Mendelson do to him?" Hael asked.

"He won't tell me," Fuki said.

The women showed Hael the neighborhood layout in case something in the plan went awry. At night, Hael watched the women carefully remove their makeup and hair clips. She helped them with their kimonos and slippers. Under Fuki's tutelage, Hael learned how to properly adorn and accessorize a kimono along with how to disrobe from one. She learned how to tie an *obi,* a decorative bow for the back of the kimono, as well as apply her stage makeup. She asked the women why she had to learn all of this. It seemed odd to Hael to do this since she was staying there for only a few days.

"He knows," Fuki said quietly as she brushed her hair. "Mendelson knows everything about us. Thank God he's not intimate."

"You work in a brothel. How can he not know you intimately?" Hael asked.

"We don't get attached to our clientele," Fuki replied. "That would be too risky. Too many girls get hurt. Some of them get lucky, get a husband, and have babies." There was a weary look in Fuki's eyes. "But, a lot of them get hurt. We service the men, make them a king for a night, and then they leave. I've known a lot of men, too many. Many of them thought that I was attached to them. Others didn't. But, Mendelson is different."

"He's too personal?" Hael asked.

Fuki shuddered. "He's territorial."

Every story Hael heard had the same morals and warnings. The women had something to say. Listening to their lives was like drowning in hidden tears. Observing how they painted their bruises and kept smiling amidst the most vulgar crowds, Hael marveled at how these women went about their day so fluidly. Yes, they were seen as the filth of the fairer sex. They were the soft faces of lost souls, but their resilience to strive for the next day was both powerful and tragic. The tortures they went through were ungodly. The scorches of judging tongues they endured and the heartbreak of glass promises was unbearable. "Fuki, I know you've been asked this question before," Hael said. "Why do you continue to do this? This world is misery."

Fuki had a smile on her face, but even her soft gestures couldn't mask the underlying flood of pain. She told Hael her story. "I was born in a stack of hay on my aunt's chicken farm. The first memories I have are the sight of dirty flattened feathers, and the cold sweat on my mother's face. My father was the son of a rich family. But, because my mother wasn't in the hierarchy, neither she nor I ever existed in the eyes of my grandparents. I grew up raising chickens with my feet in the mud. My aunt treated us like animals. She made us sleep in haystacks in the storage shed. My aunt believed we would bring bad luck into her house and her profits. She reminded me of this every day. I snuck into the house one day to grab some food. Afterwards, when my aunt found out what I did, I saw her beat my mother outside the shed." Fuki sighed. "I guess she was right about the bad luck." Soon after beating the mother, Fuki's aunt was attacked and killed by a gaki. Her aunt fought the gaki in the kitchen, and spilled the gaki's blood over a bowl of fruit. Fuki's mother decided to flee the property with her daughter to travel back to her grandparent's house. It was a long journey. Fuki took some of the fruit for the trip. By eating the tainted fruit, Fuki gained the powers of the gaki. Her mother beseeched her parents to keep her daughter. They refused.

The grandparents worked on a merchant dock where they met Kale. They told Kale about Fuki. He asked them if there was anything wrong with Fuki. They told him about the incident with the tainted fruit. They assured Kale that Fuki was an excellent worker and an exceptional listener. After seeing Fuki, Kale paid them handsomely. He took Fuki to Eastern Europe. With no family and no ties to any work or housing, Fuki's only guarantee of safety was with Kale. "I never saw my mother again. I can't tell you if she's alive or not," Fuki said, wiping her tears. "That morning, the moment I saw the sun rise, I felt my mother's heart breaking."

"Kale said that the village he visited was terrorized by a gaki," Hael said.

Fuki giggled. "Do you really think he would tell you the truth? He'd maybe tell his friend the truth. Not a woman."

Hael cracked her knuckles.

"You can't trust him," Fuki told her.

****

Friday came. Like cyclones, the Mendelson's name twisted around every corner of the brothel. Kale received a message from Mendelson. He read the letter to his employees:

> "*Kale,*
> *I'm sad to announce that I won't be visiting as long tonight as I previously intended. Something came up, and it's too much of a nuisance to ignore. But, don't fret! I would never miss any of your geisha nights.* –
> *Mendelson.*"

Kale sweated profusely. Fuki placed her hands on his shoulders. "*Danna,* what's wrong?"

"Fuck!" Kale yelled. He knocked the lamp off of the table. "This wrecks the whole timing!"

"I'm sure we could work something out," Fuki said. "We need to be on a tight watch."

Hael watched Kale's limbs shake. His face was sweaty. His hands jittered. "I'll think of something. Just give me time." He addressed the rest of his employees. "Get ready for work as usual. We can't seem conspicuous. The flow has to be seamless." He wiped his brow and retreated into his opium room.

Fuki tapped Hael on the shoulder. "He's really thrown off right now. You need to go speak with him."

****

Toppling books and shattering glass sounded from the back room. Hael slid open the door. The room was dim. Faint outlines of books, tall dressers with golden handles, and wide arm chairs could be seen. The musk of opium and rum coated Hael's tongue once she stepped inside. Kale slumped against a large armchair. Smoke rose from his nostrils and mouth like a dragon. He adjusted himself. "What's troubling you?"

Hael closed the door. "Nothing. The same can't be said about you."

Kale giggled. "Good eye. Ah, good eye, Hael. What gave it away?"

"I don't care what troubles you."

"Then, what are you here for?" he asked through the smoke.

"What's the new plan?" she asked.

"Plan?" He laughed. "Simple! The plan's simple! There is none! Mendelson is extremely aware of cycles. He knows the rotation of each geisha. We always show a new girl first. He's not going to be there for first show. When this happens, he just comes for the food and drink."

Hael seethed. "So, it's either first pick or none at all?"

"Yep," he replied.

"He's your best patron, right?" Hael said. Kale nodded in agreement. "He's wants first pick from every show, right?"

"Yep," he replied.

"Well, give him a special show," she said.

He took a deep inhale from his pipe. "I can't do that."

"Why not?"

"He'll be suspicious. He sends me a letter telling me that he's going to be late, and, 'Hey! We have something special for you!' That's not suspicious?" He rubbed his temples. "I'm not going to do it."

"You don't have to," she said. "I'll do it."

"No! This is my place," Kale bragged in a condescending voice. "You do what I say."

She punched Kale across the face, cracking his opium pipe in two. She grabbed his face and tilted his head back. As she glowered down at him, darkness swirled violently inside her irises. Her nails fastened into his skin.

"I'm not one of your whores," she growled. Her teeth sharpened. "You don't tell me what to do." She tightened her grip. "I've been waiting to kill this man for a long time. Unless you're his replacement, you do what the fuck I tell you to do!" She glared at him. "Are we clear?"

Kale couldn't move. He darted a glance around the room. Trembling, he sank deeper into his chair. "Fuki!"

She shook his head. "Are we clear?"

"Yes!"

She smiled. "Good boy." She let go of his face.

He rubbed his jaw. "What the hell are you?"

"That's a good question," she replied. "Now, listen closely. Mendelson's been coming here for a long time, correct?"

"Yes. So?"

"Since he's been such a wonderful patron to your establishment," she said, "you have decided to organize a private presentation for his viewing pleasure."

Shaking, Kale rubbed his face. "You're comfortable stripping for this man?"

Her eye twitched. "If I can finally gut this pig, yes."

He thought it over. "This is going to take some last minute preparations," he said. "However, it's feasible."

"He's going to arrive later on during the night," Hael said. "By that time, the dinners will be in full swing, and the second half of the shows will be performing. Wait until the girls go off of stage. He should've already enjoyed his eye candy. While he's still eating, go up to him, and ask him how he's doing. Small talk him. Tell him that, because of his patronage, you've arranged a treat for him. He won't refuse it."

"I know he won't," Kale grumbled.

"Trust me," she said, handing him his broken pipe. "This is going to work."

Kale grimaced as he remembered the loss of his eye. He rubbed his eye patch. "I hope it does." He sighed as Hael walked away. "Where are you going?"

"To get ready," she told him.

"Wait, what's going to be your stage name?"

"Fuki will let you know," she said. She closed the door.

Kale hunched over in his chair, eyes on his broken opium pipe. His memory of Mendelson burrowing his fingers into his eye socket like a rat haunted him. He rubbed his eye patch. "God, help me."

Kale got up from his chair. His legs wobbled. He began the evening's preparations.

****

Crowds of men flooded into the brothel. Some men were graceful in their steps while others trampled onto the floor pillows. As the girls' whisked from guest to guest, Kale watched the interactions from his office. He chewed his thumbnail. "No sign of him yet. Fuki!"

"You called, *Danna*?" Fuki responded.

"What's the plan for tonight?" he asked.

Fuki straightened her kimono. "Same as usual."

"Good. Wait. What?"

"Tonight is the usual. Is something wrong?" she asked.

"Didn't Hael give you any new plans?"

"I asked her what she was planning to do tonight. She said that after the conversation she had with you, she decided to plan an outside job due to the hesitation about his arrival," she said.

"You're serious?"

"Yes," Fuki replied. "That's exactly what she told me."

Kale sighed in relief. But, his hands were still fidgeting.

"I need to apply the rest of my makeup," Fuki said.

He kissed her on the forehead. "Good girl." He sat in his chair and reread the letter from Mendelson. "Fuki?"

"Yes?"

"Where is Hael?" Kale asked.

"Oh! Hael told me that she checked back with Josef," Fuki told him. "She said that they were going to catch Mendelson after the brothel closes. She didn't say how they'd do it."

Kale smiled. "As long as it's not in here, I'm happy."

"I can tell." She left and continued with her routine.

****

Hours passed by. The entire brothel was packed. The

bold red lights blended against the mist into different hues of orange, purple, green, and gold. In the brothel, there were two types of geishas: the server and the Geisha. Servers were the waitresses of the brothel. They zipped through the crowd to deliver food, drinks, and cigars. The Geisha title was for the women that preformed on stage. These women had the title of Geisha at the beginning of their name. People addressed Fuki as: The Geisha Fuki. The servers dressed to match the theme of the brothel, but the kimonos they wore couldn't compare to the elaborate shining robes of the titled women. The geishas' faces were painted pale white with vibrant colored lips. The servers wore masks.

Kale greeted more of his guests at the door. "Fuki!" he called. "What time is it?" He didn't see Fuki in the crowd.

A voice spoke, "Quarter past ten."

Kale jumped. "Herr Mendelson! I'm glad you've made it!" He shook his hand. "How was your day?"

"Late," Freudric replied.

"I can tell. Please, take your seat. The girls will be right out with your regulars."

"Actually," Freudric said. "I had something to eat before I came. Tell them to only bring my drinks."

"Yes sir. Hana! Momo! Table fifty-nine!" Kale said. Two women bustled behind the kitchen window as they gathered the bottles. Kale handed Mendelson a complementary pack of cigarettes. "Enjoy your visit."

"I will." Mendelson leaned back into the pillow and lifted his feet onto the table.

The two women hurried to his table, and placed his drinks around his feet. Momo massaged his neck. "Is there anything else you would like at this time, Herr Mendelson?"

"*Nein*," he said. "*Alles ist gut.*" He told her that everything was okay. They bowed their heads, and hurried back to their posts.

Five geishas preformed before him. Fuki was the start of

the second half. During the intermission, the servers came around with sweets and dessert liquor. Unimpressed, Mendelson sat back against the high pillows in the corner with his hands clasped together on his lap. He scanned everything in the room.

In an orderly fashion, the women came out from the kitchen holding large golden dessert trays. Other servers approached with smaller trays of miniature fruity drinks and small wine bottles. Mendelson kindly refused their offers. Instead, he asked for refills of his first drink.

Hana placed the empty tray under her arm, and bowed her head. "I'm sorry, Herr Mendelson," she said, "but your drinks will be briefly delayed. We're in the middle of a rush. We'll get them out as soon as we can."

"Take your time, girl," he said, grinning. "I'm not going anywhere."

People knew Mendelson as Big Eyes because of the large golden glow of his irises. It was impossible to forget his gaze. However, Mendelson never fully opened his eyes. Always, his eyelids were either halfway open or three fourths shut. The reflected luminescent glow gave the appearance of a wide-eyed stare. His full stare was said to be nothing short of a nightmare. Mendelson was never interested enough give his full attention. "Just make sure that they're cold," Freudric said.

"Yes sir," Hana said. She zipped back into the kitchen. "Zen! Table fifty-nine. Bring the regulars!"

He took a swig of his remaining drink and hummed to himself. Scanning the area, he noticed everything from the stumbling visitors to Kale chewing his thumb. Kale was always nervous in his presence. Everybody else was, too. People who heard of Mendelson paid close attention to details. People who saw Mendelson surveyed their surroundings. People who knew Mendelson watched their backs.

A small voice spoke beside him. "Herr Mendelson?"

He looked over his shoulder. "Huh?"

A server wearing a black and white porcelain mask kneeled down by his table with drinks. "Your regulars, Herr Mendelson."

He thanked the server.

"You're welcome," she said.

"Place them where the old ones were," he told her.

"*Jawohl*," she replied.

Mendelson's eyes gleamed. "Are you the one Hana was calling?"

"*Jawohl*," she said.

"Your name is Zen, is it?" he asked.

"Correct." She made no eye contact with him as she placed his drinks around his feet.

He examined her attire. "I've never seen you here before."

"I started working here this past week," she said.

"I see. Does Kale approve of your work ethic?" he asked.

"Kale doesn't know that I'm employed here," she replied.

"Oh? Why is that?"

"When a girl wants to work here as a geisha, she talks to Kale," she told him. "When a girl wants to work in the kitchen, she has to talk to Fuki. Fuki studies the work ethic and speed of the applicant for an entire week. Afterwards, if she likes what she sees, Fuki sends the girl to Kale to discuss payment."

"You're not getting paid right now?" Freudric asked.

"No sir," she answered.

He smirked. "Well, that just won't do." He reached into his pocket and pulled out his wallet. "How many days have you been working here?" he asked.

"Five days now."

"Five, ten, fifteen, here," he said, handing her a wad of money.

"No," she said. "Sir, I can't accept that."

"Nonsense," he said. "Take it."

"Sir, I'm working here like every other applicant. I don't

deserve any more attention than the next server."

His eyes traveled across her body. "Oh, yes you do."

With a deep sigh, Zen reached for the money. "If you insist, sir."

When her fingers touched the cash, he snatched her by the wrist. He didn't hurt her, but his firm grasp made sure she stayed put. She kept her voice calm. "Is there something wrong?" Zen asked.

He chuckled. "Do you have to serve any more tables tonight?"

"Yes, I do," she replied.

"No, you don't." Still gripping her wrist, he slid back into his pillow.

"Sir, I should get back to work," she said nervously.

"Zen, for every table you were supposed to serve tonight, I'll match the price."

"That's over nine hundred marks!"

He rolled his eyes. "So?"

She counted the bottles on the table. "Pardon me, sir, but I believe you should take a rest from your drinks."

He pulled her towards him. "Do these eyes look out of focus, my dear?"

The color shift of his eyes alarmed her. Her muscles stiffened as she caught her breath. "No, sir." His stare was soft, but it packed the intensity of a loaded cannon.

He led her down next to him. "Sit with me."

Zen nodded her head and obeyed.

****

Zen sat next to him throughout the intermission. Resting comfortably in his pillow, Freudric took a swig from one of his bottles. "So, Zen, where do you come from?"

"My family owned a small farm far in eastern Europe. The countryside is lovely, but I've always wanted to see the city. However, my timing couldn't have been worse."

"Why is that?" he asked.

"Well, the war, sir. I could've saved a lot of money if I would've moved sooner than later due to the war."

"I can see that." He offered her to partake in his drinks. She politely declined. "I'm not one for drinking, sir."

"Don't have the head for it?" he asked.

"No," she replied. "I don't have the conscience."

"Do you feel guilty if you have a few drinks?" he inquired.

"No," she replied. "I'll be lucky if I feel anything if I get drunk."

He smiled. "Really?"

She asked Freudric how he could afford this constant special treatment. He grinned. He told her that luxury and pleasure shouldn't come with a price or regrets.

Kale walked onto the stage. He waved his hands to quite the ruckus. "Everybody, the second half is about to start!"

Mendelson wrapped his arm around Zen's shoulders. He whispered into her ear, "Look at this clown."

"I can see all of you enjoyed the intermission!" Kale said. "You must be ready for the performance, yes?"

The crowd cheered in response.

"Excellent!" He proceeded with the introductions. "Coming to the stage is a radiant beauty from the mists of the Far East! She's a fanatic for danger and, given her nature, she's prone to bite. Lucky for you, she'll happily show her true colors and more for your fancy. Please, welcome to the stage, my favorite pretty plum blossom, The Geisha Fuki!"

There was a red flash, and a blast of smoke. Kale was gone. The lights died down to a plush, majestic purple. Pale plum blossom petals floated down onto the stage. With a gorgeous white fan as wide as her arm, Fuki emerged from the imperial light. In wooden sandals and a long flowing kimono, Fuki, like a crane, stepped towards the crowd. Her face was milk white. Skillfully, she danced, revealing her form fitting dress. Her dress had slits on the sides to show her delicately bending legs. The beads in her hair twirled in sync with the rest of her body. Her pale lips shimmered with silver like the shadow on her eyelids. Her nails glistened with color like the light behind her. The crowd, along with Kale, ogled and fondled her curves with their gaze, except for one.

Mendelson drank the rest of his lager. He turned his gaze towards Zen. He watched her eyes following the falling petals. He placed his drink on the table and slid Zen close to him. She flinched. She looked at Fuki. "Lovely, isn't she?"

"You can say that," he said.

She turned to him. "Is she not to your liking?"

"It's not impressive," he replied.

The scenery mesmerized Zen. "How can this not be impressive to you?"

"My dear," he said, "when a child plays with the same toy, learning its ins and outs, he becomes disenchanted and bored with his plaything."

"Miss Fuki is not a toy," she said.

"To you she isn't. But, to us," he said gesturing to the room, "she's just another one of Herr Drosselmeier's dolls. She's a high quality one, yes. But, she's still a doll."

From the corner of her eye, Zen looked at him and the rest of the crowd in hate.

He noticed her slowly distancing herself from him. "If you ask me," he said, "I'd pass up the majority of the women in here."

"Really?"

"Absolutely." Mendelson moved his feet off the table. "My tongue wants something different. What's the word they use? *Umami.*"

Zen crossed her legs. Her tone sharpened. "Fuki isn't savory enough for you?"

"No, but you are," he replied.

Zen paused. She looked at him through her peripherals. She said nothing.

"Yes, the geishas are beautiful with their painted lips, manicured hands, and styled locks. However, the real beauties are the ones behind the mask."

"Sir, we wear these masks as a job requirement," she said.

"I know. But, let me explain." He pointed at Fuki as he coiled his arm around Zen. He pulled her closer to him.

Something shiny flickered around his neck. Flushed against him, she peered down his shirt. As he adjusted himself, Hael saw a ring on a gold chain. At first glance, it appeared to be a wedding band. *Was he married?* Hael wondered.

Freudric rubbed her shoulder. "You see her dancing on that stage? She looks like a porcelain doll made flesh. But, that doll has been cracked and scuffed so many times to get her that way. It's ridiculous. That, my dear, is a broken woman. Her mind and the minds of all the geishas performing here were weak or already chipped to begin with. In that state, it makes it easier for a man like Kale to refashion them to his cravings. It's nice to surround yourself with the company of these women, letting them entwine themselves all over you. But, those women in there," he pointed to the kitchen, "cannot be made to roll on their backs for money."

He studied the women coming out of the kitchen doors. "If that wasn't true, then why are you working for a whole week without compensation? Hell, when I handed you money earlier this evening, you denied me more than three times. If I left the money here for you, you wouldn't touch it. Would you?"

"I'm not here for tips," she said.

"Exactly! You're self-disciplined." He placed his hand under her chin. "This is why I'm more impressed with you."

"Why be a devoted patron if they're not your preference?"

He laughed contently. "Who wouldn't want an easy fuck?"

She glowered at him.

"Besides," he said, whispering in her ear, "I believe that

the real reason you have to wear this mask is so the geishas won't feel threatened."

"By what?" she asked.

He sipped his drink. "By a gorgeous woman like you."

She grabbed a chopstick from the table and hid it under her kimono. "You don't even know what I look like," she said.

His eyes traveled her body. His smile broadened. "Well, I'm about to find out." His arm coiled around her entire waist. He began to lift her mask.

Behind her back, Hael cracked the chopstick inside her kimono sleeve. Across the room, Fuki glanced towards Hael. Fuki twirled, stumbled, then fell, twisting her ankle. She fell hard onto the stage. Her fan flew into the crowd. The stage lights were shut off. The darkness put the crowd into commotion.

Hael plunged the broken chopstick into Mendelson's side. His flesh ruptured as she dragged her weapon upward. Blood spattered across her mask. He howled painfully; his eyes glowed in fury as his teeth sharpened. He clenched his fist and right-hooked Hael across the head. He snatched her by the collar, and flung her over the table. She stumbled getting up, but managed to grab a knife from the table. He was gone.

She looked around the brothel and the floor. The pillows were drenched with blood. Small puddles of blood trailed from the corner to the front door. She hurried to the entrance. A bloody handprint covered the doorknob. Hael sprinted out of the brothel, and down the hallway. At the top of the stairs, she pulled the lever to open the nutcracker's mouth. Sawdust from the top floor blew over her feet. She ran into the toy shop. Nobody was there.

Hael inspected every corner with the knife clutched in her hand. Mendelson's footprints and blood coated the floor. The front door was open. Another bloody handprint was splattered on the glass. The neighborhood was silent. Residents were asleep in their houses. Hael was infuriated. The knife started to bend in her grip. When she heard the knife creaking, she crunched the blade in her hands and dropped the metal shards.

Back in the shop again, she closed the door. She glared at the bloody handprint. "How could you let him get away?" she asked herself. She wiped Mendelson's blood off her neck.

The shop was quiet. The clocks ticked. She returned to the nutcracker. She drew first blood. She smiled remembering him writhe in pain. She had him exactly as she designed. And, he slipped away from her. Her plan was defeated. "Josef is going to kill you when you tell him this," she told herself. She stopped, and looked at the nutcracker. The carving's bayonet was ripped from the wood.

Something tapped her shoulder. "You don't have to tell him you failed." She turned around.

Mendelson plunged the bayonet through her abdomen, forcing her against the wall. He twisted the weapon like a stubborn corkscrew. He pushed the bayonet farther into her. "Like I said," he said, staggering, "you don't have to tell him. You can just die right here."

He crashed his hand onto Hael's mask and pushed it down against her face. He was suffocating her. Her screams faded as she thrashed her limbs. She tried to land a critical blow into his open side.

Before he could maim her again, Mendelson heard voices travel up the steps. He removed his palm from Hael's mask. "Whenever I'm getting happy, somebody always has to fuck it up." He yanked out the bayonet. Hael screamed as her blood dripped from her mouth. He held her up against the wall by her throat. He smiled. His eyes were wide open.

"I hope you get the job. I would love to see you again." He lifted her mask up to the bottom of her nose, and kissed her full on the lips. "*Schlaf gut,* Zen." He wished her goodnight, and let go of her throat. Her body plummeted to the floor. Mendelson disappeared.

Fuki ran upstairs. At the sight of Hael's body, she screamed. She knelt at Hael's side. "Kale! Kale! Get up here quick!"

Kale ran through the opening.

"Is she dead?" Fuki asked.

Kale pushed Fuki out of the way and felt Hael's wrist for a pulse. He ripped her mask off and pushed his fingers into her neck. There was no pulse. He grabbed her head and slapped her cheek to make her focus. She didn't respond. Kale placed his ear against her lips to feel for breathing. He felt nothing.

"Fuck!" he yelled. "Josef's going to slaughter me for this."

Fuki cried alongside the wall.

He shook Hael by the shoulders. "Wake up! Hael, wake up!"

Hael gurgled and spat blood on his face.

"Agh!" he yelled. He stumbled backwards. He wiped the blood from his face.

Fuki slid over to Hael and held her. "Hael? Come on, sweetie!" she said. "Wake up! Wake up!"

Hael's chest rattled as she inhaled. "Fuki?"

"Yes! Hael, I'm right here. What is it?"

"Fuki." Hael coughed roughly. "Your ... your voice is fucking loud."

Fuki laughed. She cried, laughing, and held Hael closer to her.

"Fuki! Fuki! You're crushing me. Stop! Fuki!"

"Oh, I'm sorry!" Fuki wiped her face. Some of her makeup was smudged. She smiled at Kale. "She's alive!"

"I can see," Kale said in disbelief. He gawked at her gaping wound. "What the hell are you?"

Hael coughed, then smirked. "I told you that was a good question."

Chapter Eleven
Responding to the Grapevine

Back at the hotel, Josef stayed awake the entire night with a searing pain under his ribs. There was neither an open wound in his side, nor faded scar to indicate a major injury. However, his muscles burned as if something rendered his flesh. He walked about the room rubbing his side to ease the pain. The pain began to slack as the dawn came. With the exception of gnashing his teeth and grunting, Josef remained silent throughout this ordeal. As the morning's light crept through the window, he sat in the chair away from the light. Silent and still, he held his aching flesh while the sun rose. He thought of Hael, and smiled. The phone rang. He grabbed it, shouting, "*Hallo*?"

Kale's voice ushered in from the other end. His shallow breath bombarded the receiver. "Listen, you need to get over here fast."

"What happened?" Josef repeated.

"Nothing! Something just came up, and I think you should know about it."

Hael shouted to Josef over the phone, "He's still alive!"

Kale continued, "Something went wrong, and —" Josef slammed down the phone. Kale tapped the receiver. "Josef? Hello?"

Immediately, Josef rushed to the toy shop. Fuki tended to Hael in the back office. Kale sat on top of the register when Josef arrived. "Where is she?" Josef asked.

"She's in the back with Fuki," Kale said.

"Is she hurt?"

"She just needs some rest right now," Kale replied. Josef looked at the blood on the ground. "Hael had a big confrontation with Mendelson. Things spun a little out of control."

Josef right-hooked Kale in the throat. Kale tumbled over the register. He stood over Kale. "What happened?"

Kale crawled away from him on the floor. "I had no idea what was going on. I thought she went back to go get you after we received the letter from Mendelson. She said she was going back to get you."

"Shut up!" Josef kicked Kale against the wall. "Do not move until I come back."

Josef raced downstairs into the brothel. There, he found Hael's blood streaked over the floorboards. The more blood he saw, the faster he ran. When he opened the door, he saw Fuki, Momo, and Hana cleaning the counters through the kitchen window. "Fuki!" he hollered.

Fuki jumped at his voice. "Where's Hael?" he asked.

Fuki gasped. She steadied herself. "Josef, you shouldn't go back there. She just fell asleep."

"Back where?"

"She really needs her rest," Fuki told him.

"Back where?" he persisted. Fuki flinched. She dropped Hael's bandages into the sink. He saw the bloodied wraps. "Oh, God!"

Fuki limped behind him, favoring her twisted ankle. "You shouldn't go back there."

He looked at Fuki. She stopped following him. Josef's gaze pierced through the shadows. Fuki's heart pounded. She backed away from him, and returned to the kitchen. Josef opened the door to the back office. His eyes were hardened with anger, but they melted into worry at the sight of his companion. Hael lay on her back across the day bed. The sides of her face and forehead were badly bruised and reddened from the mask's indentations.

Josef closed the door behind him. He crept to Hael's bedside. Her breathing was steady. Fuki had washed her beforehand, but the acrid, iron aroma of blood was potent. Hael's hair was damp, and she was dressed in a cotton robe. The trashcan was stuffed with bloody gauze. He felt the warmth of her cheek. He smiled. "You're getting your blood back. That's a good sign."

He smiled in relief and sighed at the sight of her system repairing. But, seeing the aftermath, he was regretful. She was recovering, but he hated himself for letting her take on the mission alone.

Hael was a tough and headstrong woman. Even if he demanded that he would stay at the brothel, she would refuse. He didn't know why.

Hael groaned in her sleep. She flinched trying to scratch her sides. He sat beside her and scratched her side. She smirked briefly as she drifted back to sleep. She was unaware that he was in the room. She tried to move, but the pain kept her stationary. She groaned again and clenched her teeth. Josef kissed her cheek and rubbed her shoulder until she stopped wincing.

He combed his fingers through her hair, and looked down at the covers. He had to see the damages. He carefully pulled back the blankets to reveal her wraps and small patch of dried blood in the center of the robe. This small blood patch was the tip of the iceberg. When he pushed the robe to the side, a huge blotch of blood covered the entire surface of her abdomen. The gauze was wrapped tightly around her. Mumbling, she shifted her head. He closed her robe. At first, her speech was an inconsistent entanglement of ramblings. After a few moments, he could decipher three words: "… so, he's, and ran." He leaned in closer. She continued muttering.

There was a knock at the door. "Josef?" Fuki said lightly. He opened the door. "I came to redress her wound."

"Did you give her anything?" he asked.

"Why? Did something happen?"

"No," he said, emptying the trash. "Did you give her any painkillers? Morphine?"

"We had to give her an opiate. She was conscious before, but her afflictions were excruciating. I couldn't let her continue like that."

"Which opiate did you give her?"

"Oh, I didn't administer it. I told Kale that she needed an immediate painkiller and he gave her something. I don't know what it was."

"Thank you for tending to her, Fuki."

Fuki smiled at Hael. "She's a very brave woman. It would be wrong not to help her."

"Can you tell me what happened?" Josef asked. He sat alongside the bed. "I need to know."

She sat across from him, and placed the new gauze on the desk. "Kale really didn't know what was going on," she said. "He thought things were going smoothly until he received a letter from Mendelson."

"Was it bad?" Josef asked.

"No," she replied. "Mendelson informed him that he was going to arrive sometime after the first half. He didn't say why, except that he was dealing with some kind of annoyance. Kale was furious. It threw off our timing. Hael talked to Kale about an alternative. She purposely told him a fake plan to calm him. She told me the real plan."

"Why didn't she just tell Kale the truth?"

"You know as well as I do that Kale is a nervous wreck when he keeps secrets from Mendelson."

Josef nodded with agreement. "True."

"Hael couldn't risk that. She told me to perform as scheduled. Instead of being a performer, Hael decided that it was best if she played the server role." Fuki remembered her earlier conversation with Hael:

"Why are you so upset about this? You're a new girl," Fuki

said. *"Mendelson always picks the new girls."*

"Kale's lost his mind if he thinks I'm stripping for that pig."

"Hael didn't want to be a performer, but she needed my help," Fuki told him. "She told me to listen for a chopstick snap from his corner of the room."

"What was that supposed to do?" Josef asked.

"After I heard the snap, I was to immediately twist my ankle. My injury would create a huge distraction. No performer has ever fallen on stage before. And, with Kale completely oblivious to the situation, Mendelson won't get anything from him about the incident."

"What about Hael? How'd she get hurt?" Josef asked.

"Kale led the guests out the bordello's back exit. We heard a huge bang," she said. "When everyone left, we ran to the toy shop. Mendelson was gone when we arrived. Blood was everywhere, and Hael was maimed against the wall. The nutcracker's bayonet was covered in her flesh. I thought she was dead. Kale searched for her pulse until she came to. She spat blood all over him. You know the rest."

"That's all?"

"That's all," Fuki replied.

He thanked her. "You're welcome." She shook his hand, and unraveled a gauze roll.

He stopped her. "You go rest. I'll take care of her."

"Do you know what to do?" she asked.

"Trust me," he assured her. "I've done this before."

She bowed her head. "Call us if you need anything."

****

After washing his hands and forearms, Josef took the covers off of Hael. Her mumblings grew louder. "It's okay," he said.

Josef was very diligent and precise when tending to injuries. He removed her robe, revealing her bruised arms and lower back. The skin had turned green and purple. He took off his shirt for better maneuvering. Securing his hold on her, he removed the bloodied towels from under Hael, and replaced them with new ones. After laying her onto the clean towels, he unpinned the bloody gauze wraps. She flinched as the fabric brushed against her raw skin. "I'm sorry," he said. "I know it hurts."

As the gauze layers fell into the trash can, he noticed the change of texture in them. The top layer was dried over with blood while the underlying layers were sticky and marinated. They made a wet plopping as they landed in the pail.

Hael moaned in her sleep. "I'm cold," she said.

Josef called for Fuki to bring him warm water and towels. He cleaned Hael's wounds. Goosebumps reappeared on her skin. "I'm so cold," she grumbled. Hael was unconscious, but she usually talked in her sleep.

"I know. I know," he said, stroking her face. Josef slid his hand under her, and held her at a slant. He didn't want to sit her upright since the muscle contraction increased the pain. The hole that Mendelson burrowed through her abdomen had closed. Her back had healed, too. But, her abdomen was still gouged open four to five inches deep. He smiled at her recovery, but the bruises from Mendelson's handprint enraged him. He cursed in Czech. He dressed her wound with antiseptic ointment, and wrapped her in fresh bandages.

"Fuki!" he called. "Come get this."

Fuki retrieved the used wraps. He thanked her.

"You're welcome." Fuki watched Josef tend to Hael's wounds.

He turned around. "Close the door, please. I don't want the heat to leave the room."

She sat in the desk chair. "What?" he asked.

"I suspected something," Fuki said.

"What?"

"You love her, don't you?"

Josef cleared his throat. He lowered his head. "She's the best partner I've had in a long time. She's diligent and smart."

"Pretty."

"She's crafty."

"She's caring."

"She knows how to properly organize infiltrations, and--"

Fuki interjected, "Take care of children, cook, and treat people nice."

He bit his bottom lip. "She's a unique marksman, strategist, weapon's specialist, and apothecary."

"And," Fuki said, "Hael's the loveliest thing you've ever seen."

With a reddened face, Josef rubbed his temples. She walked over to him. "I may be a courtesan, but I'm still a woman. I've seen time and time again the true eyes of love. She's more than just a partner. You're heartbroken seeing her like this."

"How can you tell?"

"You have some of the coldest, hardest, most unfeeling eyes I have ever seen on a man. Even when you're smoking opium with Kale, your eyes still remind me of nothing more than stone."

He scoffed. "Thanks."

"I can tell," she persisted. "When Hael entered the room, your eyes turned into the most full hearted gems I've ever seen. Your aura was joyful like a child's after he found his lost toy."

"She's not a toy," he told her.

"Of course she's not. She's your love." He cut his eyes at her. "Be mad all you want. I can see right through you." She walked to the door. "I don't know what you're afraid of. Who knows? She may love you back." She waved goodbye. "Sayonara."

Josef glared at Fuki. "You have to rub it in, don't you?"

Hael groaned. She shivered in the bed. "Why is it so cold?"

"Don't move," he said, placing his hands on her shoulders. "Your wounds haven't healed enough in the front yet."

Hael opened her eyes. "Josef?"

"It's me."

She lifted her head. "The whole plan went haywire! He got away. I don't know where he went."

"It's okay," he said. "I understand."

She stared at him. "Wait, you're not mad?"

"I'm mad at what he did," he said. "I'm not mad at you."

She rubbed her eyes. "Truthfully?"

"There was a good chance this would've happened, but I didn't think that he would have done this much damage to you."

She sighed and laid her head back.

He poured himself a glass of water. "Anyway, I can tell that he didn't leave here unscathed."

"How did you know?" she asked.

Looking at the glass, Josef rubbed his side. "Kale told me."

She laughed. "I cut at least four inches into him. He felt like a pot roast." She held her wound. "I didn't know a human could be that thick."

"Really?" Josef asked.

"Compared to past enemies, he topped the list."

He patted her shoulder. "You got him good. I don't think he'll fully recover from that." He looked at her bruises. "Did he see your face?"

She snickered. "No."

"You gutted him, and he doesn't even know what you look like." Josef laughed. "You really got him good."

"I have no idea where he escaped to."

"Don't worry about that," Josef said.

"What? You found something?" she asked.

"I did some digging while you were here. I found some interesting stuff," he replied.

"Like what?"

Cleaning some of her blood off his fingertips, he remembered returning to the hotel room. "Why were there two passed out men and water all over the bathroom?" he asked.

Recalling the incident, Hael averted her eyes. She cracked her knuckles. "I forgot. I was really tired. I stumbled. It's not important." She pushed the memory of the past nightmare deep into her mind.

Josef sensed something off about Hael. Everything about her, even the way she cracked her knuckles, was frazzled. But, due to the fight she endured, he remained silent. While he was away, through other connections, he gathered new information about Mendelson. "You remember Kirk?"

"Yes."

"He's dead."

She shrugged. "It was going to happen sooner or later."

"I found out that he was Mendelson's assistant. He was his *main* assistant."

Hael stopped cracking her knuckles. Her brow furrowed. "Who told you this?"

"I heard it through the grapevine. I followed a suspicious shipment from outside the *stadt* we ran from. It traveled halfway back to Dresden. The guards were gossiping about Mendelson offing his assistant because of a delivery delay. Apparently, Kirk was stealing money from Mendelson for the Nazi border patrol. Nobody knows where Kirk's body is."

Throughout their travels, Josef was secretive about how he came across some of the information about Mendelson. Even though his findings were highly detailed, Hael never questioned him about it. In her own weary paths, she encountered her share of unsavory bunches. She understood Josef's want for privacy. "What good will this do us?" she asked.

"He's looking for a new assistant," he told her.

"Great! You'll be perfect for the job!"

"Not me," Josef said. "You."

The pain from her injuries was still prominent. However, with her body swiftly healing, her pain was manageable. She leaned forward. "You were hesitant about me being next to him in here. You want me to be his assistant?"

"I don't want you anywhere near him. But, my wants aren't reality. I can't apply."

"Why not?"

"He'll know my face!" he said. "I'm in the system, remember? He looks for wanted criminals and vigilantes just as much as the Nazis do. I had a bad encounter with him a long time ago, and he never forgets a face."

She adjusted herself in the bed. "I suspect there's a deadline?"

"No. Thank God."

"Where are we even going to find him?" she asked.

"Kale will know where to go." Josef looked at Kale's picture on the wall. "Kale's had some scuffles with Mendelson in the past. But Mendelson eventually puts all of his pigeons in their holes. For now, Kale is still in the green zone. With some negotiation, I'm sure Kale will help us."

Hael pointed to her wounds. "Even after the attempted assassination?"

"Yes. If Kale can get in contact with him, he'll say that he has a good candidate for the application. And, Kale was oblivious to your plans. When Mendelson looks for information, he'll get nothing."

"That's some insurance. So, I heal, dress up, and play the eager young woman."

Josef shook his head. "No way. You're going in as a man."

"The job position is for men only?"

"Yep."

"Whatever." She pointed to the pitcher on the table. "Can I have some water?"

"Sure." He handed her a glass of water. "The job application is for men only because he's a complete lecher."

"That's important because?" she asked while taking a sip.

"He's knocked up every female assistant he's had."

Hael coughed up the water. "He raped his assistants?"

"No. It was consensual. I'm serious."

"I don't believe it," she said.

"I heard it myself."

"From whom?" she asked.

"Kale told me. And, before I met you, I was sneaking around getting evidence on this guy. I heard from the guards and his past flames that women chase after him."

Hael gasped.

"Take it all in," he said.

She put the glass down. "I don't think I want to."

Josef laughed. He poured himself some water. "It's shocking."

"It's fucking disgusting."

"But, it's true." He finished his glass, "I'll ask Fuki to help with the disguise. The application is for men between ages from twenty to thirty years old."

"No older men?"

"He doesn't want anyone at the age of his last assistant."

"Does he have any other preferences?" she asked.

Mendelson's application stated that the entries didn't need to possess anything particular. However, if an applicant could demonstrate something that was unique, that person will have the best chance of being hired. Hael tapped her fingers against her kneecap as she jotted down the details in her memory. "Any thoughts?" Josef asked.

"I need to heal quickly." She thought about whatever supplies she would need. "For the disguise, I'll need bindings, thick bindings, and a really good wig. Fuki should have that."

"Anything else?" he asked.

She leaned back. "How am I supposed to kill this guy?" She scoffed. "I'm going to be next to this man for a long time. And, I'll be in the dead center of his territory!"

"You'll have a better chance to kill him."

"I'll be in his territory. He can do worse to me!" Hael cringed. "Mendelson is paranoid. He keeps a close eye on everyone surrounding him."

"So, how did you get close to him last time?" Josef asked.

"He knew I was a chick and he wanted to fuck me!" She shivered in disgust. "I'm going in as a guy. He's more lenient towards women because they're women. He's brutal with his male subordinates. After what I did, he's not trusting anybody."

"It's not all bad," he said.

"This is like walking blindfolded into a no man's land. Survival is unknown, but somebody's getting shot."

"This is true," Josef said after rethinking the situation. He dreaded the idea of Hael venturing with Kale. But, with his past haunting him, it would only take the faintest trace of Josef's scent to spark a catastrophe on Mendelson's turf. He didn't want to jeopardize her first meeting. "You're right, but I'm not going back on my original idea. Let's wait a while until the commotion simmers down. The rumors about the application just started. We can afford a few weeks to get everything ready." He picked up her glass. "Just rest. I'll take care of the details."

She thanked him.

He walked outside, and handed the glasses to Fuki.

"Is Kale still up there?" he asked.

"He hasn't come down yet," Fuki replied. "I wonder why?"

Josef tied his boots. "You'll find out."

****

Kale walked around his toy shop. Angrily, he pushed his shoe through coagulated puddles of blood, and assessed the damages. He yelled to himself, "Son of a bitch! Why did I agree to this?" He kicked a marionette across the room. "They broke my nutcracker. The floor's ruined. I need a fucking contractor!"

Josef tapped Kale's shoulder. "You need to turn around."

"Josef!" Kale cried. "How is she?"

"Hael's better, thanks to Fuki," he replied.

"Fuki's always there when you need her." Kale laughed sheepishly. Josef glared at him. "But, really, it's a shame what happened. Really."

"What did I tell you before I left?" Josef asked.

"Stay in the toy shop?" Kale replied.

"I told you to take care of her."

"Okay, fine! I admit it. I fucked up. But, you can't blame me for this!"

Josef grinned. "Oh, yes I can."

"That's not fair!" Kale shouted, stamping his foot.

Josef kicked the broken bayonet aside. "Something tells me that you don't want Mendelson dead."

"Now I don't. Look at this place. Where else am I going to get the money to clean this mess?"

Josef cracked his knuckles. "Your life insurance if you don't shut up."

Kale was quiet.

"I'm sorry about your shop," Josef said. "But, you have to help me."

"Why should I?" Kale hissed.

Josef wrapped his fingers around Kale's neck. "Because," he said, "you don't want me as an enemy."

"Josef! Come on! We're friends! Remember?"

"Friends help friends. Remember?"

Kale sighed. "What do you need?"

"I need to know where Mendelson's guards loiter."

Shaking in Josef's shadow, Kale laughed at the thought. "If one guard sees you, you'll be shot on sight."

"With one trace of my scent, they'll shoot me," Josef said. "Not Hael."

"You're sending her in there after that kind of scrap?" Kale asked.

"No," Josef replied. "I'm sending her in there with *you* to find out where to apply as Mendelson's assistant."

"Kirk was a ruthless bastard. Mendelson's going to want someone as cutthroat as Kirk was along with some devious skills. I don't think you should put her up to this."

"You underestimate Hael. You have no idea what she's capable of."

"I never underestimate Mendelson," Kale said.

"Neither do I." Josef walked back downstairs. "Find out where they gather and pry for as much information as you can get. This needs to be done clean. Don't fall apart."

"Whatever. You better back me up on fixing this place!"

Josef agreed. He walked back up the steps. "Oh, Kale?"

"Yeah?"

"Fuki told me that you administered an opiate to Hael. Which opiate did you use?"

Kale scratched his neck. "Opium?"

Josef rolled his eyes.

"It's an opiate," Kale said. "It got the job done."

****

Three days passed. Hael's wounds healed, but her injuries took their toll. From the fight, Hael's scars were the first to fully fade, but the nerve endings in Hael's abdomen were severely crushed, making her abdomen a highly sensitive area. Once rested, to harden her up again, and build up her endurance again, Josef engaged Hael in spurts of fast paced combat. Fuki also gave Hael a concoction of herbs to help deaden the nerves. The whole of her damages couldn't be reversed within that short of a time. But, the marathon of sparring sessions with Josef brought her back to pace.

Fuki agreed to help Hael with her disguise for the application. Fuki fashioned a short, blonde wig from human hair. To kill the scent of the previous owner, she washed the wig with the bloodied bandages from Hael's wound. This would enhance Hael's cloaking skills. Fuki wrapped thick bandages around Hael's chest, waist, and hips. Due to Hael's endowments, it proved harder to conceal her figure. However, realizing she had a high pain threshold, Hael ordered Fuki to pull the wrappings as tight as possible. The constricting bandages wrung the air from her lungs. Hael adapted quickly to the pain as she regained

control of her breathing. The wrappings forced her into a milita-
rized walk. This suited perfectly for Mendelson's disciplinary
standards. As they traveled through the underground, Kale told
Hael the rules of their meeting's destination. They went through
the west side of Berlin.

"Until we get back to the brothel, you never leave my
side," Kale instructed. "Speak when you're spoken to, and keep
all answers to either a yes, no, or a direct sentence. Don't make
eye contact with anybody and don't look at anyone funny. Keep
your gaze straight ahead and do not turn soft under any circum-
stance. Understand?"

"Perfectly," Hael replied.

****

They exited the brothel through a hidden tunnel that led
them to the outskirts of Berlin. Kale made numerous escape
routes under his shop in case of an immediate evacuation. During the trip, he repeatedly asked Hael about her persona, "Now,
who are you?"

"Gabriel Erzengel," she said.

"Archangel? Is that really your last name?" he asked.

"No."

"What's your real last name?"

"I don't know," she replied. "I ran away from a foster
home when I was a child. I don't remember my real last name."

"How old were you?" he asked.

"Five."

"Why choose the name Erzengel?"

"My favorite Archangel is Gabriel. Since my name is Gabriel, I thought it seemed befitting."

"I see. Where did you go after you ran away?" he asked.

They continued practicing trial conversations until they
exited the tunnel. Kale explained that the majority of tunnels
were built by thieves. These thieves saw Berlin as a perfect hot
spot for heists. "How did they make these tunnels?" Hael asked.

"The thieves who built this were Alps. Each vampire species has power over an element. The Nosferatu's element consists of the manipulation and infiltration of shadows, and the Khang-shi of China controls air. The Alp has earth." He continued to give examples. He explained that Alps fed from their host through one of two ways. Whichever methods they chose was their preference. To avoid detection, Alps stayed away from streets and rooftops. Alps burrowed underground to infiltrate their victim's house from basements and cellars. "Mendelson's guards usually dwell in some of these tunnels," he said. "By being underneath Berlin, they receive plenty of confidential data."

"Mendelson's guards are all Alps?"

"No. They're human," Kale replied.

"How come they're not dead yet if they stay close to these vampires?" The details didn't sound right to her.

"No sane person would dare mess with Mendelson's property." Kale lit a cigarette. "When he pays you, he owns you."

As she bit her tongue, Hael's eye's twitched at the thought about her future employment.

"Anything else you want to know?" he asked.

"Why doesn't he hire vampire guards?"

"That's a reason you don't want to know. Anything else?"

"What's the other thing the Alps consume from their victims?" she asked.

Kale cringed. "You really don't want to know."

****

Their destination was hidden beneath a cluster of boulders inside of a small grove within a large pond. Kale told her to wait at the edge of the pond as he walked to the boulders. "I thought vampires can't cross bodies of water," she said

"Vampires cannot cross *moving* bodies of water. Unless the vampire is experienced enough, that detail does not apply." The water was up to his elbows. His nails elongated. He dug into the boulder and scaled the surface.

"What vampire are you?" she asked from across the

pond.

"An Alp," he said, standing on top the boulders.

"What turned you?"

"My mother was stalked and attacked by an Alp while she was still pregnant with me. She survived, but a vampire's venom seeks out the most susceptible target."

"Is the majority of Germany's vampire population Alps?"

"No. Actually, there aren't that many Alps around to begin with. We all stick together in specific areas. This hideout is the largest gathering of Alps. Vampires sometimes share the same areas of origin. Germany and the rest of Bavaria can mingle together without a territorial conflict. I'll tell you more about it later. Follow me." He pushed the top boulder to the side. "You don't have a problem with getting wet, do you?"

"No. I'm alright," she replied. She walked deeper into the pond. When she reached the boulder, she lengthened her nails. Tiny sparks fell from her claws as she climbed the surface.

Kale's eyes widened. "Holy shit."

Hael shook the water off her pants. "What's that?"

He looked at her claws then his own. He mumbled to himself climbing down the hole, "Remind me never to piss you off."

"What?"

"Nothing. Remember what I told you."

"I'll remember," she said.

"Oh. There's one more thing."

"Yes?"

"Watch your head." He pulled her down the hole.

As they fell deep into a cavern, the smell of cold compacted dirt and rock surrounded her. The glow from Kale's eyes trailed down into the darkness the deeper they fell. The steep drop angled into a short incline. She plummeted onto the dirt below and rolled to a stop. Rubbing her head and back, Hael looked atop her side. She was on the edge of a long downward staircase of carved rock. She shook the debris from her head. She looked towards Kale. He landed on his feet and brushed the dust off his clothes. "How was it?" he asked.

"I could've broken something!" she shouted.

"No. I wouldn't have let that happen."

She looked up into the hole they fell through. "A slide?"

"Ha, that's right. I forgot to tell you. We Alps are one of the most territorial vampire breeds in existence. We carve structures like that slide to make sure that people who aren't supposed to be here never come out again."

She dusted her pants. "Maniacal things, aren't you?"

He grinned. "When we want to be." He dusted her back. "This way."

****

They descended the rock steps. Deep into the tunnels, the steps became more and more gravid with precious stone and mineral deposits. The tunnel walls at the entrance were lined with hard dirt, but, like the steps, they shifted into the hardened precious stone. Vampires entered from different tunnels. Some tunnels were burrowed into the walls while other vampires dropped down from the ceiling.

At the bottom, there was a large semicircular opening hidden by a waterfall veil. Intricately carved ditches in the floor led the water out through the side walls. Kale stepped halfway through the waterfall. "Welcome to *The Hidden Caverns*."

Hael walked through the waterfall, her eyes widening. Her jaw dropped. "Whoa."

Hael envisioned that the tunnels would be like a miner's cavern, but these tunnels were magnanimous in both size and stature. The height of the tunnels stood ten stories tall and two hundred feet wide. In different locations, smaller compacted tunnels were built to accompany small businesses and taverns. The main tunnels and walls were the host for trading, vendors, and transportation. "I had no idea Alps were capable of all this," she said.

"This took hundreds of years to complete, but here it is,"

Kale said. "Beautiful, isn't it?"

Hael was breathless. "Extraordinary! This is the most beautiful architecture I've seen in my life."

Kale chuckled. "Other vampires think we just dig in the dirt." He dried his hair. "Stay close to me. People have gotten lost for months in here."

She gazed at the mineral deposits. "I believe you."

Gargantuan segments of precious gems littered the cavern walls. They glistened brightly in the lights of the establishments. Gems of amethyst, ruby, fire opal, sapphire, and emerald reflected multicolored rays of light onto the walls and vendors. The light continued reflecting from vendor to vendor. In the top stories of the cavern, vampires jumped from window to window of different institutions. The flow of traffic was never one speed. Some creatures strolled casually to their destinations while others leapt over the crowds. The clanking of utensils and pots from the vendors clashed with the vampires' screeches.

"I thought vampires couldn't eat human food," Hael said.

"Veteran vampires can eat human food, but not too often. Fledglings and young vampires can't eat human food. They're only allowed to eat what's permitted to their breed until they surpass one hundred years old, a full lifetime. Human food is like a luxurious substitute for hunting. Didn't Josef tell you this?" Kale asked.

"No," she replied. "He doesn't like discussing details."

"I suspected that." Kale spotted the tunnel the tavern was located in, "Do you know how to jump?"

"Yes."

"Good. Follow me and don't drag your feet." Kale launched off the ground into the air. Hael followed him. Being in midair was a sobering and transcendent chord. They leapt from a large granite deposit and landed at the entrance of a small tunnel. "Half a block down this way is a small tavern."

"Why is it so far away?" she asked.

"The makers of this tunnel learned a long time ago not to

permit the building of taverns along the main walls. An intoxi-
cated vampire being thrown out of a tavern into traffic is a nasty
sight."

The tavern's tunnel had an uneven ceiling. Occasionally,
they had to duck and dodge sharp slabs of granite.

At the end of the tunnel, a green light illuminated a broad
wooden door. Mist seeped from under it. The wood around the
door's handle was chipped from being replaced multiple times.
Kale knocked on the door.

Built into the door, a dark rectangular slit opened. An old
man peered through it. His voice was deep and raspy with age.
The old man spun a riddle. "Why does the lonely wanderer
make haste to his impregnable sanctum?"

Kale answered the riddle, "*Denn die todten reiten schnell.*"
He told the man that the dead traveled fast.

The old man grinned. "Well said, Herr Drosselmeier."
The window closed. The man spoke again. "You may enter
when ready."

Kale nudged Hael. "Hat down. Hands behind your back
at all times." She nodded. He opened the door.

The old man behind the door overshadowed them as
they entered. His voice was even raspier up close. "Welcome to
The Ragged Homestead."

Like a vulture, the old man hunched in the chair and
twiddled his long blackened fingernails on top his bony knees.
His cheeks were sunken and a deep scar traveled diagonally
across his brow. With his sharp uneven teeth, he smiled, and
waved at Hael.

The Ragged Homestead was the largest gathering of the
most notorious vampire assassins, thieves, and drug peddlers in
Germany. In the corners of her eye, Hael observed a multiplicity
of underhanded swindlers. From pitching sales for bags of im-
ported hallucinogenic drugs to pickpockets, Hael moved
through the thick of Europe's most infamous creatures.

Kale sat at the bar. "You're not carrying anything valuable in your pockets, are you?"

Hael sat next to him. "No."

"Good," he said, waving down the bartender.

A brawly Nachzeher emerged from behind the beer kegs. A large portion of his right bicep was mutilated and scarred over. The bicep looked as if it was chewed on. His nails were thick like garlic cloves as he picked gravel from his sleeve. "Herr Drosselmeier!" he said in a jovial voice. "It's been a while since I've seen you. How's the business?"

"Smooth as ever. How've you been, Dieter?"

"I'm pissed. I got into a scrap with a B.E.D." According to Kale's employees, Mendelson's nickname spread throughout the underground. In the Ragged Homestead and the rest of the taverns, Mendelson's guards were given the acronym B.E.D. B.E.D stood for Big Eye's Dog.

"What happened?" Kale asked.

"They think they own the place," Dieter said.

Kale shook his head. "Not again."

"The dog skipped out on his tab. I'm sick of them paying whenever they want. They think that everything should be on the house since they work for Big Eyes."

"That's tough, man," Kale said. "I'm sorry that happened."

"I should've strangled him. If Jürgen didn't hold me back, I would've killed him." Jürgen was the tavern's doorkeeper.

"We don't want that."

"I'm glad he stopped me," Dieter said. "The last thing I need right now is Mendelson hunting me down."

Kale clasped his hands together on top the bar. "Speaking of which, has he been around as of late?"

"Why do you ask?"

"I've been hearing rumors lately about him looking to hire a new assistant. My friend Gabriel," he said, gesturing towards Hael, "wants to apply for the job."

Dieter stopped wiping the glass. He slapped the rag on

the bar. "Did Reinhardt sell you a bad batch?"

Kale laughed. "I'm sober, man. It's not the opium talking."

"I don't believe you. For God's sake, look at that boy!" Dieter said, gesturing to Hael.

"I'm recommending Gabriel myself. He's a hard worker and a pretty good analyst."

"He'll be a pretty good corpse if he applies for the job. He's a Dhampir!" Dieter shouted. "No vampire, even the ones in here, would ever consider working for him. You want to vouch for a half-breed?"

"I know he's young, but that's one of the qualifications. He's good. He knows what he's getting himself into. I just need to know where I can get the application."

Dieter sighed. He pointed his finger at Hael. "Boy, you got a death wish."

"Well?" Kale asked.

"Mendelson isn't here. He hasn't been here for over three weeks now, but his guards just left for something to eat. They'll be back." He shook his head at Kale. "You can wait in the back room. I'll tell them where you are."

"Thanks Dieter," Kale said. He turned to Hael. "You see that back door with the bullet holes? Wait in there until I get back. I need to meet someone."

"Okay."

"Hey. Before you go back there, grab yourself a drink." Kale put some money on the counter, "Dieter! Ring up a Red Mead." Red Mead was the tavern's signature mixture of calf blood and honey wine. "It's good. Trust me. He makes it himself." Kale always vouched for Dieter's home brews.

Hael crossed her arms on top the table. Dieter sneered at her. He began mixing her drink. "What?" she asked.

"You got a death wish?"

"Pardon?"

"Do you have a death wish?" he repeated.

"I'm just looking for a job," she said.

He slid the drink hard to her. "I don't like your kind."

"And, what exactly is my kind?" she asked.

"Dhampirs." He moved closer to her. "I don't like any of you. Every time one of you half-breeds arrives, trouble follows."

"Your bar is filled with a lifetime's supply of ransoms in wanted criminals. I'm the one who's bringing in trouble?"

The doorkeeper's long fingernails draped over Hael's shoulder. "Actually, it's my bar. And, my friend here does have a point." Jürgen sat next to her. "Every time a dhampir comes here, it's never for good business. These customers aren't saints in the slightest, but they don't bring the whole house down with them."

"I'm not going to denounce your tavern," Hael said.

"Your kind usually does," Jürgen replied. Jürgen was a very old Alp. Throughout centuries, he prevented the collapse of *The Hidden Caverns* along with other underground societies. "Your kind brings the humans in here by infiltrating and distributing our secrets. To retain order, we have to comb through the entire city to insure that any human who saw us receives amnesia."

"What makes you think I have human friends?" she asked. "The same speech you're giving to me is the same accusations humans have about dhampirs."

"That may not be the case, but you are associated with Herr Drosselmeier. We've been friends with Kale longer than you've been alive. We don't want him killed," Jürgen told her.

"Nothing's going to happen to him," she said.

"For your sake, I hope so. He's given a lot of these people very good business. They would be exceedingly cross if you brought their good friend to danger."

"I couldn't bring him to any more danger than he's already dug himself into."

Jürgen knew that Hael meant no harm, but her aura was too dominating for a dhampir. To his own befuddlement, deep down, Jürgen's instincts identified her as a threat. He smiled at Dieter. "I like this kid. He's not like other dhampirs. He doesn't know his place." The old Alp ruffled her hair. "Be good, now."

He snapped his fingers. "Dieter, cut this one some slack. He's already throwing himself to death. The least you can do is slide a cool drink his way."

Dieter took the mead and poured it into a frosted mug. He sneered giving Hael her drink. Hael sipped the mead. "Jürgen's good people," she said to Dieter.

A door opened. Hael looked over her shoulder and saw Kale enter the room. Kale walked over to her and placed his hand on her shoulder. "Ready to go?"

"Yes," she said.

"Mendelson's boys are coming back. I heard from Jürgen that they won't stay for long. We have to make this count."

They entered the back room. The room was a small dwelling with a large round table in the center. Small towers of poker chips and card decks littered the table along with various sized coin bags.

"Take a seat in the corner. Don't talk until I tell you to," Kale instructed. Hael finished her mead and waited.

****

Thirty minutes passed. Hael counted the cobwebs in the corner. The stench of sweat and dirty shoes wafted into her nose. "How long will they be?" she asked.

"I don't know," Kale said.

"Are they even coming?"

"Yes."

"When?"

"I don't know," he replied.

"How do you know that they didn't just brush us off?"

"They didn't," he said.

"Are you sure?" she asked.

"Yes."

She continued, "So, when are they coming?"

"I don't know!"

The door opened. Four brawny men in padded vests strolled through the door. Portable oxygen tanks were strapped to their backs. Being below underground, the henchmen carried small oxygen tanks to help them breathe. Looking at Kale, they laughed at him. "What are you doing in here?" one of them asked.

"I've heard that your boss is looking for a new assistant," Kale replied.

They laughed again. One man walked up to Kale and looked him over. This dog was cynical. Snickering, he cut his eyes at Kale, and pushed his dirty fingers against Kale's forehead. "You want the job, old man? I don't think so."

"Oh, no. You've got it all wrong. You see I'm Herr Drosselmeier. Herr Mendelson--"

"Wait! Wait! Wait!" the man interrupted. "You're Herr Drosselmeier?"

"Yes," Kale answered.

"So, you're the clown he's been talking about?"

Kale paused. "Excuse me?"

The dog chortled. "The Clown of Berlin. I've heard about you and your dry Japs."

Kale lowered his eyes. Hael saw his face redden and contort.

The man continued mocking Kale. "Ha! He knows it, too! Look at him!"

Hael stood up. She put her hand on Kale's back. "It's alright, man. Sit down."

"What are you doing?" Kale asked her.

"I got this," she said. She glared at the henchman.

The henchman spit out his toothpick. "What are you staring at, half-breed?"

"I'm here for Mendelson's assistant application."

The men burst into raucous laughter.

"Something funny to you?" she questioned.

"Kale, you really are a clown!" the henchman said, wiping spit from his chin. "This is a joke?"

"I don't joke," Hael said.

The man pointed his dirty finger at her face. "Nobody's talking to you, boy. Sit the fuck down!"

Hael snatched his finger and twisted his arm from the shoulder cuff down. She broke his wrist. "You sit down."

Another man unsheathed his knife. "Who the hell you do think you are?" He slashed at Hael.

She grabbed his wrist and twisted his arm around, too. She stabbed his knife into his hip. The other henchmen launched at her. She broke the man's fingers, pried the knife out of his hand, and threw the first henchman into the others. They grabbed their pistols from their holsters and aimed them at her. She locked the man's arm behind his back, and held his knife to his jugular. She spoke in a calm, cold voice. "My name is Gabriel Erzengel, and I came here for the application. Are you going to tell me what I have to do or not?"

"Mendelson doesn't want any trash in his operation," one henchman said.

She pressed the blade against the man's skin. "Ah. Then, you won't mind if I dispose of this."

"No! No! Wait!" they shouted.

"I will do it."

The man sighed, and grabbed the side of his face. "We'll tell you what to do," he said reluctantly.

"Are you lying to me?" she asked. "I swear I will end him."

They men holstered their pistols. "We're not lying. Just let him go!"

She felt the man's pulse quicken under her fingertips. She smiled. "Deal." She dropped him. She examined his knife. "I'm keeping this." She slid the knife behind her belt. "Can we get to business?"

Disgruntled, the henchman balled his fist and sat at the

table. "Have a seat." He took off his face mask. "I hate wearing this stupid thing." A huge scar ran diagonally across his face.

"Give me the paper to sign," she said. She was tired of his empty words.

As he started to laugh, Hael could smell the rot from his discolored yellow teeth. He pulled a paper from his satchel, and tossed it at her. "Here."

The application was one page with one line on it. She examined the paper. "This is it? It's just a signature line."

"Sign it," the henchman said.

"What's going on?" Kale asked.

"This is the job application," the man answered. "Sign it, and I'll tell him everything he needs to do." He handed her a pen. She signed the application and pushed it back to him. He placed the paper into his satchel. "Be here at a quarter past eleven tomorrow night. Weapons and methods of communication are prohibited. Report to this room. Eight other people will be here for the job as well. Come alone."

"Anything else?" she asked.

"Until three days pass, no matter what happens, questions are banned."

"I'm like a dog sometimes," Hael said. "I have no sense of time. How will I know it's been three days?"

He snickered. "You'll be alive." He joined the rest of the group and left the room. She heard the men gossip outside. "He'll be dead before the first sundown," they said.

Kale sighed in relief. "That went well."

"I almost killed someone. That went well?"

"The last dhampir that bucked up to Mendelson's men was found face down dead in a sty with boars chewing on his legs. Yes, this went well. They know not to cross you."

"Why are you so jumpy?" she asked.

Kale adjusted his gloves. "I'm just getting over the brawl you had."

"Let's get back," she said. "Josef has to hear about this."

****

Back at the brothel, Josef sat on the couch in the back office. Hael came into the room, and removed her wig. "I hate that thing," she said. "It's so itchy."

Josef sprang from the couch. "Did you get the job?"

"My application isn't over with yet," she answered.

"What else do you have to do?" Josef asked. Hael told him that she had to return to the tavern tomorrow night. The other applicants would be there as well. She didn't know what they would be doing. She explained that the henchman said the application took three days to complete. "Let me know what time and I'll be there," Josef said.

"I have to go alone."

Frowning, he shook his head. "Forget it."

"Those are the rules, Jo. I have to abide by them."

"You're not going alone."

"Jo, I have to. We're this close to getting him."

"You're breaking your own rule. We never let the other go alone without backup."

"They may have people watching the caverns. Do you really want to risk it?" she asked.

"No," he grunted. "Can you take anything for communication?"

"No. I'll be totally solo."

He kicked the trashcan. "Fuck."

"I'll get this job," Hael said.

"If you can gut Mendelson with a chopstick, I don't doubt you." Worried about her security, he sat down and rubbed his temples. He looked up at Hael. Through her tightened fists and fiery eyes, he saw how adamant she was about this mission. But, everything that could possible go wrong bulldozed his mind. He smacked the side of his head. There was no room for paranoia. "No weapons allowed, right?" he asked.

"I'm not worried about weapons. I'm all I need."

Josef smiled. "He'll never see you coming."

"Damn right he won't." She removed her shoes. "I'm not going to the hotel tonight. I don't want any more scents on me."

"Good idea," he said. "Fuki told me that before you go, she'll make sure that your wig and bindings are secured."

"Thank you."

The following night, she left for the application.

****

Hael followed the path Kale took to the caverns. Heavy rain dominated the weather for the rest of the week. The combat boots she wore sank five inches deep into the mud and softened leaves. Other deep footprints imprinted the soil leading to the grove. The pond's water level rose, and caused the area to flood.

The water was black. The ends of the banks mixed with the silt. She moved steadily into the pond. The texture of the water seemed odd to her as she moved inward. The water was like viscous slime as it swirled and wrapped around her.

Something caught her foot. She moved her hand down her leg to grab her boot. She couldn't decipher what latched onto her. It seemed like an old root. It wrapped around her ankle. Its edges were hard and pointy. Her fingers kept slipping because of her gloves. She pulled her glove off between her teeth and pushed her hand under the root. The rain fell harder. "Come on!" she said jerking her arm. She snapped the root in half and pulled her leg to the surface.

She climbed up the boulder and tried to push away the top rock that concealed the entrance. It didn't move. She tried again. The rock would not budge. She kicked the rock and shouted, "Is anyone down there? Can anybody hear me?"

The rain fell harder. She shouted again, "Can someone push from the other side?" Her voice dissipated under the rain.

Someone screamed, "Help me!"

Hael darted around. A gargled voice strained from the other side of the rock. "Help me!"

She slid down the boulders. Her legs sunk into the ground below.

"Please! Where are you?" a man cried. "I need help!"

"Hang on!" Hael searched around the boulder. No one was there. "I can't find you!"

"I'm over here!" he called out.

She ran back around. From the furthest corner of the rocks, a man bobbed in the water. He was struggling to keep his head above the oozing mud. He waved to her. "I'm here!"

She moved closer to him. "I've got you!" she said, grabbing his arms and shirt collar.

His mouth gaped open in terror. "Wait! Wait! Wait!" he screamed.

"What?"

"I can't move any farther," he told her. "I'm stuck!"

"On what?" she asked.

"Under the rock," he replied. "I'm stuck under the rock!"

"How did this happen?"

"Never mind how! Listen carefully. I need you to dig under me and pull out my legs."

With a fervent nod, she slid next to him. She clawed her hands through the mud. "Did you reach them yet?" he asked.

"Not yet."

"Please hurry."

Hael was up to her ears in mud. She felt his pant leg. "I got it!"

"Pull!"

She pulled hard. "My hands keep slipping." The man's legs were wedged deep under the rocks.

"Please!" Pleading, he twisted his fingers around her sleeve. "You can't give up!"

"I can try something, but it is going to hurt."

"Do it!" He gave her the green light.

She dug her claws into his leg. His voice cracked from screaming. She secured her footing and pulled him slowly towards the bank.

"Wait!" he cried. "I can't do it! It's too painful."

She let go. His body slowly receded back into its original position. "What do you want me to do?"

"I need to think," he replied.

She kneeled in the mud and waited for his request. He drummed his fingers frantically on top his head. His chest trembled as he sobbed to himself.

The area was a deluge. Hael watched the pond swell as the water engulfed more and more of the bank. "If you keep stalling, you're going to drown!" she shouted. "Let me pull you up!"

Air bubbles popped alongside the boulder's surface. The man shuddered at the sound. He looked behind him. "Did you hear that?" he asked.

She shrugged her shoulders. "An air pocket must've ruptured below the mud." She looked at the surface of the water. The mud continued to bubble. The water level rose rapidly. "Please, let me pull you up!"

His eyes bulged like soup plates at the sight of the bubbling mud. The mud stopped moving. He turned towards her. "Leave."

"What about your legs?"

"Forget about my legs!" he shouted. "Just get the fuck out of here!"

She ignored his statement and waded towards him. He unsheathed his Bowie knife and swung it wildly in the air. "Go away! Damn it. Go away!" he threatened.

"Are you crazy?" she shouted.

He began to cry. "Please! Just leave!"

A gurgling sound erupted from beneath the water. It was deep and loud. The man gaped in fear. With his face paled to a paper white, his mouth opened and closed in horror like a dying guppy. The noise increased in volume, morphing into a horrid watery groan. He tossed his knife at her feet. She grabbed onto his arms to pull him out.

The man made no effort to move. She sank her feet into

the mud and pulled. "Please! Help me help you!"

He lifted his head up to her. His eyes were drenched in tears and wide with anguish. His mouth quivered sorely. "If you want to help me, heed the words of this old fool. Leave this place. Forget about me. Forget you ever came here. Forget your reason why, and get to the closest source of concrete." He grabbed her hand. "Take the knife! Stay away from the water banks!" Those were his last words.

His body was yanked underneath the boulder. The pull's tension and the sharpness of her claws severed the man's hand from his body. She flew backward. The severed hand fell into her lap. The air thickened with danger. She flung the hand back into the water. Something swallowed it from beneath the surface. Screaming, she grabbed the knife and ran from the boulders.

The hard rain loosened the soil around the trees. Roots were exposed over the ground. She bounded over them to avoid getting caught. A lightning bolt crashed in the distance. She tripped and plummeted to the banks. An exposed tree root slammed against her head when she hit the ground. Half her face sank into mud.

She nearly stumbled back into the water as she hoisted herself out of the sludge. She searched for the knife. It was lodged underneath a tree root. The mud bubbled around her feet. The ground swallowed the knife. She jumped back and ran.

The earth caved in everywhere she stepped. The further she ran out of the grove, the more the ground sank around her. She vaulted over new forming holes big enough to fit a torso.

Her foot was caught. She struggled to pull herself out, but the force of the suction engulfed her entire leg. She searched for something to free herself with. She reached over and grabbed an entanglement of roots. The roots snapped down onto her palm. Her bones crunched. She yelled. Globs of soil and gravel clung to her. Something sucked her arm deep into the earth.

Her limbs were captive under the ground. She was rendered helpless. She looked towards the night sky, a prayer forming on her lips. "Help me, God."

A groaning emerged from below. Gobs of mud popped in her face. A deep voice spoke to her, "I was beginning to wonder when you were going to beg."

A hand rose and clutched Hael's ribcage. Mendelson emerged from the ground. Clumps of black soil fell from his hair and face. He cracked his knuckles and grabbed the back of her head.

"It's funny," he said. "At first, I thought it would be amusing to hear another dhampir beg for its life." He squeezed her head. "But, hearing you plead sours my taste buds."

She spat on his face.

He chuckled. "Inches away from a potential death, boy, and you still aim to disgruntle your attacker. You'll do perfectly." He slammed her forehead against a gnarled tree root. She blacked out.

****

A lamp swung loosely over her head. The static whining of a radio pestered her ears as she awoke. As she regained consciousness, the voices of men grew sharper and louder around her. Outside, the wind whistled against metal. She was in a bunker. Groaning, she rubbed her head. A man climbed to the top bunk. "Hey! He's up!"

The man helped her sit up. "Easy now," he said. "You've had a rough journey."

"I did?" she asked. "I don't remember it."

"I suspected you wouldn't," he replied. "You took a rather nasty blow to the head. Mendelson flung you into the back of the truck. You were knocked out for the whole drive."

"Where are we?" she asked.

"I don't know. None of us do," he said. "The best guess I've got is that we're in an abandoned military camp." He hopped off the top bunk. "I have to admit. I'm impressed."

"At what?" she asked.

"You." He sat down next to two other men. "I've never heard of a dhampir surviving anything by Mendelson's design."

"Who are you?" she asked.

He extended his hand and smiled, showing his fangs. "Nicholas Weiss."

Observing his fangs, she shook his hand. "Gabriel Erzengel. What vampire species are you?"

"Nachzeher," he replied.

"How did you know I was a dhampir?" she asked.

"I didn't know. You're covered in blood and earth. No one could decipher your scent. Mendelson said you were a dhampir."

"Why?"

Nicholas chewed his toothpick. "I think he wanted to see if we would kill you." He flicked his toothpick into the trash. "It would've been a waste of energy. You're on borrowed time. Besides, your smell isn't bad like we thought it would be."

"Shut up, Nicholas," another man said. This other man had the same eye color as Nicholas. He climbed off another bunk. "You talk too much."

Nicholas smiled. "Had enough beauty sleep?" He turned back toward Hael. "Don't mind him. He's quite nice once you get used to the teeth."

"My name is Harold Weiss," the other man said, adjusting his cap. I'm Nicholas's brother. Astoundingly, Gabriel, I agree with Nick. Even with training, a dhampir has never survived for this long."

"Training? I thought there was going to be an interview."

"Oh, there's an interview once you survive his trials," Nicholas said. "Mendelson is as twisted as he is thick."

"What? Am I supposed to expect beatings on the regular?"

"He may beat you," Harold said. "But, his mind games slice deeper than a trench spike."

Hael adjusted her neck. "I'd like to see that."

Nicholas raised his eyebrow. "I think I can see why Big Eyes didn't kill you."

Hael crossed her arms. "Do tell."

"Every dhampir I know that's heard of Mendelson flees with their hands guarding their neck."

Harold chuckled. "If they were women, they'd be clasping something else."

"You spat in Mendelson's face and lived," Nicholas said. "We'd actually feel remorse if he had you cornered."

"Does anybody know if we're on his main base of operations? How many times has he spread assistant applications?" she asked.

"That doesn't matter," Harold said. He looked at his watch. "Our lineup is in four hours."

****

Sore and riddled with headaches, Hael didn't sleep that night. She stayed up to search the small bunker for any clues or past remains of applicants in the bunker. There were no traces. The dwelling was peculiar. The bunker's outside was weather abused, but the inside was immaculate. The floor was free of scuffs and stains. The mattresses were new. Remembering his ways, Hael knew how tactical and devious Mendelson could be. After the experience she endured at the pond, the clean atmosphere improved her night. But, the stage propped up before her exhaled a fouler and more insidious air that fogged the senses. As she looked about the bunker, she couldn't shake the sensation that something lurked beneath her feet.

Nicholas's brother stayed awake as well. Harold told her that he rarely slept, and, in that bunker, he wasn't going to nod off any time soon. "Even if you know where he is, never let your guard down around Mendelson," he said.

"I couldn't sleep if I tried," she said.

"Good." Harold looked out of a small window. "Stay up for as long as you can."

"You let your brother go to sleep," she said.

"This is a competition," Harold clarified. "Every player that falls is another win for me."

"So, why did you warn me not to sleep?" she asked.

"Why not? You won't be here for much longer."

She examined Harold's face. His nose was crooked and his right cheekbone was slightly lower the left one. "What happened to you?" she asked.

He spat his toothpick on the ground. "You're wondering how I got so pretty?"

"Never mind," she said

"Good answer." He sharpened his claws. "You do know how to hold your own, right?"

"I do. Why?"

He felt the edge of his nails. "Oh, you'll see."

****

A storm blew through the encampment that night. The wind raked and screeched against the metal. Hael listened to every corner of the bunker. Hael was in one of four bunk beds. With the other three taken, the rest of the applicants slept on the floor and chairs. It looked like a kennel. They didn't fight her for her bed since they thought the gesture would be her last gift of mercy.

She watched the end of Harold's cigarette smolder and die. God knows how much she wanted sleep. As her head swayed to and fro from weariness, Hael yawned and rubbed her face to stay awake. The weather made it harder to stay awake. The raindrops against the windowsill aided in the persuasion. She ignored their honeyed words and stayed alert.

The ground softened outside. Drenched weeds limped into the mud. The urge to sleep was relentless. She slapped her head to keep focus. She looked outside. Now and then, with the help of lightning, she could see past the fallen weeds. But, the darkness was insatiable. It ate everything beyond the boundary of the bunker's lanterns.

The storm grew closer. The wind was fierce. Lightning

bolts multiplied in their ranks. The bunkers vibrated with each boom of thunder. Harold fell asleep. His cigarette dropped from his lips. The odor of sweaty clothes and smoke was prominent. She had to get some air. She opened the door.

Small puddles of mud ran inside. The outside lantern was thrown against the next bunker. She suspected it was tossed by the wind. Freezing rain drenched her shoulders. She walked outside and unbuttoned her collar. She tilted her head back, and let the rain shower her face clean. When she reached the other bunker, she stopped. The lantern was broke. Blood was streaked across the glass.

A voice called out behind her. "I knew you'd be curious."

She turned around. A tall man looked down on her. "It's been a long time," he said.

"Since what?" she inquired.

"Since I've dissected a dhampir," he replied.

"I'm not dead," she growled.

He circled his finger around her heart. "Who said you have to be?" This man was dressed in a dark gray trench coat with his hands folded behind his back. Unlike his previous encounters, he realized that Hael wasn't fearful of his presence. "Bold, aren't you boy?"

She dismissed him. "I'm not in the mood for Nazis."

"Nazi?" he exclaimed. "Not all Germans are Nazis."

"It's really hard to tell right now," she said.

"Where are my manners?" He laughed. "My name is Dr. Alrich Strauss. I'm the head physician of this encampment as well as the lead mortician and medical examiner."

Hael froze in shock, speechless. Her arms hung by her sides like dead weights.

"I must thank you, boy," he said, walking closer to her. He circled her as he studied her stance. "It's been a real drag in the mortuary for years. But, thanks to you, I'll have a new gadget to pass the time with." He gnawed at his thumb knuckle. "I know that this is an abrupt first impression, but I had to see you before you get too mangled. You actually survived Mendelson's recruitment!"

She growled at him. "Get away from me."

He looked her over once more before leaving. "You dhampirs are interesting things. With them being mixed with the most stubborn species on this planet, it's never easy to guess what makes them tick." She watched him as he walked away. His narrow footprints disappeared in the rain.

She picked up the lantern, and threw it into the woods. His words enraged her. Hael didn't know why she was a dhampir. Except from the fact that she couldn't hide her fangs, she shared nothing in common with her breed. She couldn't even decipher what species she was. Yet, how people addressed her existence tested her tolerance beyond belief.

Alrich was still alive. How could this be? After all these decades, she thought Alrich would be a withered corpse. He hadn't aged. Vigorously rubbing her temples, she calmed herself. As she tilted her head up towards the sky, the cold cascading rain numbed her face. She evaluated the situation. It didn't matter if the doctor was alive or not. Compared to Mendelson, Alrich was a minor nuisance. She refocused on her main target. If Alrich got in her way, she would end him as well. She was more awake than ever.

****

Morning came. The rain stopped. The black mud that clung to the bunkers dried to a chalky residue. Hael's eyes were itchy and dry. Hopping off the top bunk, she landed on Nicholas's hand. She quickly jumped away. Nicholas did not respond. She called to Nicholas and nudged him with her foot. He didn't move.

"Don't waste your time," Harold said. "He's dead."

"How?" Hael asked. "I was awake the whole time."

Harold flipped over his brother. "I know."

"You were asleep," she said.

"I was pretending to sleep," Harold clarified. "I felt that something bad would happen, but not like this." He chewed another toothpick. "Why did you leave the bunker last night?"

"I needed some air." She looked at the dead bodies. Out of the full bunker, only Harold and she were awoke that morning. "Shit."

He stooped down to his brother. "Poor Nicholas." Harold placed a sheet over Nicholas's body. "Be happy for them. They're the lucky ones."

Hael shook her head in disbelief. "Harold, he was your brother. Your family. Doesn't this bother you?"

Harold stood up. "There's no place for warm hearts in hell. It's just going to get colder the deeper you go down."

Alrich's voice boomed over the intercoms. "All applicants must report to the center of the encampment within the next five minutes. That is all." The other applicants from the neighboring bunkers stumbled out, weary and confused.

Harold sighed. He adjusted his hat. "Here we go. Come on, Gabriel."

Hael covered the rest of the dead men with sheets before she left.

****

In the center of the encampment, there was a brick building with two large double doors. The windows were high with white blinds. The doors were closed. Alrich spoke again through the intercoms, "*Guten morgan,* everyone. When the doors open, please proceed to the mess hall. Breakfast will be served shortly."

Hael looked at the crowd. They were starving. They salivated like hounds waiting for their master to open the screen door. When the doors opened, the applicants flooded the hallway towards the mess hall.

A buffet of food served in hot trays was presented to them. The white of the plate disappeared underneath generous food portions. Eggs, bacon, bratwursts, oatmeal, waffles, pancakes, crepes, strudels, blood sausage, flanks of steak, muffins, bread, and toast were piled into mountains next to a lineup of various syrups, teas, coffees, creams, sugars, juices, and milk. Hael cringed at the drool hanging from an ocean of hungry mouths. The applicants stuffed their faces.

"That buffet doesn't stand a chance," she said.

"They don't stand a chance," Harold replied.

"Aren't you going to eat anything?" she asked.

Alrich spoke over the speakers, "You have less than an hour to eat your fill. Don't dawdle."

"Are you going to eat?" Harold asked.

"I don't know. This doesn't seem right." She scanned the buffet. "It seems odd that Mendelson would kill off sleeping applicants only to reward the survivors like this. This isn't sitting well with me."

"I get what you mean," Harold said. "Let's just eat light."

She sat down. "Agreed." The slurping, smacking, chewing, and swishing jaws echoed in the mess hall.

"They're like animals," said Harold.

She stirred her oatmeal. "Maybe that's what he wants."

Harold's neck tensed. His arms fidgeted.

"What's wrong?" she asked.

"The walls are watching me," he replied.

She looked around the room. All she saw was a bobbing sea of dirty faces.

"See anything unusual?" he asked.

"No."

Unlike the others, Hael and Harold cautiously ate their small breakfast. She consumed milk and a small saucer of oatmeal. Sipping from her glass, she closed her eyes and concentrated. She honed her focus on the corners of the room, sifting through waves of clatter.

Something caught her attention. Her eye twitched. A splintering crunch shot out from across the room.

Harold gave no indication of hearing the sound. He cupped his ears to silence the eating noises.

"I know that sound," Hael said to herself.

"What sound?" Harold asked.

"Somebody's tearing up a bone," she said.

"Where?"

She tugged on Harold's sleeve. "There. It's coming from

the far corner."

"Keep your head down," he said. He drank the rest of his juice. "Mendelson could be here."

She listened to the sound. "Why is he here?" she asked.

"I don't know. He wouldn't want anybody to know that he's here." Harold lowered his eyes. "Breakfast is almost over." Lowering her head, Hael grabbed the knife from the table, and hid it in her clothes.

Mendelson sat in the corner of the room and downed a fish head. He locked onto Hael. He watched her stack her empty plate with Harold. He licked his thumb. "You can hear me, dhampir?" Mendelson pushed his plate to the side. "You may have more notes to you than I thought."

Shrouded within a dark corner, Freudric remained undetectable to the crowd. He glanced at his watch. "I have time for another fish."

****

The applicants slumped over the tables after breakfast. Full with all the liquids and matter they could shove into their stomachs, they leaned against one another and talked contently across the tables. Alrich entered the mess hall. "Attention, applicants. In five minutes, report to the infirmary for examination."

The men lined up in an orderly fashion.

Harold walked on his toes as he peered over the crowd. Hael lowered her head and searched for Mendelson. They approached the infirmary. The infirmary door opened. Dr. Strauss walked outside. "Thank you for being orderly. One at a time, please step into the room for your examination."

The first man walked in and closed the door behind him.

****

The examination was longer than the group anticipated. No one heard any voices from the room. "What's taking so long?" Harold asked.

"What do you think they're doing?" Hael inquired. She tried to decipher the shadows behind the glass.

"I can't tell," he said. "It can't be that thorough."

"Oh, God no!" a man screamed. The group backed away from the door. The applicant cried for help from the room. Hael pushed her way to the front and grabbed hold of the door knob. The door was locked. The man continued to wail. He sounded like he was drowning.

Harold grabbed her shoulder. "What are you doing?"

"I'm going to ram it."

Mendelson opened the door. She ran into him. He didn't budge, but Hael was sent tumbling to the ground. A sour smell wafted out of the room and gagged the other applicants. Mendelson stood in the doorway looking down at her. "Alrich, clean up the chair for the next one. That smell is sickening." Dr. Strauss dragged the first applicant to a room down the hall. The applicant was unconscious. His wrists were blistered and he was covered in vomit from his chin to his lower stomach. Mendelson washed his hands in the sink. "Alrich!"

"Yes?"

"Bring the dhampir!"

Alrich snatched Hael by the back of her neck. The doctor grinned wickedly. "Tried to break down my door, did you?" He shoved Hael into the room and shut the door.

Mendelson put on a new pair of gloves. "You've managed to survive this far, dhampir?"

"My name is Gabriel," she said.

Mendelson cleaned his glasses. "Did I ask you your name?"

"No."

Mendelson approached her. "You will be known as dhampir, you will be called dhampir, and you will respond to dhampir until I've deemed you worthy of a name. Understand?"

"Yes, I do."

Freudric cleaned his glasses. "If you act accordingly during this examination, I'll consider letting that previous stunt pass."

"Sit down," Alrich ordered.

She sat in the chair.

"Show me your wrist," he instructed. He searched for her pulse. The doctor being this close to Hael gave her the advantage. By him touching her for a brief moment, she was able to create the illusion of a successful examination. With this skill, along with the wig Fuki gave her, hiding her gender was the easiest part of her mission. "The examination's complete," Alrich said.

Mendelson raised his eyebrow. "That fast?"

"There wasn't anything wrong with him," Alrich said. "He checked out fine."

"Everybody checks out fine in part one," Mendelson reminded Alrich. "Administer the serum."

With leather belts, Alrich strapped down her wrists and ankles to the arms and legs of the chair. Emotionless, she didn't wince. He took out a thin syringe and injected a serum into her arm. Freudric sat down in front of her.

Hael became instantly lightheaded. Her throat quivered. Her arms exploded with goose bumps. The skin on her wrists chafed against the leather as she tried to release the grip. Her surroundings became blurry. She shook her head in the hope that her vision would improve. Mendelson and Alrich sounded like they were talking through a pipe.

Mendelson put his hand on her shoulder. "Are you still with us, dhampir?"

She nodded.

"Can you hear me clearly?"

"Yes."

Freudric tapped her forehead. Her eyes flew open. Her hands trembled at the sight of him. His face was demonic. Mendelson smirked. "This one is holding out longer than I thought."

"What the hell is going on?" she exclaimed.

Alrich laughed. "I knew it was going to be any time now."

"They all lose it eventually," Mendelson said.

"I'm not losing anything!" she yelled. Her breath shallowed as tremors coursed through her limbs. "What the fuck is wrong with your face?"

"He's still talking in complete sentences," Alrich said.

"What did you put into me?" she demanded. She strained to keep her composure. Horrible visages raked her mind. Twisting shadows screeched and howled at her. The walls oozed with black sludge as foul pustules bubbled and popped on the ceiling. Gaping maws gnashed their crooked, slimy teeth at her feet from the cracking floor. As the darkness spiraled closer, the pale yellow glow from Mendelson's sunken eyes illuminated the manic contortions of his face. It was madness.

"He didn't lose it, Freudric. He passed the test."

"Indeed he did. Give him the antidote."

Alrich administered the solvent. Mendelson unstrapped the belts and gestured to Hael. "Call the next one in line when you leave."

Hael's arms flopped like noodles. "What did you inject me with?" she asked.

"You're done in here, dhampir," Alrich said.

"Alrich, leave him be." Mendelson walked up to Hael. "Go call in the next applicant."

After she left the room, Mendelson closed the door. "He did well. He lasted longer than I thought," he said to Alrich.

Alrich cleaned his goggles. "Are you really considering hiring a half-breed?"

"If he proves himself, he may have a chance."

"Those things aren't reliable, Freudric," Alrich said. "Dhampirs are great at first, but they have a short fuse."

"And, I have a shorter tolerance," Mendelson said. "It's pathetic that he's the one of the few applicants who doesn't reek of mediocrity."

"What if he does become your assistant?" Alrich asked.

"Then, he'll be my assistant."

"And, if he loses his mind?"

Mendelson shrugged. "Kill him like the rest."

****

Harold waited for Hael in the hallway. "What did they do to you?" he asked.

Steadying herself against a wall, she looked back at the door. "They're going to inject you with something."

"What's the injection?"

"Psychotic shit," she said. "It makes you sweat, your heart races, and your vision goes blurry. I felt like I was going to puke." Cringing, she remembered Mendelson's face. "I don't want to think about it." She walked down the hall. "I need some air."

As the examinations ended, Hael paid attention to the descending numbers. There were about thirty-seven when the trials started. After the first night, that number dropped to twenty-two. As the examinations progressed, Hael inspected the people coming in and out of the room. From her observation, eleven people managed not to vomit.

Hael, Harold, and two other men were placed into the same bunker after they passed the examination. Before dusk, Alrich made an announcement over the intercoms, "A complication arose in the list of those who had to leave the encampment. Therefore, to maintain organization, everyone will remain in the bunkers until the corrections are made." In the bunker that night, Hael tucked the knife underneath her mattress.

****

Two days passed. The applicants were still in the bunkers. Someone had locked the bunkers remotely from the outside. Restless, Harold paced back and forth throughout the nights. "What's taking them so long?"

Yearning desperately for sleep, Hael steadied her thoughts. As the bunker's air thickened, thinking of Josef was the only thing that calmed her. She gestured to Harold. "Just open a window and chill."

"The windows are jammed," Harold responded.

"Then stop talking." She rubbed her head. "Relax. They'll give us our orders soon."

****

The days ran on. They breathed each other's air for two and a half weeks. In Hael's bunker, there were three different species: two vampires, one human named Herman, and Hael the dhampir. Harold paced from his bed to the door. The other vampire, George, watched Herman's every move. Hael stayed on top of the bunk bed and gazed out of the window. Herman weakened. Licking his dry lips, he wrung his fingers. "We haven't had any food in weeks."

Hael turned on her side in the bed. "There's water."

"But, there's no food!" Herman shouted. "God, my stomach feels like it's eating me from the inside!"

Harold turned to him. "Calm down, Herman. Don't let this get the best of you."

"Shut up, Harold!" Herman scowled.

"Keep your voice down," Hael told Herman.

Herman foamed at the mouth. "You don't fucking tell me what to do, dhampir!"

"I'm not telling you what to do," she said. "I'm fucking ordering you!"

Harold grabbed Hael's shoulder. "Don't entertain him. Let him have a panic attack. He'll pass out soon enough."

Herman sneered at Harold. "You'd like me to do that, wouldn't you?"

Harold stared him down. "What are you implying?"

"I'm implying that you're all limey blood suckers that want me dead!"

George grabbed Herman's collar. "If I wanted to have the stink of your blood under my nails, you'd be dead by now."

Hael grabbed George's wrists. "George, let him go!"

"Why?" George asked. "The little man says we want to kill him. We don't want to make a liar out of him, do we?"

"Fuck you!" Herman shouted. "You think you're tough

shit because you're a vampire! I've done in twenty of you in my lifetime."

Hael looked underneath her mattress for her knife. It was gone. She swore she'd hidden it underneath her mattress. She passed her hand under her mattress frame, then yanked it back. Something sliced the back of her hand. Turning the mattress over, she saw a small chipped microphone. Herman continued to shout, "I'll make it twenty-one!"

"Shut up!" George sharpened his nails and sliced Herman across the arm. Blood spewed against the wall.

Hael jumped on George's back. She grappled him around his neck. "Let him go. This is just what Mendelson wants."

George elbowed her in the ribs. He yanked her off. "Fucking half-breed! Who do you think you are?"

She pinned George to the wall. George's hand loosened its grip on Herman's collar. "Mendelson is listening to us!" she said. "This is just what he wants."

"Get off me!" George jabbed Hael three more times in her ribs.

Pale and clutching his arm, Herman broke the window. He launched at Harold with a glass shard.

"I'll be damned if I let you things get the best of me." George pounced onto Herman's back. Blood pooled down Herman's arm. Wheezing and frenzied, Herman thrashed about the bunker to throw George off his back.

"Get off!"

George twisted Herman's wrist backwards. His bones nearly broke through the skin. Hael shot up from the floor. George tore half of Herman's throat out. She wrapped her fingers around George's neck, sliced his jugular to pieces, and tossed his body against the wall.

Sliding down onto the floor, George bled out. Panting, Hael held her ribs. "Are you okay?" Harold asked.

She took a deep breath. "Yeah. Yeah, I think I'm alright."

"What about your wound?" he asked.

She applied more pressure on her injury. "He cut me deep." She felt the gash beneath her fingertips. "It'll be fine."

"What happened to Herman was inevitable," Harold said.

"It shouldn't have happened. It's what *he* wanted." Hael sat down. "Look under my mattress." Harold pulled the mattress up. He saw the microphone.

"He locked us in here so we could take down the number of applicants ourselves," Hael continued. "Herman was the first man to throw up, remember? He was the weakest link out of the four of us."

"No," Harold disagreed, "Mendelson is the type to take care of the dirty work himself."

"He's sick," Hael said. "He likes to see people tear each other to shreds, and we gave it to him. He heard everything." She bit her lip. "He's probably laughing it off with that botch doctor of his."

"It's over," Harold said. "Mendelson won this round." He hung his head. "Mendelson wins everything."

She stormed over to the mattress and grabbed the microphone. She screamed into the speaker, "Are you satisfied? Did you get your jollies tonight?"

"Gabriel! Stop!" Harold shouted.

She strangled the microphone. "You fat happy bitch!"

"Stop!" Harold yanked her back. She pushed him off and crushed the microphone in her palm.

"Have you gone completely insane?" Harold grabbed her forearm. "You don't mouth off to Mendelson!"

"I don't care!"

Harold wiped his brow. "You need to get some air."

"Harold, I just got thrown, jabbed, and stabbed because of Mendelson's sick games. What I need is for that pig to plop his fat ass over here so I can tear the fuck out of his side."

"Don't you want this job?" he asked.

"Yes!" she said. "But, why like this? We're not animals."

Harold grabbed her shoulders. "Yes, we are."

****

Another week passed. The stench of blood and dead flesh polluted the bunker. Her gash across her ribs was fully healed, but her bones and joints ached. Maddened with insomnia, her mouth salivated at the thought of rendering Mendelson's flesh from the bone. Rotting fumes fogged her senses. As she gazed at the dried blood and pieces of flesh on her fingers, the memories of Josef pooled into her mind, and cooled her rage. "Josef," she whispered. "Please, stay safe for me. I'm almost there."

In the morning, Alrich made an announcement over the intercom. "Attention to all remaining applicants. In a few moments, the locks on your bunkers will open. All applicants must report to the main building and enter the front doors. But, be aware. Herr Mendelson has informed me that due to new developments in his schedule, the space for applicant reviews has decreased to six. The main doors have been programmed to open six times. No more. No less. Those who do not enter will be disqualified." Alrich smiled holding the microphone. "You have five minutes."

The people who survived burst from their bunkers and ran in frenzy to the main building. Hael and Harold opened the door. They watched everyone tear each other to pieces. Harold took off his hat. "They've all gone mad. Gabriel, we have to go."

She wasn't in the bunker.

"Gabriel?"

Hael ran outside. She picked up a flintstone from the ground and hummed it against the bunkers. Sparks flew off the metal. The stone ricocheted through the crowd and sliced the backs of the applicants' legs. Four men fell. Grabbing Harold's arm, she threw him in front of her. She rammed her way to the front. She grabbed Harold from off the ground, and pulled him along.

Harold spat out gravel. "You could've told me you what you were going to do."

She panted. "Keep running!"

They made their way into the building. Harold was the last one to enter the doors. Another man tried to pry his way through. The alarm sounded and the door slammed shut. The man's hand was cut in half. His severed fingers fell to the floor. Hard footsteps sounded behind the men outside. Dressed in black uniforms, a firing squad mowed down the failed applicants.

The gunfire stopped. Hael pulled Harold back and watched the men die against the window. "We made it. Harold, we made it."

Harold was against the wall. His face blanched.

"Harold, what's wrong?"

"Oh, shit."

"What?" she asked.

Harold pointed to a vampire standing in the corner. "You see that guy?"

"What about him?"

Alrich entered the hallway. "Good job, everyone. You are the six final applicants. I have to admit, I didn't believe that there would be more than four. I was wrong!" He laughed. "Any questions before we proceed?"

The hall was silent.

Hael raised her hand. "I do."

The applicants and Dr. Strauss looked at her.

She stepped forward. "Why the hell do we have to go through these trials? I was told that this was a fucking job application."

"This isn't just a job application," Alrich replied. "Yes, the pay is exponential and the advantages are numerous, but look around you. The applicants here are wanted felons. They're undesirable to the public. Nobody wants them alive."

He paused and relished in their misery. "Once you become Mendelson's assistant, you are allowed to ask one favor. The favor you ask, no matter what it may be, will be fulfilled to the fullest extent. So, if you are a fugitive with a despicable track record, the thing you covet is a clean slate. Mendelson has rewarded clean slates before. To him, it's a very easy procedure."

The applicants lowered their heads. All of them were fighting for a chance to start over. They were ashamed that their lives boiled down to this.

Grinning from ear to ear, Alrich twiddled his fingers. "Now, follow me."

Hael turned to Harold. "Is this true?"

"It's entirely true," Harold replied. "I've been a fugitive ever since I was a teenager. I'm wanted in four countries with a death sentence in two of them. This is my last chance to walk through the streets without a gun in my back." Harold kept watch of the vampire walking behind Alrich.

Hael walked in front of Harold. "Why are you staring at him so hard?"

Harold took a deep breath. "Keep your eyes on that guy when they're not on Mendelson."

The six were led to a black door. Alrich shoved his key into the lock and turned around. "You will enter side by side in pairs of two. The person already next to you will be your partner." He unlocked the door.

The center of the room was bright. A large light illuminated an elevated portion of the floor. On top of the higher ground, a circular wooden table with two chairs on opposite sides was fastened to the floor by long screws. Beyond the light, the room was in darkness. Alrich stood next to one of the chairs. Three papers were placed in the center of the table. Alrich stepped up to the edge. "Gentlemen, I congratulate you. You are the first six to make it to this stage of the application in many years. These papers hold the continuation of your progress."

He handed every applicant a pen.

"Thank you. Now, if you would, please line up alongside one another."

Hael stood next to Harold. Harold stared at the vampire

from the hallway. Alrich pointed to the pens. "Pay close attention. The pens you now hold in your hand must be kept on your
person until the application is complete. Remain quiet until Herr
Mendelson has made his choice."

He's here? To Hael, the room seemed empty. Except for
the doctor and the other applicants, she didn't sense anyone. She
looked into the darkness. A pair of smoldering eyes stared back
at her.

Mendelson sat contently in his chair. He spoke in a sing
song voice. "Who to choose? Who to choose?" He drummed his
fingers together. "We have an interesting spread this time. Don't
we, Alrich?"

"Indeed we do, Herr Mendelson." Alrich's mind raced
with ideas. *This ought to be quite the spectacle.*

Freudric leaned forward in his chair. The glow in his eyes
dimmed once he entered the light. Hael's fixed her eyes on
Mendelson. As he tapped his fingers against the armchair, Hael
noticed a ring on his finger. It was the same golden wedding
band that he wore around his neck at the brothel. Mendelson
lifted his finger, and pointed at each one. "Two Nachzehers, an
Umpier, a Nosferatu, a human, and a dhampir."

Hael looked at the man Harold was staring at. The
Nosferatu was one of the world's strongest and most deceptive
vampire breeds. From books and legends, Hael had read about
the Nosferatu, but, until now, she'd never seen one. Mendelson
sat back in his chair. "How fun!"

He snapped his fingers. "The Umpier and Nosferatu. Step
forward. The rest of you can wait outside." Alrich escorted the
four out of the room and locked the door behind them.

"What was that about?" Harold asked.

"You don't know?" Hael inquired.

"No," he replied. "Put your ear to the door and try to
hear what's going on."

She pressed her ear onto the door. "Nothing's happening."

"Concentrate!" Harold said.

"Damn it," she said. "I told you. Nothing's happening."

The door opened. Strauss cut his eyes at Hael. "Bad habits die hard, I see."

Alrich pushed her back. The Nosferatu stepped out of the room with blood dripping off his fingertips. Strauss stepped to the side.

"The two Nachzehers may enter the room."

Harold stepped forward, and gave Hael his hat to hold.

Hael shook his hand. "Good luck, Harold."

The doors closed.

Hael turned to the Nosferatu in the corner. "Hey. Can you tell us what happened in there?"

The Nosferatu turned his eyes away from her.

She waved at him. "Hallo?"

He rolled his eyes. "I can hear you."

"You can't answer a question?"

"You should be lucky that I haven't finished you off already, dhampir," he snarled.

"You're just a moody little bitch, aren't you?"

"Hold your tongue, half-breed!"

She scoffed. "You got a problem with me?"

"The whole world has a problem with your kind."

She toyed with him. "Max Schreck's the best vampire."

His fangs sharpened. "You disgusting abomination!"

Before she could choke him, Harold exited the room. Alrich followed him. "Congratulations, Harold. The human and the dhampir are next."

Hael handed Harold his hat back. The human and Hael walked behind Dr. Strauss. Hael looked at her opponent. The man stood straight as he walked evenly. They stood on opposite sides of the table. "Both of you are one step closer to finishing your application," Alrich said. "Herr Mendelson has chosen you two to fight to the death to proceed to the final round."

The rules were straightforward. The large ring around the desk was the boundary. The one who crossed it was the loser and was put to death. On the desk, there was one application form. The objective was to kill the other applicant to gain the form upon the opponent's death. If the person's pen was cast out of the ring, he would lose and die.

"At the sound of Mendelson's snap, the battle shall commence," he finished, smiling. "Fritz and Gabriel, shake hands. And, wait for the signal."

In a show of good sportsmanship, she extended her hand out to Fritz. "I don't know what's to be the outcome of this, but good luck to you."

Fritz spat on her palm. "Abomination."

Her eyes hardened. "I've heard that twice today."

Mendelson snapped his fingers. Hael hopped over the table, and kicked Fritz in the face. He almost fell backwards out of the ring. Hael stomped on his groin and lifted his neck up. She threw him onto the table and pulverized his face.

Fritz kneed her in her ribs and stabbed her stomach with his pen. She curled over. He rolled on top of her and stabbed repeatedly into her abdomen. Hael couldn't catch her breath. She gasped and recoiled in agony. He grabbed her wrists. He pushed his knees into her hips. "Tell me something, dhampir. Will I get to see the soul leave your eyes, or is this all you are?"

Her fangs and back teeth sharpened under the light.

Fritz laughed. He spat in her face.

Her roar boomed in Fritz's ears like the eye of a hurricane. She turned feral! She kneed him between his legs. Streams of blood trickled down his thigh. She pushed his head upwards and choked him on his own vomit. She flipped him on his back. His pen flew from his grasp, over the table, and across the room. She strangled him with glee. Her nails penetrated his skin.

Alrich walked up to the table, clapping his hands. "Bravo, Gabriel! Well done! You've won the round."

Averting her eyes, she ignored Strauss.

Alrich gestured for her to walk down. "Gabriel, you can rest now."

Focused on Fritz's anguish, Hael continued to puncture his skin. She was having too much fun. "Is this all you are, Fritz? Where's your soul, you bastard?"

Fritz gagged.

Hael's right eye flashed a dark red.

A gunshot went off! Hael's eye reverted to its dark brown. She was hunched over her opponent. Fritz was covered in blood and vomit. Mendelson shot Fritz through the ribcage. Smiling at Hael, he lowered his gun. "That will do for one performance."

She gathered her paper and hopped off the table.

Alrich walked behind her. He was uneasy. "Congratulations, Gabriel. You've earned your application form. Please, exit the room and fill out the rest of the questionnaires."

Strauss did not follow her out.

****

Three applicants were left. Hael filled out her form and waited in the hall with the other two. Harold kept his eye on the Nosferatu. Hael shifted towards Harold. "You're sweating like mad."

Harold wiped his neck. "When we get in there, once we start fighting, we're not friends anymore. Don't hold back. I sure the hell won't." He glanced at the Nosferatu. "And, neither will he."

The Nosferatu grinned. "Are you nervous, Harold? Or, are you remembering the day I broke your muzzle?"

Hael snarled at the Nosferatu.

"Listen to your friend, dhampir. You just may last a breath."

"Going after the dhampir?" Harold asked. "I thought your breed would pick a challenge. Not pussy out."

"That thing isn't a challenge, Nachzeher," the Nosferatu responded. "It's an eyesore like a stain on my clothes. I don't keep stains around."

Hael leaned her head back. "You'll have more than stains when I'm done with you, bitch."

Alrich opened the door. "The last three applicants may now enter the room."

After they walked in, Alrich closed the door behind them. "Sorry for the constant back and forth orders. The place gets crowded with all the bodies after a while." Alrich stood in by the table. "Front and center! Line up with your papers."

"Excited, Doctor?" Mendelson asked.

"We have a gradient of applicants competing today. Think of all the tactics! How can I not be excited?"

"Indeed, my friend." Mendelson regarded the three. He extended his hand. "Papers."

They handed him their applications.

He examined them. "Harold Weiss. You're wanted in four neighboring countries with a death sentence in two. Brother to Nicholas Weiss. You've been running from justice for your entire life. I see that your skills are as ruthless as your fraternal instincts are absent. Ignoring the chance to save your brother's life! I can use a man as cold as you along with the benefit of gaining an expert weaponsmith."

He addressed the Nosferatu. "Stephan Constantinescu. The full-fledged Nosferatu titled The Devastator of Health. With your reputation and cunning, you're very welcome here." Mendelson tried to decipher Stephan's handwriting. "Your talents include: elite assassin and battle planner."

Freudric turned to Hael. "Gabriel Erzengel." He sat back in his chair and said nothing more.

"Is something wrong, sir?" she asked.

"I'm waiting," he said.

"Waiting for what, sir?"

Mendelson examined the form. "On this paper, the only thing you wrote was, 'Check your coat sleeves.'"

"Yes, I wrote that. Did you check your sleeves?" she

asked.

"I'm not doing anything until you give me a proper answer," he ordered.

Hael removed her hands from behind her back. She held Mendelson's steel skewers in her right hand. When gathered around other vampires, Mendelson hid a pair of meat skewers in his sleeves.

"I'm trained in armed and unarmed combat. I know how to speak several different languages."

She scratched her back with his skewers. "I can be a leader, a follower, or a second in command. I can read ancient literature."

Mendelson's eyes widened.

She continued, "I'm a professional archer, swordsman, and equestrian."

Mendelson clapped his hands. "You're a professional thief. Marvelous show, boy! I've come across a slew of thieves in my lifetime, but no one has ever been able to steal me blind."

He beckoned Hael. She returned his skewers.

"I wish you good luck on the next challenge," he said. "It would be sublime to have a genuine thief under my wing. But, here's the dilemma. I only need one assistant, and a duel consists of two people. Yet, three people stand before me. I have a killer, a strategist, and a thief."

For a moment, Mendelson sat silently in his thoughts. As the three waited, the ground began to vibrate beneath their feet. The lurking sensation Hael has in the bunker returned as she looked at the floor. Mendelson cut his eyes at Harold. "I have no need for your skills."

The ground broke beneath Harold's feet. Hael and the Nosferatu jumped back from the cracked floor. Dark globs of soil bubbled up from the ground, and raced up Harold's legs. As it wrapped around him, the earth hardened and clamped down on Harold's body. Immobilized, he gasped for breath. The earth encased Harold up to his shoulders.

Mendelson tapped his feet. "Let's have some fun. The first man to kill the Nachzeher will get to use a personal weapon in the duel, or ask me a favor before the fight begins."

Stephan walked forward. "Sir, I will gladly accept your offer."

There was a loud thud. Stephan looked behind him. Hael had slit Harold's throat. Hael approached Mendelson with blood covering her forearm.

"You cheated!" Stephan yelled.

"You wouldn't stop talking," Hael said. She looked at Mendelson. "I don't want to use any personal weapons."

"Then what do you want?" Mendelson asked.

Hael sensed herself weakening. Her ability to maintain her illusion was becoming unbearable. She didn't know how much longer she could continue her disguise. She made her request. "If I win, no matter what happens during the course of this fight, I expect to be treated the same way with the same benefits presented to me as in the beginning. No back stabs, no catches, and no questions asked."

"If you win, I promise all these things," Mendelson said. She walked back to her place in line. She hung her head, looking at Harold's body. Her voice sad, she whispered, "I'm sorry."

Dr. Strauss walked up to the side of Mendelson's chair. "The final match is decided. The dhampir Gabriel Erzengel and the Nosferatu Stephan Constantinescu will compete. Gabriel has earned the advantage. Therefore, Gabriel will take first blood."

"The hell he is!" Stephan bellowed. He rammed his hand into Hael's ribcage. Blood gushed onto the floor. She collapsed. Stephan kicked her across the room. He turned to Mendelson. "When do we start discussing my award?"

Mendelson laughed. "What award? He's still alive."

Hael propped herself against the wall.

Stephan crashed his arm against her throat, and kneed her relentlessly in her diaphragm. She coughed up blood, still conscious. He threw her on the floor. The wood cracked on impact. Her face was pallid. Scowling, Mendelson watched Stephan with hate.

Alrich tapped Freudric's shoulder. "You should say something. Stephan cheated."

"Gabriel cheated, too," Freudric replied.

Alrich watched the beating. "Stephan will slaughter him."

"Do you have any faith in the underdogs or the outcast species?" Sitting back into his chair, Mendelson clasped his hands on top his lap and reveled at Hael's resilience. "When an animal is near death and cornered by the enemy, it has two choices: defend the life it has left or die miserably."

"You'll see an animal be put down today," Alrich replied.

Mendelson chuckled. "Yes, I will. But, which one is it?"

A cruel and sadistic creature, Stephan loved to see his victims writhe in their last breaths. He prolonged his victim's anguish to the point where the poor souls were reduced to tears, crying for their nightmare to end. His methods failed this time. Stephan kicked, stabbed, clawed, cut, and beat Hael with every inch of his strength. But, she refused him the satisfaction of one tear.

Wondering who would give in first, impatient, Alrich chewed his cuticle. "How much longer is he going to draw this out?" he asked.

Mendelson didn't answer.

For the sixth time, Stephan grabbed Hael by the ankle and flung her on the floor.

Enraged, Stephan seethed at her impassivity. Emotionless and limp, Hael hung in his grasp like a marionette with the strings cut. Before Stephan could strike again, Mendelson raised his hand to stop the fight. He was silent as he watched Hael.

"Freudric, this has gone on for long enough. Look at him!" Alrich said, pointing to Gabriel. "It's like watching a hound chew on a dead fox. It's got to stop."

Mendelson sat quietly. With halfway opened eyes, he

agreed with the doctor.

Alrich stood up. "Stephan Constantinescu, as determined by Herr Mendelson, you are the victor of the final match. You have proven that not only are you skilled in the ways of combat, but you are ruthless in your methods of extracting life. To obtain your place as the assistant, you may now take your opponent's life."

Stephan smiled wickedly at Hael. "Did you hear that, dhampir?" He spat on her face. "You finally get to die."

He approached Mendelson. "Herr Mendelson, I thank you for giving me the privilege to demonstrate my skills to you."

Mendelson made no response.

Stephan continued, "I would also like to ask about my conditions as your new assistant."

"You talk too much," Hael said. She leapt up from the ground and coiled her arm around Stephan's neck.

Mendelson's eyes gleamed with excitement.

Stephan's face turned blue. Hael was twisting his neck. He snatched the side of her shirt and yanked her off. She rebounded from the floor and tackled him. They wrestled on the ground. Hael kneed Stephan in his back. He screamed. He twisted her arm behind her back. He stood up as he kept her on her knees. He grabbed her hair and held her face upward. Stephan's sweat dripped on her cheek. "Look at me!" He yanked her wig again. "You don't yell. You don't scream. But, your soul will beg as the light leaves your eyes!"

He aimed for her throat. His claws extended like trench spikes. She caught his wrist and flung him over her shoulder. Her wig was thrown across the room.

While flinging Stephan in midair, Hael's black hair swung around like a tempest of ink. Mendelson was on the edge of his seat, his eyes wide open, and his arms shaking. With sweating hands, he removed his gloves as he watched Hael in amazement.

The Nosferatu's bones cracked with every whip. Sweat

streamed down her face, traveled over her lips, and flew off the tips of her fangs. Time slowed down in Mendelson's mind. With her long black hair trailing behind her, her fangs bared, and her eye flickering red with anger, she was a dark water dragon. Breathless with a slight bow of his head, Mendelson was humbled that he could witness this creature drag her victim into the abyss.

A hellish roar shrieked from her mouth. The last of Stephan's bones broke. She slammed Stephan into the floor at the foot of Mendelson's chair. Stephan was still alive. She pointed to Mendelson's jacket. "Check your sleeves."

Stephan yelped. When Freudric looked down, Stephan's throat was slit, and both of Freudric's skewers were lodged into the Nosferatu's heart.

There was a great silence in the room. Hael stood with her shoulders back, looking at her bloodbath masterpiece. Freudric was taken aback by the battle. The Nosferatu laid in ruin.

Alrich broke the silence. "Aren't you going to say anything?" he asked Freudric. Shaking with fury, he boiled at Hael's revelation. "She lied!" Alrich said.

Mendelson watched her anxiously as she removed the skewers from Stephan's heart.

With half cut eyes fixed on Mendelson, Hael wiped Stephan's blood from the skewers.

He snickered.

She flicked the blood off her fingers. "Something funny?"

Mendelson erupted into laughter.

She flinched at his outburst.

His voice shifted from a hearty laughter to a fiendish cackle.

"Are you going to sign my contract or not?" she asked.

He calmed down. He wiped a small tear from his eye. "Don't be so fussy, *fräulein.* I'll sign your contract."

She handed him her papers.

"But, first we need to talk." He snapped his fingers. "Alrich."

"Yes?"

"Go get some gauze from the back. We can't let her bleed out, can we?" Freudric instructed.

Scowling at him, she held her arm. Blood trickled between her fingers.

He chuckled, lightly.

"What?" she asked.

"Gabriel Erzengel. Gabriel the Archangel: the entity of life and death, and the only angel who is depicted in numerous cultures as man or woman. You're a clever girl." He pointed to her arm. "Doesn't that hurt?"

"No."

He laughed. "You're so unaffected! It's extravagant!"

"Excuse me?"

"Aww, come on! You fooled me with one of the most brilliant cross dressing illusions I've seen. You survived my tests, murdered the competition with no remorse, and now you're sitting emotionless in my chair, bleeding like a horse with its head cut off."

"Will you sign the damn contract or not?" she repeated.

He took out his lighter, and lit his cigar. He held up her contract. "You're damn right I'll sign it."

Eyes widening, Hael felt her pocket. How could she not notice him take the form from her?

"You're not the only one with fast hands, my dear," Freudric said.

Alrich came back in and tossed the gauze to Freudric. He caught the gauze and handed it to Hael. "I'll happily sign your contact. However, there will be some changes."

"Hold on. We had a verbal agreement stating that whatever happened from that point on, nothing would change."

"I'm sorry. I didn't mean to say change. I just want to add on a few things."

"Like what?"

"I'm adding on three things to your agreement. You don't have to be so tense. I'm not going to kill you."

She relaxed her arm.

"These additions are neither severe, nor do they possess any extreme difficulty."

"How do I know you're not lying?" she asked.

"I'm not lying to you. Actually, I'm glad you're a woman."

Recalling Josef's descriptions about Mendelson's history with his past female assistants, she gazed at Freudric with wary eyes. "Really?"

"Yes. There are some jobs that women can do that put men to shame. And, with your durability, you're more than capable for this." He slid the paper to her. "Please, look it over."

She scanned the paper. "This is it?"

"That's it."

"Nothing else?"

"There's no catch," he replied. "Along with being my personal assistant, whenever your assistance is needed in strict professionalism outside of the lab, office, or surgical vicinities, you are required to stop any current tasks to respond accordingly to my demands."

"What's your definition of 'accordingly'?"

"It means you don't have a choice," Alrich said.

Mendelson fiddled with his pen. "I thought I told you to go, Alrich."

"You have an important phone call," Alrich said.

Freudric rolled his eyes. "Can't it wait?"

Alrich shook his head.

Mendelson sighed, glancing down at his ring. "I know who this is. I'll be back in five minutes." He extended his hand to Hael. "Do we have an agreement, Gabriel?"

She stood up and shook his hand. "When can I begin?"

He grinned at her handshake. Her grip was firm and unshakeable, but her palm was warm and soft to the touch.

"Rest for now. Just be ready to work in two days. My employees will show you to your quarters."

She put the extra gauze in her pocket.

He finished his cigar. "I'll contact Kale to let him know that you were accepted. I'm sure he'll want his part of the payment. Is there any message you want me to pass on?"

"No," she replied.

Mendelson left the room.

When the door closed, Hael fell back into the chair. Limp and battered, she slid down the chair onto the floor. Staring at the remains of her opponents and the wounds littering her body, she sighed in relief. While the blood clotted around her as the dead flesh turned cold, Hael gazed at her reflection within the dark pools of blood beneath her. A tear fell down her cheek. She smiled. "Josef," she whispered gleefully, "Josef, I'm in."

About the Author

Born in 1993, L. M. Labat stems from New Orleans, Louisiana. From the struggles of a broken family and surviving life-threatening events, Labat found refuge within the arts while delving into the fields of medicine, psychology, and the occult. While combining illustration and literature, L. M. was able to cope with endless nightmares as well as hone in on artistic techniques. From confronting the past to facing new shadows, this author gladly invites audiences into the horror of THE SANGUINARIAN ID.

Made in the USA
San Bernardino, CA
18 September 2016